The Stripper Diaries

The Stripper Diaries

A Novel About Passion

N. Kathryn Howard

Tenth Street Press
El Segundo, California

First printing 2004

ISBN 0-9755645-4-4   LCCN 2004109179

TABLE OF CONTENTS

DEDICATION

To all the powerful female personalities I've been surrounded by throughout my life. We've loved, laughed, fought, hugged, and survived it all. I thank you for the strength, drive, and tenacity you've instilled in me. You are all in my everyday thoughts: Mitzie, Marvy, Dorothy, Dawn, Alison, Suzanne, Christa (pita), Laura, Katrina, Kathy, Shelly, and Jenny.

To my mother for being the backbone of our family. Thank you for your selfless commitment, and for believing in me, and rooting for me unconditionally.

To my honey bunny Alexi, who may prove to be the strongest one of us all. I thank you for giving me the ultimate purpose, and for helping keep my priorities intact. I love you more than life itself. Friends forever.

A NOTE TO READERS

This story was inspired by experience and information gathered by the author. However, *The Stripper Diaries* is a work of fiction. The situations encountered and characters involved are products of the author's imagination, and in no way reflect any true life occurrence. Any resemblance to actual events or persons is purely coincidental.

This novel is not intended to endorse or otherwise encourage young girls to engage in the occupation of exotic dancing. On the contrary, it is the author's objective to expose the field as detrimental to one's physical and emotional health. It is her wish that young women would never consider such an option to make a living.

ACKNOWLEDGMENTS

I wish to thank: Everyone at About Books, Inc. I have a feeling this is the beginning of a long and prosperous relationship. Jaysun McMillin of Jaysun McMillin Photography for his valuable time and unique vision. Garby Leon for giving me the idea, and pushing me toward it. Fantasy Island, West L.A.'s premier bikini bar, for all the entertaining stories that will stay with me for a lifetime.

In addition to the commanding female presence in my life, there are a few special men without whom my accomplishment may not have come to fruition. You know who you are: TH, I couldn't have done it without you. Thank you for letting me be me. RC, for getting it all started, and being a true friend when I needed one most. CBM, I'm eternally grateful for reconnecting. Thank you for freeing my mind. JM, we may never know, but I thank you for the inspiration. BJ, for keeping my passion alive. MM, for not getting mad when I didn't call for months. NV, for letting me do all the talking. And PJS, for being the brother I never had.

I'm a better person for knowing you all. Thank you for enduring my endless dreams.

1

The Background

If a psychic had told me that at age thirty-three I would be dancing in a strip club for a living, I would have shoved her crystal ball up her butt and reported her to the Los Angeles County District Attorney's Fraud Department. I believe in psychic ability, and have successfully consulted those with special talents of accessing futuristic information. After a particularly validating session, it's quite difficult to repress the urge to change certain circumstances in your life, which presumably will alter the forecasted outcome. I often wonder how my life would be different had I seen one before October of 1997.

It's not that I personally viewed strip clubs as grungy, smelly, drug-infested, Mafia pervert hangouts like those that have been depicted in every movie ever made about the business; I just didn't have any opinion or any thoughts about them whatsoever. I had never been in a strip club, other than one time in Arizona with an old boyfriend who wanted to go for fun. I wasn't completely naive about the business and knew pretty much what to expect—a few pairs of huge, fake boobs hovering over some poor sap, who was happy to empty his wallet to continue the suffocation. Not something couples should really be sharing, right? Nonetheless, my boyfriend assured me, "It'll be fun, something new, and I've never been here before, so let's check it out."

We were barely through the front door when this stunningly beautiful bleach blond, size zero, with a rack that would make a playmate blush, halfway through her contortionist act on the stage, peeks her head out from between her legs, waves at my boyfriend all giddy-like, and squeals, "Glenny's back!" With that as my only experience, I think I mentally blocked out all thoughts that the fantasy world even exists, at least for the next decade.

I, like most people, shared the common belief that girls that take their clothes off as an occupation are such dramatic, adult head cases largely due to tortured childhoods, abusive relationships, and lack of education and resources (all leading to poor self-esteem, resulting in only one option for putting food on the table). That may very well be the case for some strippers, (referred to as *dancers* from this point on). But having worked in or otherwise become knowledgeable about a myriad of occupational fields, I can say I've encountered people of the same backgrounds appearing to function as lawyers and prominent real estate brokers, all the while sucking clients into their internal dysfunction, and wreaking havoc all over the lives of those they are not personally involved with. At least the *dancers* that do seem to be sanity-challenged keep to themselves, and don't misrepresent what they have to offer. What you see is what you get, literally.

As much as I want to acknowledge the business of exotic dancing as one of many professions that employ all types of women, there are certain personality characteristics that must be present to be successful at the art of seduction for hire. Most of which I did not have.

I grew up in a suburban, Midwestern small town outside Chicago. A notable city whose name means Vale of Paradise. Most worldly people wouldn't associate this town with the word Paradise. (One imagines tropical birds and sandy white beaches, surrounded by quiet, attractive tourists sipping Mai Tais out of a straw with a colorful plastic umbrella stuck to it.) However, for me and my three sisters, childhood there was just that. We were smart, athletic, popular kids—more like boys than girls. Being aggressive leaders meant that when the neighborhood moms would call a meeting to find out which one of their kids was behind whatever teenage prankster mayhem that caused local law enforcement to wake up and leave their Mayberry-like office, my mom would conveniently have a last-minute obligation rendering her unable to attend. Ahhh, the good ol' days!

We definitely took for granted some of life's simpler things, like leaving the doors unlocked at all times without even a hint of worry. Come to think of it, I never had a key to the house I lived in for eighteen years. Our house was typical Midwestern. Tri-level, four bedrooms, huge yard—front and back. A friend of my mom's was an executive at Bethlehem Steel. He brought some of his guys out to build my youngest sister her *own* house in the backyard. It was nine feet off the ground, carpeted, insulated, and could hold about six to eight people. A ladder was extended through a hole in the floor, and could be pulled up when you wanted no one else's company. It was the coolest little hangout, and served more of a purpose as hosting late-night impromptu parties for us older siblings than pre-adolescent, Barbie-doll-playing get-togethers, its original intended use.

During the construction, my mom's friend had a heart attack and spent three months at the Mayo Clinic. We held a special candlelight vigil for him, and always felt his dedication to the project—although we never saw him again.

You know your upbringing was fairly healthy when memories include your friends always wanting to be at your house. We had fun, and my mom liked the idea of knowing exactly where her children were, so she didn't mind being the after-school supervisor. When boy suitors came calling on one of her girls, she'd lead them to the garage, citing, "She's in the shower, it'll be a few minutes. Why don't you rake the backyard while you're waiting?" Then she'd hand him some gigantic, metal, raking apparatus.

It wasn't uncommon to see four or five pubescent young men mowing, painting, shoveling snow, or cleaning out drain pipes on our roof. She had found a way to get some of the most annoying household chores done, and test their determination to date her daughters. We figured better them than us, so it worked out for everybody. Despite her efforts to recruit my would-be boyfriends as landscapers, my mom easily won their respect. They confided in her and maintained relationships with her long after I had gone to college.

All families have some dysfunctional attributes, and we were not without our share. My father was a criminal attorney, and a very powerful personality. He was charismatic, tall, dark, and handsome. Everyone thought so...everyone. It's hard for a man to resist so much temptation, and women are as guilty as men when it comes to throwing themselves at the opposite sex. Not that I'm defending his actions. I'm just giving him a chemical imbalance excuse. Excessive testosterone could be perceived as a double-edged sword. A driving force in achieving certain levels of success, but at a price that I suppose most men wouldn't complain about.

Luckily, none of us knew how appealing he was to the female population, and my mother never led on to his infidelities until we were grown adults. They divorced after a long separation when we were young, during which time my mom met yet another lawyer. She always said lawyers were great mates.

"They make clear, articulate arguments in a non-emotional tone, are willing to hear your side, and can easily agree to disagree." We took her word for it, and welcomed our stepfather into our family.

Having recently attended my twenty-year class reunion, I was reminded numerous times throughout an evening that was supposed to be entertaining but was not (Who nominated that reunion committee anyway?), about how much of a class clown I had been over the years in that little town. All of my good friends in high school had known me through grade school and junior high. Astonishingly, some are still my very close friends, and we get together frequently. Which is good and bad. It made for some incredibly genuine long-term friendships, but also gave way to years of telling stories about my attention-seeking, comedically driven, entertaining antics, all of which I would have liked to forget as I evolved into my adult body and post-dancer seductive aura that I now carry with me forever.

Nonetheless, everyone still thought it was funny how I made tediously boring history and social studies classes hilariously tolerable by making fake fart noises for an entire semester, torturing our teacher who had never entertained the possibility that the offensive sounds were coming from a girl, and repetitively punished one of the usual trouble-making boys, who vehemently denied the wrongdoing onto deaf ears.

Another anecdote making the reunion rounds was an imitation *Saturday Night Live* skit that a girlfriend and I had somehow worked into a creative writing class. We dressed as men, sat behind a long desk, and acted out our rehearsed version of "Not Necessarily the News." This was at a time when *SNL* was actually funny. The late seventies, early eighties, Gilda Radner, John Belushi, Chevy Chase days. So the skit was well received. I can't remember exactly what we wrote, but I know we thought it was funny, and seemed to get laughs from everyone in the class, *sans* the teacher. Of course the highlight was me making fake fart noises throughout its entirety. I had figured out a way to do that discreetly that won't ever be divulged. We fit them into the act as punctuation at the end of the one-liners.

It was hard to keep a straight face, and I can't imagine how we got through it. I don't know why, but fart noises and even just the word fart always cracked me up—still does. What came out of that simple assigned performance was a great desire I subsequently realized I had. The need to entertain.

Growing up a successful child athlete leaves one with a painstaking void upon reaching one's early twenties and realizing all that glory is gone for good. We tend to relive those exhilarating high school moments over and over all through life, exhausting those close to us, until someone's had enough of the embellished version of the stories, blurts out that "You're a has-been!" and tells you to "get over it already!" No one did that to me, but I suspect a few wanted to.

I had been a competitive gymnast since I was nine. A pretty good one for that time. I won't bore with specifics, but I have a lot of blue ribbons. Ok, I was a state champion. I had always loved to dance, and like most kids, took ballet and tap as soon as I could walk. I dreamed of being a world-renowned ballerina, and was strong, dedicated, and capable. Although, once I began tumbling classes at the local YMCA, I quit taking dance, and focused completely on being the next Nadia Comaneci. I had found my passion as a performer, and loved being the center of attention. Winning was everything. After all, I am a Leo.

Time is a funny thing. The intangible, universal dictator of all aspects of our lives. My mom used to say, "Live every day to its fullest, 'cause one day you'll look back and wonder how thirty years could go by so fast, without realizing where or how that time escaped, and then it's gone forever." Those profound words never hit home until I experienced lost years of my own.

I went to college at Arizona State University...for seven years. Since I had the ego-stroking, super-athlete distraction all through high school, the idea that I should be thinking about what I wanted to do with the rest of my life never seemed to cross my mind.

I knew that I would go to college somewhere in a Sunbelt state (the Leo thing, and I had shoveled snow for fifteen years longer that anyone should have to), but beyond that my mind was a blank. I guess I figured I would ride the athletic scholarship route as far as it would take me, and whatever came my way after that, so be it. I mean if all else failed, I could follow the family tradition and be a lawyer.

My stepfather had become the county prosecutor, and would go out on late-night raids. We didn't know what that meant, but from what we gathered from episodes of *Dragnet* and *Hawaii Five-O*, he was chasing drug dealers, pimps, murderers, and car thieves. Sounded kind of interesting, and piqued the excitement-seeking side of my personality. So by default, I studied criminal justice, with a minor in beer drinking, party throwing, and pizza eating. I logged more hours on academic probation than actually attending class. The 0.0 GPA (Mr. Blutarski) spring semester of 1985, cost me three years of anxiety in the re-admissions office of the Tempe campus, and ultimately led to a beg-and-plead session with the Dean of Liberal Arts.

"Give me one reason why I should let you back into an educational institution you obviously have *no* respect for, and at which you have clearly demonstrated your inability to exercise *any* self discipline whatsoever?" he barked.

You know how the words coming out of your mouth are completely contradictory to the ones racing through your head? What I heard was, "Look, Baldy, your lecture on respect and discipline is about as effective as the one I'm mentally giving you on your chocolate-eclair-eating, Scotch-drinking diet!" What then came to mind was a line from one of my favorite comedy films, *Stripes*. "I'm pacing myself. Now get off my back!"

Luckily, the words that came out were a combination of suck-up compliments, a "Please, please, please" sentence, and an "I'll do whatever it takes to finish in a year" mission statement. The follicularly challenged one saw some promise in my relentless efforts, and did finally allow me the opportunity to complete my degree program. I was happy to have graduated in under a decade.

My mother's words about time echoed in the back of my head, about as loudly as my own internal voice that tortured me for blowing off my gymnastics scholarship so that I could be free from physical obligation. When I had first arrived at ASU, the thought of hibernating in the gym six hours a day while the sun beamed brightly in the clear blue sky, and the pool at my co-ed campus housing unit magnetically pulled me toward it, was far outweighed by the newfound freedom and social life I had within hours of unpacking. The eight floors of my building were occupied by some of the most radical, partying Sun Devils the campus police had ever seen. The drinking age in Arizona back then was nineteen, and obtaining fake IDs that made us one year older wasn't too tough. Although the age was raised to twenty-one two years later, we were all grandfathered into the local bars, and spent most week nights getting drunk on a quarter with penny drink specials catering to all us starving students. We took Monday nights off, and would gather in Danny's room to watch the first syndicated season of *Soap*. Danny was a cute, rebellious, blond, baby-faced guy with one leg, and my first boyfriend in college. (Yes, the one-leg thing was a little weird. The lights were always kept off.) It was a fun group, and we were never without laugh material. I had a knack for surrounding myself with genuinely good people that just wanted to keep smiling.

During my forced hiatus from ASU, I worked as a cocktail waitress in a posh nightclub in Scottsdale. It was a spectacular place. My two roommates, who shared a huge three-bedroom townhouse with me in Tempe, also worked there. I think our entire rent for the 1500-square-foot, vaulted-ceiling palace (to any twenty-year-old) was $500. I distinctly remember my share being around $175 a month. I paid more since I got the master bedroom with an enormous remodeled bath, walk-in closet, and private entrance to the carport. The girls and I made roughly eight hundred dollars a week each slinging cocktails to Scottsdale's rich and famous. It was amazing I ever went back to school after making almost forty grand a year in cash at such a young age.

The DJ at the club was a good friend of mine. He was seven years older than I, a total horn dog, and a frustrated wannabe comedian. He couldn't carry a conversation without delivering a series of jokes at the end of which you felt obligated to finish with a cliched *"ba dump bump."*

We bonded one summer while training for the "waitress olympics." A local club promoter had made a name for himself, and a lot of money, putting together a competition for the wait staff of desert bars and restaurants. The grand prize was usually a trip for the team to Hawaii or some other desirable destination. Some of the events included the three-legged race, in which you were tied together at the inside legs of you and your teammate. You then had to delicately place drink garnishes onto a stick, put them into completely full glasses of water that were carried on one tray that you both held with your inside hand, sashay across the field without spilling a drop, and hand off the tray to your other teammates to do the same. To further the humiliation, we wore swim flippers on our outside feet, and chef's hats that nearly covered our eyes. These were timed events, and our team was the team to beat, as we had won the gold medal the previous two years in a row.

My DJ friend was our coach that final year. I'm not sure if it was when I was bobbing for a pickle in a bowl full of whip cream wearing a Donald Duck pool flotation device, or spinning around in circles trying to keep my forehead centered on the standing baseball bat after chugging a Kamikaze, that he looked at me differently and said, "I want to marry that girl."

Michael and I were engaged well over a year before either of us mentioned that the date we had set to marry had passed. I guess it was my job to plan the wedding, and the fact that I didn't should have been a pretty strong indicator of where I was at emotionally with him. They, the proverbial "they," say that an ideal mate should be your best friend. When the romance dies, the kids are grown, and the jobs have been fulfilled, all you're left with is a friendship anyway. So, it's the most important thing, right?

I've ruined more great friendships entering into romantic relationships using that logic. What I've learned over the years is that passion better be on your list of necessary relationship attributes or you're likely to end up alone and unhappy. That is, if you're the type of personality that needs, craves, and has experienced what being passionate about something can do for you. I loved Michael, but I had no passion for him.

We did, however, share a colossal amount of laughs, and I'll always be grateful for the time we spent together. Michael had quit spinning records in clubs, and decided to take a chance and live his dreams. I admired him for his risky attempt to develop and produce comedy acts. He had solicited three unknown, slightly raunchy, up-and-coming male comics that were regularly booking club gigs in Los Angeles. The five of us set out on what would have been a three-month performance tour throughout popular ski resorts in Colorado. We drove from Phoenix to Vail, with stops at Copper Mountain, Steamboat Springs, Keystone, and Telluride with four over-zealous, zany comedians, all firing hilarity at once, measuring who was the funniest by how many times they made me spit diet Coke on the dash. There was no down time during the eighteen hours in the car, and despite many opportunities to jump in on the competition, I was too intimidated by their expert timing and delivery. Their constant need to entertain made me forget all about mine.

By the time we arrived at the third resort, my face hurt so bad I couldn't watch the show without fear of permanent wrinkling. The common denominator in all their acts was the extended use of profanity. The substance and delivery by each was completely unique, but none of them would have had an act at all if it weren't deluged with the chronic use of four-letter words. This was acceptable for the L.A. adult crowd, and seemed to fly at the first couple of shows, despite one resort entertainment director boycotting the early show, insisting they not go on stage until after 10:00 p.m.

The problems began when nobody screened the crowd in Keystone, and the first of our foul-mouthed standups perpetrated his obscenities onto an American Martyrs Catholic Church young adolescent retreat group. The show came to a screeching halt, and not only were we not asked back, the resort spread the word throughout the mountain communities, and Michael's dream of being the Don King of comedy was squashed.

Back in Phoenix, still on indefinite sabbatical from ASU, I was facing once again what to do with my life. Michael became increasingly difficult to live with. He was going through tough financial times, and harbored deep embarrassment about his failed business pursuit. It was evident our relationship was rapidly deteriorating when he began insulting me at every available opportunity. During happier times, his quick wit had always been an asset. Once he allowed the self-inflicted pressure and disappointment to rule his life, his clever tongue bordered on abusive.

When we went out for dinner, I carried a bag with my running shoes just in case I had to jog home from the restaurant. He'd fire some derogatory comment at me, and halfway between the salad and main entree I'd go to the bathroom and never come back. He'd spend hours looking for me until he finally clued in that I had left. After a few occurrences, I can only assume he expected me to leave. It's funny how we subconsciously push people out of our lives, even when we think we want to be with them.

Most people are lucky if they have one person, other than their mother, that they know beyond any hesitation or doubt they can count on. In the nine years I spent in Arizona, I met three women I instinctively knew would be unconditional friends for life.

Kathy was one of my roommates at the townhouse during college. We worked at the Scottsdale bar, and pretty much did everything together. We were exercise addicts and loved spending all our hard-earned tip money incessantly shopping for the next trendy ensemble to wear out clubbing on our only night off during the week. Since we worked in the hottest club in town, it was hard to make a case to go anywhere else on our Monday nights. We knew everyone, and could get free drinks, and we both liked flirting with a couple of cute male bartenders that we were not privy to working with. I ended up dating both of them over the course of the next year, while Kath opted for a few of our regular customers.

In 1984, Toyota manufactured a brand-new design for the sporty Celica. Kathy had bought her first new car. It was metallic navy blue with all the necessary perks: sunroof, AM/FM cassette player, power everything, top-of-the-line chrome wheels. It only had twenty-two miles on it before it would become our new girls-night-out limousine. We had been carting around town in my two-seater Fiat Spyder, commonly known as Fix-It-Again-Tony, so the Celica was a welcome improvement. One Monday night we valeted the car as usual in front of our club. After a long night of drinking and dancing, we exited the club and waited patiently at the curb for her car to be pulled up. We sported a healthy buzz, and Kathy was cracking jokes to all the other patrons as we waited for what seemed to be an unusually long time. Finally, the valet whipped into the space in front of us, jumped out of the car, and held the door open for us to get in.

"Is he kidding?" Kathy's first response. We both stared in disbelief as the valet stood waiting for his tip next to this vehicle that had been driven off the new car lot earlier that day, and now had two flat tires and a bent antenna that appeared to have scratched the paint along the entire driver's side. She looked at me, smiled and said jokingly, "It wasn't like that when we came in here, right?"

We laughed about how idiotic the valet guy was. I mean did he not notice that something was wrong as he drove on the flat tires for a mile, or did he really think we were so drunk that we wouldn't notice the noise, the off balance, and the severe pull to the left? We never did figure it out, and the club paid for all the damage and then some. That story always stayed fresh in my memory because Kath was so calm and cool, and found the humor in an otherwise dismal situation. She remains one of my closest friends to this day.

Trina and I met a year later while working in another nightclub. I had advanced my skills in the service industry, and was now bartending. She was a couple years older than I, and married. I don't know if it was her Australian accent, her bold personality, or the uninhibited way she carried herself that made us click right away. Her husband was the DJ at this popular Phoenix club, and would play whatever we wanted to hear all night.

I'd practice dance moves behind the bar, and she'd reciprocate in the waitress station. It never seemed like work—waiting on the Phoenix Suns basketball players, listening to great music, making a ton of money while hanging out with my good friends, but somehow the club owners deemed us two of the hardest-working employees there. I outpoured most of the bartenders, and would lap the bar so many times, I'd have to wring out my soaked socks at the end of the night. She was waitress-extraordinaire, and a cocktail hustler. We found common ground as go-getters in our club life, but soon realized we were both filling voids.

One late night over super birds at Denny's, Trina and I discussed the possibility that we were not reaching our full potentials. She wanted to start a family soon, and needed a more stable career. I was still playing the waiting game to get back into ASU, and it was going to be at least another year. I could only make up my deficiencies during the summer sessions.

Trina had done some research on freelance careers that pay a lot, and found a local trade school that offered accredited courses in court reporting and paralegal studies. My knowledge of paralegals was null, but from what she said, "They can do the same thing lawyers do except represent a client in court."

That didn't sound right to me, but I was all about cutting corners to get to where I needed to be, and it was about that time to crack down and get serious about life. Within a week we were both enrolled at the American Institute, and I was back on track scholastically. It felt good.

I graduated with a 4.0 ("In your face, Baldy!"), and an American Bar Association paralegal certificate, proving I did possess the ability to focus my intellectual energy in a positive direction. During the year at the Institute, Trina's husband haphazardly discovered a recording device that he then patented, and its sale took off like brush fires in Tucson. Subsequently, she quit, got pregnant, and moved to Beverly Hills, leaving me at the Institute friendless, unsupported, and surrounded by a bunch of wannabe legal gurus, who started each day with a what-are-we-going-to-learn-today pep rally. Under the circumstances, I was exceptionally proud of myself on graduation day.

The director of the career placement department at the Institute failed to adequately inform us that the really good jobs in the paralegal field, which was rapidly gaining respect in the legal community, required a certificate *and* a four-year college degree. No accident I'm sure. Trade school recruiters have a way of painting an elaborate picture of what your life is likely to be like after you obtain the "highly sought-after skills that are only offered by our faculty, for a nominal fee, when you consider the big picture, which can easily be deferred with government financial aid if you sign right here." Then tap the school-monogrammed pen on the dotted line.

The post-graduation emotional crash that occurred after spending four thousand dollars and a year of sweat equity only to hear the news that I was not marketable in the work field I had spent tiresome hours learning about, would have sent a weaker person searching for a room at the local asylum. However, for me, it prompted the equally insane, earlier-mentioned visit to the ASU Dean's office, and another year of collegiate discipline. Lesson for all you college-bound hopefuls: *Go to class!* You'll have plenty of time to get drunk in your thirties!

I had been a self-sufficient child and teenager. I spread my time evenly between athletics, friends, family, and academics (in that order), which undoubtedly accounted for my lengthy stay at college. When I finally got my bachelor's degree, it was like being released from prison. The long-awaited goal of getting out was now upon me. I stepped outside the gates, looked down the empty road that lay ahead, and said to myself, "I got to get a job. But I'm taking a vacation first!"

The phone conversation with my closest and most reliable girlfriend, Liza, requesting her companionship on a covert rendezvous to the East Coast went something like this:

"Hey, what do you got going this weekend?" I said with a hopeful tone.

"A bunch of work I really don't want to do. Why?"

"I need you as an alibi. Remember those guys that came into the bar last week? The ones from New York?"

"Yesssss." She replied as if she were my mother.

"Well, I kind of had this great chemistry with one of them. We've been talking on the phone a lot, and he wants me to come to New Jersey and see him this weekend?" She'd heard me make a case for cheating on my boy-friend before, and I could sense her disapproval.

"I don't have the funds nor the patience to fly across the country and babysit the hotel phone so I can deceive your boyfriend about your where-abouts!" she said harshly.

"All expenses paid, you can hang with us and his friends, and I'll 'fess up to needing a separation from Glenn?" I begged.

"Fine. But if you pull a Julie[1] on me, I'm out of there! Pick me up early, I don't like rushing to the airport. 'Bye." She hung up on me like I was one

---

[1] Pulling a Julie meant ditching your girlfriend to be with a guy, and leaving her with his idiot, ugly friend, who without any invitation globs all over you all night, forcing you to swat off his advances until she's done copulating with the cute guy. Named after our flight attendant friend. (Need I say more?)

of her grunt workers who jump at her every beck and call. Which I did on that occasion.

Liza and I had known each other for a few years at that time. I always referred to her as the ultimate statistic. She had gotten pregnant the first time she had sex, and married the Jehovah's Witness boyfriend that she hardly knew. They toughed it out for two years, but she quickly realized Bible groups three times a day wasn't for her, and became a single mom at twenty-one.

She and I are a lot alike, yet complete opposites. It's what's made our friendship last so long. She's meticulously clean and organized. I'm not. She's extremely focused, sets her sights on long-term goals, and has no problem sticking to them, however long it takes. I have no focus. She's more responsible than anyone I know. I believe the pregnancy was a result of faulty equipment.

It was particularly difficult for her to deal with the cards she was dealt, becoming a parent so young. However, her smart and aggressive personality, two of our more similar attributes, never allowed her to miss a beat. She finished school, got a master's degree, became a corporate executive for a Fortune 500 company, and now barks out orders to six hundred blue collars that report to her.

The trip was important for two reasons. First, it functioned as an example of what I was willing to do to have a passionate encounter with someone I hardly knew. Once again, I had found myself in an unfulfilling relationship with a really great guy, but was missing the necessary chemistry to keep me faithful. By the time I turned thirty, I learned it was better to leave the relationship at the first sign of loss or lack of passion, than to risk compromising the friendship entirely. It was a long and painful journey for that life lesson.

Secondly, on our flight from Phoenix to Newark, I met a man that would soon after become my boss at my first corporate job. It was seven o'clock in the morning, and the plane was near empty. Liza and I sat in the far back section of the 757 so as to spread out and not be bothered. As if the completely vacant midsection wasn't enough room. The flight attendant wobbled her way back toward us with a tray full of Bloody Marys.

"These are from the gentlemen in first class," she said with an annoyed tone for being treated like a cheap cocktail waitress.

"Right on." Liza gulped one down quickly, then replaced a full one with the empty one on her tray. "Things are looking up already," she said between swigs.

"Great, now we have to entertain these numbnuts for the next four hours," I complained, as the two men from first class teetered their way down the narrow aisle, sporting dorky smiles.

"We don't have to talk to them. It's their problem if they think they can buy conversation with cocktails," Liza uttered snidely, then snuggled into the seat, and buried her head in a blanket.

Liza has no problem accepting drinks or dinner invites from men she has no intention of going any further with. I, on the other hand, feel sorry for them, knowing that somehow men are under the impression that they have nothing to lose by asking an attractive woman out. I mean, all they can say is "No," right? Wrong! A woman can destroy a man's self-confidence beyond repair with a single blunt statement. I'd seen Liza do it many times, and couldn't bear the thought of these forty-something, obviously unhappily married corporate suits losing the only grain of self-esteem they may have had left by plopping down in our row and addressing her with a what's-your-name-cutie pick-up line. I spared them her wrath, met them halfway, and escorted them to another row, apologizing for my sleeping friend.

My belief that all people you encounter have a purpose in your life had not yet been edged in stone. Although there are no coincidences, we still have free will, and sometimes don't take the Universe up on the opportunities that are right in front of us. I'm thankful I did act on the chance meeting I had that day on the airplane.

2

The Real Job

It's six-thirty. Monday morning. My first day of work at the prestigious Los Angeles law firm that I've recently been transferred to is only a shower away. "Get up!" I yell at myself telepathically. I hear the alarm, yet I'm not moving. My head hurts as I squint my eyes open to identify the creature staring at me. A fluffy white rabbit curiously chomps on a pellet-like food item that resembles what it will look like later. Ok, it's all coming back to me now. My roommate appears in the doorway.

"It's 6:30. Good luck." She rounds up the three cats and two rabbits that have enjoyed their nocturnal existence at my expense, and closes her bedroom door.

I crash to the floor, forgetting the couch is my bed. Whose idea was it to go partying on the Sunday night before starting a new job? There's got to be someone to blame for this. Anyone? Anyone? I *had* to move to L.A. on a pro-beach-volleyball weekend!

"Hi, this is Alex Parker from the Phoenix legal office. I had some trouble on the move over here, and got in late last night. I'm not feeling well…and…and…would it be all right if I started tomorrow?"

Only I would call in sick on my first day of work. What were they going to do, fire me? They needed me. I was the only one that had knowledge of the early stages of litigation support work that had been done on the multi-billion-dollar antitrust lawsuit I had worked on for the past two years.

When I was in paralegal school, I never envisioned being a high-priced paper pusher, neck deep in documents, held hostage in the war room (the term given to the room that housed every piece of paper gathered for the case throughout years of litigation). I saw myself sitting behind some young attractive attorney in a courtroom, feeding him the smoking-gun piece of evidence he needed to get a conviction against a murderous defendant. Then we'd go out for drinks that might or might not lead to a celebratory roll in the sack, and I would get a raise and promotion. Basically the plot line for every episode of Ally McBeal.

When I first took the job in Phoenix, it was supposed to be part time and last only a few months. Two years later I'm in L.A. working for a top-ten law firm, schlepping documents, and wondering, *How did I get here? This was not what I wanted to do with my life.*

L.A. did offer a nice change from Phoenix. After nine summers in the desert, I'd had enough of burning my butt on car seats, and not being able go outside four months a year. The whole dry heat thing is no consolation, unless you're a fan of oven life. Southern California indisputably has the best weather of any region of the country, and there's something to be said about being in the center ring of the entertainment industry. The vibe of new trends developing, and the air of moviemaking are like contagious doses of the euphoric energy creative dreamers thrive on.

I moved in with two girlfriends from high school that lived near the beach, and slept in the barnyard of their two-bedroom apartment for three months before securing my own place. Anyone who lives in L.A. will tell you that it's imperative to have a free place to stay before deciding where to live. It's the most vast city in America, and can be quite intimidating if you're on your own.

"Morning. Morning. Good Morning. Nice Day." My usual greetings as I drop my briefcase in the cubicle, and make my way to the employee lounge for that fifth cup of coffee.

I never drank coffee until I started this job. It's the unwritten rule of nine-to-fivers: coffee on the hour of every hour, and a handful of hard candy from the receptionist's desk every time you pass by. The jovial phone answerer has placed the multi-colored cavity-causers in a dish that was probably somebody's grandmother's collectable, found at a neighborhood garage sale, and now functions as the reason to stop and socialize briefly with other bored paper pushers.

"How's the coding of those tedious technical docs going?" a fellow legal assistant asks.

"Swell, I only have 100,000 more to do," I say honestly, with a slight hint of sarcasm. You never know who really likes her job, and who pretends to dislike it as much as you do to give you a false sense of camaraderie, then backstabs you and tells HR you're bad for morale.

"You know, up on the forty-eighth floor we have support staff that does all that menial computer coding work for us. You shouldn't have to do it. You're a professional." Did she just insult me? "If I were you, I'd have a sit-down with Mr. Weiss, and give him a piece of your mind."

The whole job sucks, whether you read documents all day or scan key words of a document and input them into a computer! What the hell's the difference?

"Yes, I was thinking my time might be better spent organizing and labeling the boxes of documents in the war room for the thousandth time. I think I'll go do that right now. Thanks for the pep talk." I pop a piece of candy in my mouth and walk away, muttering under my breath, "Get a life." I'm not sure if I mean me or her, but somebody needs one here.

Alan is a young, fresh-out-of-law-school kiss-ass attorney, and my immediate supervisor. He's twenty-five, and on the fastest track to becoming the youngest partner the firm has ever had.

"Alex, I need you to pull these boxes of documents." He hands me a handwritten list two pages long. "Review them for case-relevant issues, then reorganize them by author, make twelve copies, and have them delivered to my office by eight o'clock tonight."

"Um…Alan, it's two o'clock. It's not possible to complete that task in six hours, and I was hoping to get home by seven tonight, since I've been putting in thirteen hour days…" He's walking away as I'm talking. Hello, I'm in midsentence over here!

There's something about newly obtaining a Juris Doctorate degree that gives one the power and balls to ignore the needs of the little people, bellow out orders to as many of them as you can, then scurry off, knowing you've delegated all the work put on you by the older JD holders and can now escape to the gym.

I head into the war room where I've set up a computer desk in the corner, entirely barricaded by tall stacks of boxes. This is my sanctuary. My hiding place. If I stay visible out there, someone will give me more work. Alan will forget he gave me that assignment, and I know after much trial and error, that if I actually do what he asked me to do, the documents will sit in his office for a month, then his secretary will toss them in the recycle bin. Of course, the $1,000 of copying costs will be billed to the client and, fairly soon after that, another attorney will make the same request, if he hasn't already, and the new copies will sit in *his* office for a month. It's a vicious cycle surrounding corporate litigation. The client gets reamed over and over again for duplicate efforts that didn't need to be done in the first place, and the attorneys that really have no purpose on the case at all, appear to be working hard for long hours so they can meet the competitive billable hours requirement.

Ok, let's see…She's A Star. Speed rating—86. Number of wins at this distance—4. Time since last raced—two months. Post position—5. I hit enter, and eagerly await my printout.

"Alex! Are you in here?" I jolt as Alan attempts to hurdle through the maze of strategically placed boxes.

"I'm back here…inputting data in the computer." I quickly change screens, and become aware of the look of panic that must be on my face. "What do you need?"

"Copies of these key docs. They haven't been Bates stamped yet, so you're gonna have to dig for them from memory." His knuckles appear over the top of my stack and drop a handwritten piece of paper into my hair.

"I need them ASAP. You have to work through lunch."

Dammit! I've spent half the morning configuring my trifectas and was almost done handicapping the pick-six. I need my lunch hour to get to Santa Anita to place the bets. I settle back into the cushy, high-back executive chair I stole from the managing partner's office while he was on his fourth vacation this quarter. My life sucks! I don't know what's more pathetic. The fact that I've become a salary junkie, and stay in this spirit-robbing, dead-end job, or that I've resorted to long-shot gambling as the only way out of it.

I taught myself how to handicap horses at Turf Paradise Racetrack in Phoenix. Michael used to take me there on "dates," then disappear with his betting buddies, and leave me to watch the races alone. I'd hang in the grandstand, bored to tears, sampling food from every concession counter I could get to while avoiding being accosted by the never clean or sober track residents who raced to the window, anxious to risk their Social Security checks. Not a lot of women spend their days at the track. The regulars assume you either must have some insider information, or you're looking to get picked up. I opted to be the former, bought the daily racing form, and spent many Saturday afternoons figuring out how to read it.

A year had gone by, and I'd finally succumbed to my existence as a professional legal assistant. I accepted that this was my life, and convinced myself I should be thankful I had the opportunity to work at a firm most aspiring corporate apprentices would kill for. I was twenty-eight, making sixty thousand dollars a year, and single. On the surface, it wasn't so bad. Inside, I was dying a slow death. Not only was the job sucking every ounce of enthusiasm I'd spent a lifetime building up, but I was getting comfortable spending twelve hours a day in the war room, completely cut off socially from all normal, human life forms.

Adding to my isolation was the apparent weight requirement for secretaries and staff workers at the firm. I didn't exactly fit it. I had been able to maintain a size four frame most of my adult life without much maintenance. I got lucky genetically, and had fairly good eating habits, with the exception of pizza and chocolate weaknesses. After years of various exercise programs, I had devised one to specifically target my life's motto: Maximum result, minimum effort.

The corpulent female support staff hated me, and it didn't help that my former boss made no attempt to hide his advances, labeling me the work bimbo who got special treatment. It was easier to hide out and keep to myself, than make friends with catty colleagues of whose motives I couldn't be sure. It's all part of the corporate faux-friends policy. No one is truly your friend at work.

I'd like to exercise bragging rights about not living my life with regrets. If I had to cite one, it would undeniably be having lost sight of my dreams and passion for performing, and taking no action to find it at that time in my life. I had become so depressed at the law firm, it never occurred to me that all I ever did was work and sleep.

"What are you gonna wear to the Christmas party?" Staci, one of our permanent temp workers, asks me during lunch in the service elevator one day.

"I'm not going."

"You have to go. It's practically mandatory. Weiss has been plugging it all week."

"I'm sure no one will notice if I'm not there. They don't even know our names down here." My usual cynical response coupled with the chronic cynical attitude.

The war room had become the war floor. The number of "important" documents to the case increased so rapidly, an entire floor had to be designated to house them. There wasn't any space available on the six floors allotted to the firm, so they rented an area of the basement that was under construction. When a lawyer issued a document request, we were like building rats, scurrying around searching for cheese in microscopic cubbyholes.

"Besides, the party is at six p.m., right after work. Intentionally timed so no one can go home and change clothes. They don't want to acknowledge life outside of this place. AND there's no alcohol. Wahoo!" I could talk freely with Staci. She wasn't a true corporate grunt. I had heard she was studying to be an actress.

"No champagne, wine, or anything?" she whines in disbelief. "Those cheapskates!"

"Liability. It's a law firm." I had an answer for everything.

Whoosh! A message has arrived in the vacuum-slide tunnel communications system originally installed for the maintenance men. It reminds me of the old days at the bank drive-through, pre-ATM machines, when you put your paperwork in the Thermos, closed it up, and watched as it got sucked into the tunnel that returned it to the teller you could see through the window. Apparently the firm didn't see the advantage of putting phone lines in for us, so this became the only means of communication, unless they wanted to travel forty-eight floors into the bowels of the building, which they never did.

"What is it?" Staci asks. I open it hesitantly and read.

"An answer to our prayers. Alan wants to take the support staff out for drinks after the party." Hmmm, maybe he's human after all.

Another of my favorite lines from *Stripes* occurs after the platoon gets caught at the mud wrestling bar, and receives their reprimand lecture from the commanding officer. John Candy speaks out to explain.

"We were on our way to the bingo parlor, down at the YMCA. Well…the instructions got all fouled up…and…I don't know, somehow we ended up—" He's cut off.

When friends ask me how Alan and I began our relationship, I always tell the story with that opening line. I should have forecasted the potential fraternization, but it had been so long since I entertained a thought about dating, I didn't see it coming. Having cocktails during the holiday season with a twenty-six-year-old cute, successful lawyer who showed a completely different side of himself when away from the higher-ups, coupled with my long bout of celibacy, seemed like an obvious combination for, at the bare minimum, an evening of passion that was desperately needed.

I'd spent many hours with Alan at work, but never paid attention to him. He was the person responsible for piling more paperwork on my desk every day. I tried hard not to make eye contact with him ever, since the longer he was in my presence the greater the chance he would delegate more work to me. I kept it short, simple, and professional at all times.

I was so consumed with my own dismal disposition, I hadn't noticed how miserable he was. At the second-year associate level, he was expected to work sixteen hours a day, and was held accountable by two of the firm's top partners. He had always wanted to be a lawyer, and strived for perfection and approval from his superiors. To us, he appeared to enjoy the work, and liked being challenged with as much of it as possible. We were all aware of his credentials: perfect LSAT score, Berkeley undergrad, top of his class UCLA law. Sure seemed like textbook overachiever to me. You'd never know he was struggling internally.

It was blissfully surprising to see him unleash that night after the party. We sang karaoke, went to four different bars, one in which we danced quite seductively together, then when everyone else left, grabbed a bite over coffee at an all-night diner in Hollywood. Around two a.m., he respectfully drove me to my car in the firm's parking structure, where I said my goodbyes, exited his SUV, and began digging in my purse for keys.

He waited as I frantically shuffled makeup, a day timer, my checkbook and wallet, and some female purse items that loosely occupy different compartments (such as the lonely, fossilized condom which always seems to flop out when searching for something in public).

I gave Alan the go-ahead to take off, embarrassed that I had to dump my purse out on the concrete. "I know I put them in here," I muttered, then shook the purse violently to locate the key-sounding noise I was sure

I could hear. Alan didn't leave, and watched as my panic grew into a frenzy. He leaned out of the car.

"Maybe you left them in the office?"

"I'm not an idiot! I know I put them in here!" I snapped while on my hands and knees raking through my stuff, looking quite idiotic.

"I'll run up and take a look just in case." He parked his car and ran up the stairs.

I proceeded to curse at my purse until it was clearly evident they were not in there, but I swear I could hear them. I've never lost keys. They're a priority item in my purse, and I'm not one of those women that loses things.

I sat on the hood of my Mitsubishi Eclipse wondering how I was going to get into my apartment to retrieve the only other set of keys I had. My mind drifted for a moment and I thought about my girlfriend Julie, the flight attendant, who was famous for losing her purse. When our girl group would get together, instead of the designated driver, we had the designated purse sitter. Julie is a petite woman who thinks she can drink anyone under the table, and will always take that challenge. She could be counted on to black out and, at some point during the night, disappear for a period of time in which she would "misplace" her purse.

One night on a layover in Phoenix, she came to see me while I was bartending at a large nightclub. She gave me her purse to hold behind the bar, acknowledging that "Somehow me and my purse seem to get separated when I go out drinking."

In my opinion, it was hardly a purse in the traditional use of the word. A single hotel room key, one tube of MAC lipstick, a comb, and a loose American Express card. My purse functions as a second apartment with all essential daily necessities, and occasionally a change of clothes if one digs deep enough. I babysat her makeshift handbag for a number of hours, and midway through the evening she asked for it to go primp in the bathroom. I wasn't concerned when I didn't see her for the next few hours. We never knew where she went or ended up during a possible blackout, but she always returned smiling and unaware she was ever missing. At last call, her head surfaced, barely making it over the top of the bar.

"This place is awesome! I had so much fun! I got to catch an early flight tomorrow morning. Can I get my purse?" Famous last words.

Julie debated that it hadn't been lost, but couldn't explain how it had somehow made its way into the hands of a lucky thief, who went to her hotel room, packed all her belongings, including $14,000 worth of clothes and shoes, passport, airline identification, and every morsel of lingering possessions lying around, then confidently walked out of the hotel with her suitcases.

Recalling the story gave me a trace amount of appreciation when Alan exited the stairwell empty-handed. He felt bad for not being able to save the day, and I sensed he'd needed to do that. Nonetheless, he was helpful, and his actions were genuine and selfless. If he had an ulterior motive that night, I didn't see it.

We arrived at my apartment around three a.m., and found out the hard way my dwelling was break-in-proof. I had done a thorough job of securing windows, doors, and all other crevices that might attract a burglar, since my ten-speed was stolen out of the garage my first night there.

After unsuccessfully trying to push my body through a six-inch open window blocked with a thick board and metal secures, I unstuck my head and made a suggestion.

"Why don't you drop me at a hotel, and I'll deal with this tomorrow. I'm sure you have better places to be," I said exasperated at the emotional highs and lows that had taken place that night.

"Actually I don't. Why don't we get two rooms, and I'll drive you back to the parking structure in the morning, and we'll call Triple-A?" he countered.

We got to Hotel Hermosa at close to four a.m. They were hosting a Christmas party for a large corporation that weekend, and only had one room available.

"We'll take it." And so it began.

Dating a co-worker made life at the firm a little more interesting over the next year. We played the amusing game of don't-let-anyone-know-we're-going-out for as long as we could, and denied it even when the queen gossipers caught us making out in the war room. Alan made the forty-eight-floor descent regularly now that we were an item.

We really didn't care if people knew. I mean it's not like there was a policy that said we couldn't date. For the most part, we kept things professional, and Alan continued to pile paperwork on my desk higher than before. I suspect he was overcompensating to make sure the staff wouldn't think he was playing favorites, which they did when word first got out. After six months, they realized we were serious about each other, supported our relationship, and teased us about how cute we looked together. All was warm and fuzzy for a while until Mr. Weiss, Alan's supervising attorney, got wind of it.

Weiss was a short, heavy-set workaholic who thought anyone putting in fewer than eighty hours a week was a worthless waste of space. He openly illustrated his opinions of colleagues that fell into relationships or developed hobbies and interests that took their focus off work. This was taboo, and totally unacceptable in his book.

His lack of support for our relationship was certainly understandable. I had worked for his seven-million-dollar-a-year client prior to being transferred to the firm. I had direct links to the people paying the bills on this case. From an attorney's standpoint, it's your worst nightmare to have a representative of the client on site at the firm patrolling the progress of the litigation. Perhaps that had something to do with my office being in the basement?

The firm had committed a number of legal blunders throughout the discovery phase of the case. I had specific knowledge of the biggest, most costly one. Discovery is the process in which both sides allow each other to review the potential evidence that will ultimately be used at trial. This includes deposing witnesses and reviewing documents that may reveal the true nature of whatever allegations are being made.

Corporate litigation is all about documents, and it's common practice to warehouse the opposing side with so much crap that they might miss the real evidence of a crime. This was illustrated perfectly in the Gene Hackman film, *Class Action*. He and his daughter, played by Mary Elizabeth Mastrantonio, were lawyers on opposite sides.

The warehouse effect is an anticipated strategy and is widely practiced, but the rules of discovery are extremely clear on the issue of document production. They MUST be produced in their normal course of business. Translation: you cannot pull out the most damaging pieces of evidence, and hide them in a literal warehouse of irrelevant documents hoping they won't be found.

Not only did the firm engage in this deception, but Alan was the lawyer ordered to give the support staff the go-ahead to participate in this practice, and I was the one that physically dispersed the documents into ancient archived boxes of documents that had no bearing on the issues of the case whatsoever.

As we neared closer to the trial date, shit started hitting the fan. The firm had been sanctioned fifty thousand dollars for the "accidental misplacement" of these key documents, and the client was finally cluing-in about the "incident." I kept quiet like a good corporate puppy, but there were a lot of questions and finger-pointing as to who was responsible for such a colossal *snafu*.

Everyone at the firm knew that the *error* made during document production provided us with a year's worth of work in order to convince the opposing side that the key docs were in fact produced in their normal course of business. We trudged through boxes and more boxes of documents for months. Reorganizing, re-labeling, trying to piece the puzzle together and avoid more court sanctions. The firm employed additional support staff, and we worked around the clock for what seemed to be the longest, most tedious year of my life. Had the *impropriety* not occurred, the case could have gone to trial a year earlier, saving the client roughly three to four million dollars in legal fees. A substantial *faux pas*, to say the least.

I'm not sure if the client ever fully knew the effect of the firm's incompetence. Weiss was blessed with the ability to keep the focus off himself, and the client was obviously preoccupied with other matters. Six billion dollars was apparently not important enough to merit an investigation. To the client's defense, they had changed general counsels midway through the case, and the new man in charge was kept in the dark by the talented Mr. Weiss and the other in-house attorneys who shared responsibility in the F-up.

By the time the case finally made it to trial, Alan and I were well into our third year together. The additional workload had made it nearly impossible for us to have any type of meaningful relationship outside of the firm. I had practically moved into the war room, and Alan spent more nights sleeping on the floor of his office than in our bed. Weiss had tried everything he could to break us up, fearing the more time Alan and I spent together, the more likely we might decide to retaliate against him, and share what we knew with his precious multi-million-dollar client. He threatened Alan's job if he didn't stop seeing me, but Alan stayed strong and acted as if it wasn't affecting him, but I knew it was.

There was nothing Weiss could do about it, and we now had sufficient cause for a wrongful termination or harassment case if he acted on his threats. That gave me a little peace during my eighty-hour work weeks.

As time went by, it became increasingly ugly, not that it had ever been pretty, going to work every day. Had I wanted to advance my legal career, I'd have taken the appropriate steps to assure Weiss that I had no interest in being a whistle blower, and proudly continued with my document piles. But the fact was, I had reached the deepest, darkest, most dispassionate existence I had ever known, and couldn't see the light to get out. I had no interest in anything.

One day I sat in the cold, concrete, solitary confining war room I had been sentenced to, and reflected on my life. I had placed a mirror over some peeling drywall to force myself to take a look once in a while.

"I look old." I examined my fine lines and hair roots. "I'm wasting my life here." My eyes teared up, and I quickly looked away. The person who said, "Don't ever underestimate the power of denial" knew what I was feeling at that moment. I didn't want to face what I had allowed to happen to my life. *I* didn't really do this, did I?

Alan was out of town, and my depression reached an all-time high. We had become roommates that brushed shoulders as we came in and out of the front door, and I was once again realizing I was in a dead-end relationship. His career as a corporate litigator would always be exactly as it had been for the last three years. I mean, look at Weiss and the other partners. They had no lives. There was no emphasis on family or friends or any activities outside of the firm. I couldn't take it anymore. My whole life, I had refused to settle for anything less than what I wanted. How could I have let this happen? Where did my dreams go? What did I want to do with my life?

I couldn't answer any of those questions, so I flopped down on the pile of sleeping bags on the floor and began to cry. I must have slept for some time, when I was awakened by Staci, who was violently shaking me, assuming I had passed out from boredom.

"Alex! Are you Ok? Wake up!" she screamed in my ear.

"No. I'm not Ok. I hate my life." I stood up. Rubbed my eyes. "What time is it?"

"Eight o'clock. Everyone's gone." She whipped out a pizza. "I brought dinner."

I grabbed a piece of pepperoni, and shoved the dangling greasy cheese in my mouth. Eating was one of the few luxuries I had left.

Staci sat at her desk, one of those junior high chair-desks that are hooked together. She opened her magazine and read, ignoring my earlier life-hating statement.

"*Drama-Logue*? What's that?" I asked curiously.

"It's an actor's trade mag. *The* actor's trade. All the good ads for non-union parts are in here. It's a must-have for aspiring actresses."

"Did you always want to be an actress?" I asked, seeking some validation for not knowing my life's direction.

"Yeah, since I was a kid. As long as I can remember I wanted to be someone else. I used to dress up and do funny voices and accents. What better place to do that than in the movies, right?" She laughed with pizza sauce in her teeth. "I mean, it's so cool being on the set. And you get to meet stars. And...I don't know, we're in L.A. Isn't that why everyone comes here?" Looking for her own validation?

"What stars have you met?" I asked, intrigued by her innocence.

"Well, none officially, but I almost got run over by Goldie Hawn." Does that count? "She was leaving the Paramount lot, gabbing with security, and her car rolled forward, almost hitting me," she recounted proudly.

"What were you doing there?"

"Oh, that's a whole 'nother story. Mostly I was dodging advances from Steven Seagal. He hits on all the extras that work on his movies. It's well known in the industry."

"So you met Steven Seagal?" I drew that conclusion for her.

"Not really. He comes out to the food line...we have to eat separate from the stars...walks down eyeing each one of us up and down, then sends his people out to try and get you to go to his trailer. They make you think you'll get a part if you do."

"You didn't fall for that?" I said, surprised.

"No way. The casting couch is the oldest trick in the book. If you lay it down for them, you're sure to *not* get a part. There's plenty of stupid girls that do it anyway."

"Wow, sounds like the same politics that go on here." We laughed and finished our pizza. It was the first time I had laughed in a long time.

Staci was a cute girl with a good heart. I admired her for pursuing at least what she thought was her passion. I didn't know anything about the entertainment business, only that the strong survived. She was young, timid, and naive, and probably too nice to make it in that industry, but I wasn't about to kill her dream. At least she wasn't settling for this heinous job as her whole life!

"I'm doing a movie this weekend," she said excitedly. "I get to play a phone sex operator that gets slashed by a psycho-crazed doctor."

"Cool," I said genuinely. "Is it for video?" I assumed that plot line wasn't going to be made by the studios.

"Yeah, actually it is. An overseas release. They buy anything made in the U.S." Who said I knew nothing about the biz.

"You should come with me! The director is a friend of mine, and I'm sure you could you be an extra. Or maybe he'd even throw you a part!"

"Oh…no, I have to work this weekend, then go home and practice my usual sulk and self-loathing. But thanks anyway."

"Alex, I'm serious. You got to snap out of it! There is life outside this place. How are you ever going to find out what you want to do if you don't get outta here?" She'd been paying much more attention than I thought.

"This job is just a job…the *real job* that you have to have until your dreams can pay the bills," she explained. "I can't call myself an actress until I'm supporting myself from acting work. But if I let this place consume me, I'll never get there, and it's all for nothin'." I find myself listening intensely to the young, wise, naive one.

"I knew the first time I met you this job wasn't for you. You're stiff—I mean, stifled here. I can see it. Get out. Do something different. The work is still gonna be here on Monday. What do ya' say?" She makes a good argument.

"You should be a lawyer." I contemplated this proposition. Why couldn't I do it? Nobody would know if I was here or not. It might be fun. Remember that word? F-u-n.

"Ok. I'll go. But I'm not taking my clothes off," I said with a slight twinkle in my tone.

Dr. Phil, the popular family therapist on TV, speaks of life as being all about five or six defining moments that take place over the years. Moments that change you forever. Events that evolve your soul, and you're never the same because of them. That weekend working on *Call Waiting, Call Deadly* was one of my defining moments.

The production was cheap. The cast was cheesy. The food was lame, and the story was weak. It was a great weekend. PAs, ADs, the UPM, the first AC—there was something cool about working with people referred to as acronyms. Maybe it was because I had finally ventured out and done something a little crazy like I used to, or perhaps it was no coincidence that I ended up there. All I knew was that no one on this B-movie production had as much fun as I did. It was new, exciting, and no matter how corny the plot line, a chance to perform again.

Staci's director friend liked my look and did *throw* me a part…with clothes. All the other girls had some kind of nudity in their scenes; after all, they do have to sell the movie. I felt special that I got to deliver my lines fully dressed. Of course I was dressed in a bear suit—it was some kind of weird dream sequence—but I didn't care. Furry arms and legs, three hours in the makeup chair, and I was on my way to stardom!

Ok, so it wasn't exactly the role of a lifetime, but just being there around actors that were so dedicated to their craft that they took *this* job, inspired me and gave me hope. Had I found the performance outlet that was missing from my life for so long? I knew nothing about acting, but the thought of starting over with a new dream that included my passion to entertain was so exhilarating I could hardly contain myself. Why didn't I think of this before? My blood boiled. My stomach churned. Adrenaline ran through my veins like oat bran in young bowels. This was it! I was back!

The following Monday morning I took my time getting to work. Slept in an extra half-hour. Dressed slowly, trying to decide what outfit would violate the ridiculously conservative dress code the most. I can't believe I was shopping at Casual Corner in my twenties. The usual traffic jam on the I-10 heading into downtown L.A. didn't bother me. I inched toward the high-rises, staying close to the bumper in front of me that read: *I owe, I owe. Off to work I go*. I smiled from ear to ear.

In the packed elevator going up to the forty-eighth floor, one of the suits asked me for the time. I raised my wrist, spilled coffee on my tank top, and dropped my briefcase, triggering its opening. Weiss' trial briefs sprawled out on the floor. I didn't flinch. We reached forty-eight. The door opened. Mr. Weiss and the other partners exited a conference room just as the elevator group trampled his briefs on their way out. He glared at the dirty footprints, then gave me a look that prior to this past weekend would have scared me. I daydreamed for a second and thought about being in that bear costume doing backflips on the bed. It made me laugh and forget where I was.

"Ms. Parker! Good of you to join us this morning!" He eyed my outfit disapprovingly. "Pick up that mess, and report to my office…ASAP!" His scream brought me back.

Staci breezed by, winked, and whispered, "Mondays are good days to quit."

"Indeed."

I can't remember exactly what was said when I got to Weiss' office. There was a lot of loud yelling and belligerent comments. I stared out the window at the breathtaking view of the City of Angels, and thought about the myriad of opportunities that were in front of me. What a beautiful day it was. I smiled during his entire reprimand, which irked him so badly all the blood rushed to his face, and I thought he might have an aneurysm. Instead he involuntarily burped, and I couldn't help but to burst out laughing. At that moment, I figured if I didn't get out of there quickly, he was seriously going to have a heart attack, and I would have to live with the guilt for the rest of my life. I contemplated whether that would be so bad, while he continued the verbal assault.

"Mr. Weiss?" He kept yelling. "I quit!" With that, I threw the briefs on his desk and confidently walked down the hall, got into the elevator, and left a stunned staff blank-faced and open-mouthed. No one had ever left Weiss' team willingly. I guess you either got fired or died a slow and painful death. I heard later that he followed me, and cursed the elevator door as it descended…all forty-eight floors.

3

The Awakening

"Whenever you're ready, uh…Alex, we'd like you to deliver the lines to the empty chair. Imagine the Rod character is sitting there…and if you could cry, that would be great."

My eyes slowly panned across the panel of casting assistants that sat around the long table full of pictures and resumes. They spoke to me while staring at my image on a video screen, as if I wasn't standing five feet from them. Was I the only one that thought this was an awkward request? You'd think for fifty bucks a class they would have taught crying on cue at the acting workshop I'd been taking for the past few months. I took a deep breath, and counted to ten. That's what I learned for five hundred bucks.

"I have some bad news, Rod." I leaned in closer to the vacant chair. "She's dead. They did everything they could. She was such a…fighter." Tears! I need tears! Think about something sad! "She managed to utter a few words before she…passed. She said, 'Tell Rod I will love him into eternity.' Oh Rod, I'm so sorry!" I faked my blubbering. Wait a minute, my face is wet! Tears are actually coming out. I'm doing this. I threw myself into an elaborate embrace with…no one and continued.

"If you need anything…and I mean anything, I'm here for you. I'm here for you." I repeat that line for a more dramatic ending, then pause in the moment staring at…no one, wipe the tears from my cheek, and face the casting director. "Scene."

"Great. Well done," he says without looking up from my embellished resume of bogus acting credits. "Would you be open to playing a different part?" he asks curiously.

"Yeah, sure...I guess. I mean, you guys are the casting professionals, if you see me in a different role, who am I to question—" He cuts me off.

"Here, look this over. If you're interested, call the receptionist and schedule another audition." He hands me a set of audition materials (sides), and waves me out.

"Oh, Ok. It was nice meeting everyone, and I'll see you soon." I crash into another girl coming in as I exit walking backward.

Well, that was interesting. I walk briskly through the parking lot feeling proud of my performance, and the progress I was making in the industry. This was the most sophisticated audition I'd been on yet. They even had an office...with all the elements of a real production company. Much better than last week when I followed Thomas Guide coordinates to a shady neighborhood in North Hollywood, and arrived at a creepy, shack-like house with the word *Casting* posted outside the door on a piece of paper. I caught a glimpse of the character inside slobbering over girls' pictures and resumes, and decided to take a pass on auditioning to be the next slain, sexually assaulted victim in some psychopath's sick fantasy.

The non-union work of the entertainment industry sucks! Any joker out there can put an ad in the *Drama-Logue* as if he's making a film, and girls will send pictures and resumes with phone numbers and sometimes their addresses on them. These ads aren't regulated, and the trade mags can only do so much to verify that they are legitimate. You have to go on these auditions to try to get a part in which you'll work for free in order to obtain videotape of yourself, so you can then go on an endless journey seeking an agent or manager that will actually promote your work, and not try to have sex with you!

I reach my car and flip through the sides they gave me for the new part. "You've got to be kidding me!" I scream out loud, then frantically page through the entire scene, hoping this was some kind of mistake.

Surely after the heart-wrenching performance I gave with no motivational help whatsoever, they can't possibly want me to be the...the...masturbation girl...who doesn't even have any lines, unless you count the moaning! This is an outrage! I toss the sides in the trash, get in my car, and slump over the steering wheel. Did I really expect this to be easy? Yes! Most of my life things came easy for me. I've always been lucky.

Been at the right place at the right time. Why should launching an acting career from scratch be any different? I lift up my head and look in the rearview mirror. This may take a bit more time than originally forecasted. Masturbation girl…ugh!

Since leaving the firm, my whole life has changed. It's harder in different ways, but so much easier in most. It's never work when you're doing what you love to do. I took an apartment walking distance from the Beverly Center in West Hollywood. I'm in the thick of it. It's awesome. Did I just say awesome?

During the move, I was packing up my closet and came across the old purse I used when Alan and I first met. I tossed it in a box and heard a jingling sound. What is it with this purse? It taunts me. The ghost of the lost keys! I pulled it out of the box, and ripped through the layered lining so aggressively I shredded the Coach label in one yank. "Ahhh ha!" I shouted with great satisfaction.

The keys were there the whole time. Turns out the defiant purse had a mind of its own. It had created a secret tunnel in which it lured not only the unsuspecting keys, but also nine tubes of lipstick that I spent many hours searching for, thinking I had Alzheimer's. Later that day, I gave the purse a proper burial, hoisting it off the Venice Beach pier next to a group of West L.A. crazies, and took my sanity back.

Despite the daily hurdles of the Hollywood pavement-pounding relay, I was loving my life. Just the idea of working toward a goal that many try and few succeed at was enough to keep me going every day. I liked the challenge, and learning about the business of acting was interesting in and of itself. Artists forget that creative talent alone isn't enough to make it in this industry. You have to be business savvy, and possess basic knowledge of the moneymaking side of entertainment, or you'll never get the exposure needed to succeed.

There are a lot of scams out there, and con artists that prey on young starlets are in more abundance than out-of-work actors. They know what the books say about the necessary tools for a successful acting career, and they devise their scams accordingly. Acting classes, casting director workshops, photography scams, *modeling jobs*—anything indicating a way to cut corners and reach the professional decision makers is usually a red flag. Since I gained all my knowledge from trial and error, and error, and error, I found out quickly what to avoid, what was real, and generally the steps to take to get noticed.

The marketing of oneself in the entertainment biz is a costly investment, and my savings account most certainly reflected it. I had been lucky
enough to spend six months making the career adjustment without having
to work, but securing an income from acting jobs at this time seemed a
bleak prospect at best. It was time to get another real job.

L.A. has a bad reputation for service in its trendsetting, fast-lane restaurants. It's a unanimous opinion that one doesn't frequent a popular
eatery here because of the friendly, helpful, and cooperative behavior of
the person taking your order. Hollywood waiters and waitresses are some
of the most disgruntled employees of any work field. I'm not sure, but I
think they're automatically ruled out of the application process if attempting to purchase a weapon.

> "Have you ever been convicted of a felony, ma'am?"
> "No."
> "Ever had anyone obtain a restraining order against you?"
> "No."
> "Have you ever worked as a waitress in a restaurant in the
> greater Los Angeles area?"
> "I do the breakfast shift at Swingers, and once I filled in for
> a friend at BarFly."
> "I'm sorry. We can't sell you this weapon. Based on your
> responses, you've been classified as an uptight prima donna, an
> out-of-work actress, who will never make enough money to ef-
> fectively market yourself in the entertainment industry, thus
> rendering you a career waitress, ticking time bomb, and imme-
> diate threat to everyone around you." He smiles as he stamps
> the word denied on the application.

Trying to get a job as a waitress or bartender without having connections to the establishment you're seeking employment from is harder than
booking an acting job. Ninety-five percent of the 100,000 Screen Actors
Guild members in this city make less than five thousand dollars a year
doing acting work. Guess where they make the rest of their annual income? Walk into any bar or restaurant in West Hollywood, Beverly Hills,
Studio City, or Sherman Oaks and EVERYONE working there is an aspiring actor, writer, producer, director, model, or crew member. No matter

how unhappy they are about not fulfilling their career goals, they never, EVER give up their *real jobs*.

I had put in applications at every busy bar in town. My resume included eight years of bartending experience in clubs that varied from slow, lounge-like hotel hangouts to loud, crowded, dance-floor types. I had worked at sports bars and catered for private parties. There was no bartending work that I was not familiar with, and I had excellent references. But no one was hiring.

The thought of taking a legal temp position out of monetary need made me sick to my stomach, but I was running out of money. I knew it was going to be a long road before I might break into the closely guarded circle of entertainment professionals, and I was in it for the long haul. There was no turning back. I had to find a way to stay free during the day, and make enough money to live the way I was used to. I was too old to be a starving artist, and I was sure there was a bartending job out there for me somewhere.

I stumbled onto a place that I thought was a Polynesian restaurant. It had been there for twenty years, and I'd driven by it many times on my way to acting class. As I approached two huge Italian doormen holding back a few well-dressed businessmen behind a velvet rope, I began to think that they must have remodeled this place, and maybe it was a new, hip club no one knew about. The doorman paved a path for me and unlocked the rope without saying a word. I thought, *Ok, this is weird. He's not gonna card me? There's no cover charge. What's going on here?*

The place was dark, and I crashed into a black sheet draped from the ceiling to function as some kind of curtain put up so you couldn't see in from outside the door. I swept the curtain to one side and entered the club. Holy shit! My eyes hadn't adjusted yet, but obviously they were not serving Tiki Pomi Chicken with specials for seniors on Tuesdays. Ok...I was in a strip club. The first thing that came to mind was the time my old boyfriend suckered me by going to that place in Phoenix. I instinctively looked for the blond with the big boobs that waved to him that night. They were all blond with big boobs! I turned to leave, but my curiosity took over and I figured, what the hell, I'm here. I might as well check it out.

How do they dance in those shoes? I'd never seen heels so high. There must be special stores for exotic dancewear. Or do they go into Macy's, requesting a six-inch pencil-point stiletto, one that's sure to put you in a back brace later in life, and send the shoe salesman deep into the back room where they keep them with legal disclaimers that relieve the manufacturer from any liability incurred while wearing the shoes? Hmm, I'll have to check into that.

The stage girl, Porsche, demonstrated extraordinary agility maneuvering her body around the brass pole in the middle of the stage floor. I noticed my head was tilted almost upside down as I followed her moves to the music. A guy seated in front of me elbowed his buddy and said loudly, "When I die I want to reincarnate as a pole." They laughed as if he'd said something original.

The girl momentarily lifted her head in disgust, then continued with her act, crawling on her knees over to the guy. She licked her lips, pressed her boobs together and whipped her legs around into straddle position, knocking their drinks into their laps. She issued a feeble apology, and crawled to the next group. The two guys jumped up from the cold shower to the crotch and made a run for the bathroom. I caught eye contact with the smirking Porsche. She winked at me.

"Can I help you?" A tall, stern, and mysterious Italian man stood behind me, camouflaged by the club blackness.

"Oh…uhhh…I was just…walking by, and…no, I'm fine. I was just checking things out for a second, but I'm leaving now." I turned to leave.

"You with ABC?" he asked in a hostile, suspicious tone. I had no idea what he was taking about, and panicked thinking that in a few seconds an angry group of Mafia goons would appear from every dark corner of the room and escort me out. Then I remembered from my bar days that ABC refers to the liquor board. I guess I should stop wearing a suit and carrying my briefcase to bartending interviews.

"No, no. Um, I was just…looking for a bartending job. I thought this place was something else, and—"

"You any good?" he interrupted.

"Um, yeah. I'm really good."

"See that girl over there?" He indicated the bartender. "She's gettin' busted tonight." My eyes got bigger. "Been rippin' us off for months. Damn lucky my cousin Vito didn't catch her." I hated to think what might have happened if he did.

"That's terrible. Try to make an honest living…and…and…your staff rips you off." What was I saying?

"I'll give you a job, but if you steal from me, lady—" I cut him off that time.

"I would never do that. I'm a hard worker, and I'm always on time—"

"Go in the back and fill out paperwork. You can start tomorrow." He gave me a once-over, then gestured with his head for me to move it.

As I walked through the club eyeing professional men that looked like they could have worked in my old office gush over scantily clad dancers, I started the process of convincing myself I wanted this job. I muttered under my breath, and tried not to glimpse hands slipping where they shouldn't be going.

"It's not like I have to work here forever. And I can make a lot of money. It's all men. No women to give me quarter tips like the old days. This is a perfect job. Get in. Get out. Make money. Pursue my dreams. What difference does it make where I work? So it's a strip club, big deal. Might be fun. Maybe I'll meet somebody interesting."

"I think they're definitely real. I'm sure of it."

"As usual, you don't know what you're talking about. I remember her years ago at the Tamed Lion. She was completely flat chested, and now she's a double D or an E!"

"So she's a late bloomer."

Fat Joe and Henry, my most regular bar customers, engage in infantile squabble over the issue of whose boobs are real and whose are fake almost every night. I can't take it anymore.

"*You* are a prominent corporate attorney, and *you*, a software genius for Hughes. Have you nothing else to debate other than breast implants! What kind of lives are these?"

I slam down their eleventh round of drinks, and decide to give them a piece of invaluable information about the female human body.

"Since you both have graduate degrees, I expect you'll understand what I'm about to say." I cup my hands under my breasts to resolve this debate once and for all.

"Gravity. Ok? No real boobs will support a teeny, tiny bikini top that barely covers the nipple." Fat Joe snickers at me saying the word nipple. "These women have boobs larger than some people's heads. Simple laws of gravity would indicate that but for some artificial substance holding them up…inside…they would be resting *on her feet!*" I walk away, thoroughly frustrated by the stupidity that overcomes men once they walk through these doors.

"Told ya' they were real," Henry gloats.

"They are not!"

I give up.

I announce that it's *last call*, and start clean-up preparations. It's been a long shift, and everyone annoyed me tonight. I'm PMS-ing, feeling fat, bloated, and pimpled wearing a short tube top and size-three hot pants. The owner makes us wear shorts a size smaller than we actually are. He thinks it keeps customers at the bar. I guess I can't really complain. In the six months I've been working here, I've averaged about three hundred dollars a night, and worked three or four nights a week. It's a pretty cushy deal.

For the most part, the dancers are cool. Since I control their level of drunkenness, an apparent necessity for the job, they're overly nice to me, and make sure whoever is contributing to their intoxication tips me at least a hundred percent of the drink order.

I can't say that I've made friends here, but I have added a lot of acquaintances to my date book. Most of them are aspiring actresses or models and have contacts that they're willing to share. A few sell real estate, go to college, or moonlight from their teaching or flight attendant jobs. Although this particular place seems fairly clean as far as law breaking goes, you can't help but wonder what the older career dancers do after hours.

I'm so tired. I worked out today, delivered a monologue for a mediocre agent, ran my Pomeranian through the park for an hour, and have been on my feet since six p.m. I wipe down the bar for the thousandth time, and glance at my watch. It's one-forty-five a.m. Fifteen more minutes, a half-hour of paperwork, and I'm out of here. I sit on the side of the sink, watching the dancers milk their customers for a final lap dance. I chuckle at the sight of all the butts moving in sync to the music. Each one sports a variation of the standard Brazilian-cut Lycra mini-short with string T-back underneath, which they make the guy think he's gonna see, even though he never actually will. This place doesn't have a full adult license. They can't show any nudity or butt cracks, or anything in-between those two designations. Yes, there is actually a law prohibiting butt crack showing.

The phone behind the bar rings.

"Hello, this is Alex."

"Hey babe. Just wanted to say goodnight." My new boyfriend Justin has the sexiest voice. "You going straight home tonight?"

"Why? Should I swing by for a nightcap?" I really don't want to, but figured I'd make him feel good.

"No! I mean, I'm real tired, and have to get up early tomorrow. I just wanted to make sure I didn't have to worry about you being out late." I notice a customer giving me the evil eye.

"I got to go. Call me tomorrow?"

"You got it. Sweet dreams."

I've been seeing Justin for about four months. He works for one of the beer companies that we buy from, and makes deliveries here twice a week. One week, he convinced the owner to hire some beer girls and try a new promotion. It gave him an excuse to be in here every day…for hours. My first thought was, Duh! What twenty-three-year-old wouldn't want to spend his workday in here? But as I got to know him, I realized he was mature for his age, and was really trying to increase sales for his company.

He didn't pay attention to the dancers and mostly hung out at the bar with me. I know, I know, twenty-three! It's ridiculous. I'm totally robbing the cradle, but it wouldn't even be an issue if a man was doing it. So he's eight years younger than me. And still in college. He's moldable. And more importantly, he's my new experiment.

My past relationships were with guys I was friends with first, and the passion, if it was ever there in the first place, was lost early on. Justin and I had fiery physical chemistry. He's got a great build, luscious lips, and knowledge of how to touch a woman that goes way beyond his years. I bet UCLA offers a course on female sexual anatomy, since I've heard some of the girls talk about their young boy toys possessing similar skills.

The failed long-term relationships of my past have led me to try something entirely different with men. Justin and I don't really have stimulating conversation. We're not the best of friends. We lack similar interests, and have grown up in completely different environments. He sweats the small stuff. I slough everything off. He's an anal-retentive clean freak, and I'm, well, we've already covered that. The most marketable quality of our new relationship? Hot, hot, very hot *sex!* All the other stuff will come in good time.

He does try hard to communicate, though, I'll give him that. This morning after a particularly pleasing wake-up session, he uttered the "L" word, and fumbled some vocabulary about how happy he was, and what our kids might look like. A little soon for such a vision, I thought, but still nice to hear. These young guys, and probably the old ones too, so often mistake good sex for love. I don't care. I like him. I'm living my life in the moment these days, and his member, I mean this moment, is nice!

I wrap up last call, wipe down the bar for hopefully the last time, and begin counting out the drawer full of money. The bouncers parade through the club, sweeping horny, drunk men toward the door, and instruct the entertainers to head upstairs. As usual, the night manager is nowhere to be seen. Ever since they installed a Jacuzzi up in the attic, he's been MIA throughout most of the nights. The word from the girls is that he picks out his favorites, puts them on his personal payroll, and frolics with them in the spa way after hours. Personally, I couldn't care less, as long as he takes a break from the orgy bath long enough to count me out, so I can get home before three a.m..

As I'm just about to intercom up to the attic, the front door bursts open, and a SWAT team of armed and aggressive cops barrels in.

"LAPD! No one move!" the leader of the pack orders.

I duck behind the bar, instinctively reacting to the sight of multiple weapons pointing in my direction. A hole under the sink allows me to observe the behavior of this force sworn to protect and serve. They frisk the few remaining utterly inebriated patrons, who seem to assume that this is not real, and that some production company must be filming in the area. Not recognizing their rights, they voluntarily surrender the contents of their pockets, each possessing that same lonely condom that occupies women's purses. Did they really think they were going to get laid in here?

"What the hell's goin' on! Can't you pigs just leave us alone! We're trying to make a livin' here!" One of the older career dancers loses it.

"If I didn't think you'd like it, honey, I'd slap these on you right now." The cop pats the handcuffs on the side of his uniform, and motions some of his team upstairs.

Now is that really necessary? It's bad enough the girls are standing in their underwear during an apparent raid that, judging by the lack of preparation and direction, had no merit to begin with, but now they're also subject to verbal abuse? This burns me up, and I want to scream out from the liquor cabinet that I'm hiding in that she's a single mother of three and...and...*a person*!

I've heard about this type of sting-operation raid on some of the nearby nude clubs, but this is a bikini bar. Nothing goes on here. Their biggest crime is most likely tax evasion. It's an all-cash setup, and I'm sure any minute the cops will be trucking down the stairs with piles of accounting documents and a computer or two, and it'll all be wrapped up in time for me to catch the late-night *Lucy* reruns. But I think I'll stay in this closet anyway.

A few minutes go by, and I can hear the sloshing noises of wet feet coming down the stairs, masked by the night manager's intoxicated pleas for clothes. I slither out of the crawl space, and pop my head out over the bar so I can see. The cop holding the girls hostage catches a glimpse of my head out of the corner of his eye, and turns abruptly. I duck down under the bar, and see him tighten the grip on his weapon as he internally questions whether he saw something or not. I pop up again, and the same sequence of events repeats itself. This is kind of comical, like one of those carnival games where you try to shoot the target that pops up every few seconds and then disappears before you can take aim. I decide to avoid being shot, and stand up slowly so he can see me. He double-takes, then nods, acknowledging that he wasn't crazy, and motions me over by everyone else.

Ten minutes later, I walk out to my car past the police barricade, which is blocking three lanes of traffic as if there had been a sniper shooting at the president. They load the computers into a van, and shove our handcuffed, near naked manager into the backseat of a car, thus furthering his humiliation. His cheap toupee drips water on the window as he inches his mouth up to the open crack, clearly feeling obligated to say something to me.

"Don't worry. Everything will be back to normal tomorrow." He smiles unconvincingly. I give him a weak thumbs-up; then the flashing entourage speeds away.

The other employees gather at the front door and read the notice the friendly policeman has nailed in: *This establishment has been shut down indefinitely and is the subject of a federal investigation*…blah, blah, blah, legal jargon…blah, blah.

That's just great! I've finally adjusted to carrying on conversations with work colleagues whose dress code is an imitation designer bra and matching thong, and now I have to find another job. I walk quickly to my car, freezing my butt off, literally!

The hip-length jacket covering my mini-shorts does little to warm my posterior, and prompts a barrage of car honks as I cross the street.

"I won't miss this uniform, that's for sure," I say out loud, validating the abrupt ending of the job. I get in my car, crank up the heat, and note that I'm not that tired anymore. Justin lives about three miles from here. I think I'll swing by, and snuggle up with him for a little…attitude adjustment.

His apartment is dark with one light on in the bathroom. Through the blinds, I can see Justin's roommate's girlfriend sleeping on the couch. I'm sure she'll be thrilled to be woken up by my late-night booty call, but I'm knocking anyway. I tap my knuckles on the door softly so as to not wake up the person I intend to wake up, but get the attention of the person I really don't want to wake up. She doesn't move. I knock again. Out cold. This is a bad idea. Something doesn't feel right. I should just go home.

As I step off the patio, I suddenly remember he gave me a key when I had to feed his cats while he went home for a weekend. We always hang at my apartment due to his roommates, cats, college-pad furniture, and twin-bed mattress, and I'd forgotten I had an easy way into his place.

I unlock the door, and tiptoe past the roommate's girlfriend toward Justin's closed door. I put my hand on the knob, ready to creep in for his middle-of-the-night surprise, but am halted by a cat's screeching meow and clawed grip on my calf.

"Shit! Get off me!" I whisper-yell at the intuitive feline, then shake him off with a subtle kick. I turn the knob, walk in, and am immediately thrown into a different world.

"You've got to be fucking kidding me!" The first words out of my mouth at the sight of Justin on the downstroke on top of one of his beer girls.

No one moves. I grab anything and everything I can get my hands on, and hoist it at them. It was the only thing I could think to do. CDs, picture frames, a gallon of water, and a phone fly in their direction like a tornado spiraling out of control. I accidentally let go of my car keys then realize I need them, and reach between their naked bodies to retrieve them off her chest. He makes no attempt to remedy the situation until I get outside. I guess he finally decided to dismount unfulfilled or perhaps she threw him off for lying about us breaking up. I found that out later. His explanation—typical guy. Deny, deny, deny.

"But I saw you," I remind him.

He continues denying any wrongdoing, blames it on the girl's power of seduction, forgets that we had verbally made a commitment, and completely discredits his "I love you" from earlier today as he left my apartment after having sex just hours before this whole incident. Men! So much for my experiment.

"For every action, there is an equal and opposite reaction." "You are what you think, having become what you thought." Sir Isaac Newton and the great master Buddha in essence defined the Law of Karma the same way: For every cause there is an effect.

I had cheated on boyfriends in the past, so I guess it was my turn to know what that pain and disrespect feels like. Of course, it didn't help that I had to see it. I spared my exes the visual, but apparently the Universe felt the need to imprint the image of Justin's butt vertically thrusting into naked female flesh into my memory in order to drive the point home. I got it. What goes around…eventually…*always* comes around.

After spending three days catatonic, staring at the walls in my apartment, the urgency of finding a new job replaces my feelings of anger and inadequacy from that late-night life-defining moment. I'm thirty-two, and I can say without hesitation that I'm done with men. Done allowing them to be a distraction in my life. Done chasing passion through sex. I want to focus one hundred percent on getting my career in entertainment off the ground. I need money. I need freedom. I need a support system.

"Liza?"

"Hey. How goes it?"

"It goes." The usual start to our phone conversations.

"What's up? How's the near-nude bar job going?"

"Going, going, gone. They got shut down. That's kind of why I'm calling. What are you doing this weekend?" I try to sound authoritative, like I've worked out this really great plan.

"The usual. Clean cat litter, hike the mountain, throw down some drinks with some moronic date I've agreed to. Why?"

"I have a business proposal for you." She's all about making money these days, and I know I can appeal to her business sense.

"Oh yeah? Does it involve me taking my clothes off?"

"Just hear me out. A few of the girls from the bikini bar were telling me about doing these Vegas runs. They fly out on Friday early evening, work like ten, twelve hours Friday and Saturday nights, then head home Sunday morning with a couple grand." Silence on the other end of the phone. She's either hung up, or she's thinking about it.

"They're topless over there, though, right?"

"Yeah, but it's dark…and…and…there's like hundreds of girls that come from all over the country to work there. A thousand bucks a night. You could pay off your condo in a year!" Another long silence; then I finally break in.

"Look, it's not exactly a dream job, but I gotta make a lot of money to get this acting thing off the ground, and the industry expects you to be completely free. I mean, if you book a week on a show or something, you have to quit the job you have in order to do it. And after the week, you're back pounding pavement again and need a new job. I don't know how they expect you to live while trying to pay your dues." Poor me.

"What do you need me for? Just go yourself," she suggests firmly. That would seem logical if I weren't such a scaredy-cat. "I'm in upper management. I can't be seen in a strip club. What if I run into one of these clowns that works for me?"

"Trust me. No one that works for you can afford these places. Besides, we can wear wigs, costumes, totally change our appearance. We had a staff meeting last week at the bar. It was ten in the morning, and I didn't recognize one single girl there. They go through this whole metamorphosis before they get out on the floor. All we have to do is put on a lot of makeup, tease our hair real big, and wear the highest heels we can cram our feet into." Another long silence.

"A couple Gs would be good right now. I'm spread pretty thin with my mortgage and new Lexus." I can hear her weighing it out in her head. "Has it occurred to you that we've never lap danced before? I mean, do you really think we can waltz into a Vegas strip club, pull down a hundred dollars an hour, then waltz right back to our regular lives?"

"A lot of uglier girls than us are doing it. What's the worst that can happen? We look like idiots, don't make any money, and laugh about it the rest of our lives."

Sold.

4
The Hiring

The next few days I spent raiding my closet and piecing together whatever skimpy, sexy, lingerie-y type garments I could find to make an outfit. I didn't want to spend any money on this venture until I knew I could do it and be successful at it. It was already gonna cost us a few bucks to get there and stay in a hotel. Plus, I had to figure in a certain amount as a gambling allowance. I was being realistic, knowing there was no way I could go to Vegas and not play.

I made a few phone calls, and got the scoop on where to work and what was necessary to get started. Because the city is full of transients, convicts, and would-be mental patients, anyone seeking employment at a bar, restaurant, or casino has to get a license to do so. It's no big deal, just an afternoon at the local sheriff's department, similar to a day at the DMV. The usual suspects are present: the very types of people you'd think they're trying to screen out. Background check, fingerprinting, picture taken, waiting, and more waiting. Then finally they give you your card, and you're legal to work in Sin City.

We cab over to a club just off the strip, confidently giving each other a pep talk.

"We're in our early thirties, our sexual prime."

"We're more experienced than these young girls. We know what men like." Despite the fact that it had been fifteen years since Liza had taken a dance class, I reminded her that, "We are both professionally trained danc-ers. This will be a snap."

The irritated cab driver dumps us off at the front door, confirming this is the umpteenth time he's been here today. I pay him, and we get out to make room for the drunken bachelor party climbing in on the other side. The club is huge. But for the naked lady ornament on top of the building, you'd never know what kind of place it is. We share a moment of silence while staring at the perfect physique of the ornament.

"So, this is what it's come to," Liza says, jokingly mimicking Marlon Brando in *The Godfather*.

"Can we just go in?" I refuse to engage in a dramatic moment here.

We walk in carrying small backpacks, each equipped with one outfit, lots of makeup, nutrition bars, and herbal energizers. Before rounding the corner to see into the club, we follow the line of girls to a podium where a short Italian man (they're all Italian in this business, go figure) sits with a cash register, scribbling on a piece of paper as each girl approaches and gives him money. We reach the front of the line.

"Stage name, sheriff's card," he says in a monotone without looking up. Liza nudges me hard in the side.

"We forgot to pick names. Don't tell him our real names," she panics. I mouth, "Relax" at her, and address the distracted money-taker.

"Hi, I talked to Nick earlier? He told us to come in around this time to get hired."

"Youse got sheriff's cards?" He looks up, and holds out his hand. We nod and pull them out. "Get dressed, and I'll put you on stages six and seven to audition." He takes our cards and waves us to the locker room.

"Audition! You didn't say we had to audition!" Liza cops a hostile tone. "What if we don't get hired, and we spent money and did all this stuff already?"

"Would you relax! It's just a formality. They hire everyone that walks in the door. There's like...eight hundred girls that work here," I reassure her.

"Why do we want to work where eight hundred girls are?"

"They're not all here at once. Just chill out, and let's get ready. This is supposed to be fun, remember?" I push the locker room door open, and am yanked in by another girl opening it from the inside. I nearly fall as Liza pushes by me mumbling to herself.

"Can't believe I let you talk me into this..."

Considering this club makes millions of dollars a month off women that pay them to work here, you'd think management would fork over a tiny fraction of the earnings to upgrade the facility where average women prepare to be fantasy seductresses for large samples of the world male population.

"This place is a pit," Liza spits, emphasizing the "P," and throws her backpack in one of the few available slender lockers tattooed with heavy metal rock stickers.

I walk through a maze of women in various stages of the metamorphosis, searching through rows and rows of lockers for an empty one. The large one-room work lounge leaves a lot to be desired. The thin, ten-year-old tweed carpet that probably hasn't been vacuumed yet this year sports unidentifiable stains, the origin of which I don't want to speculate on.

It's clear the setup was designed to cram as many people in here as possible without any regard for necessary items typically found in a locker room. No bathroom, no shower, one mirror. I guess the two hundred girls working tonight can fight over a small corner in which to catch a glimpse of their images in order to apply the suitcase full of makeup they brought, or use the one from their compact and skip the final full-body look-see before heading out.

I spot a vacant locker on the lower level between two naked girls. One digs through a gym bag full of skimpy clothes, yelling at herself for misplacing the outfit that made her the most money during the rodeo convention last year. The other perfumes her naked body, excessively spraying places that I wonder who and how anyone would ever attempt to smell (and why, for that matter). I open the locker hesitantly, fearing I might find a pair of crusty old underwear or a half-eaten, week-old shrimp salad.

"That's Damian's locker!" A harsh voice echoes from the front of the butt that's in my face. I turn away quickly to erase the visual.

"She'll cut off your lock and throw your shit outside." Her face talks to me now.

"Oh. Sorry. I thought it was a first-come, first-serve kind a thing…like the sign says on the wall." I point to a handwritten sign that says: *No permanent lockers! Any locks left on overnight will be cut off and the contents discarded. Management.*

"Whatever. It's your shit. Just thought I'd let ya' know. Here's the fucker!" She untangles a string bikini from a glob of…string things, and climbs into it.

I reach behind the locker to get my backpack, and am immediately distracted by the Satan-worshiping symbols, burning flames, and letters cut out and pasted on the front of the door. The way the letters are pieced together resembles a typical ransom note. The words, however, are a bit more disturbing: A *n* Y O n E wHo *D* a r E s tO UsE thIs LoCkER wiLL sUFFeR eTeRnAL bUrNInG HELL oN EArtH!! (I hAve cOnnECtiOns!)

"You know, I'll bet this is Damian's lucky locker. I think I'll go to the other side." I grab my stuff, and put as much distance between me and that locker as fast as I can. I round the corner abruptly, and slam into Liza, who is bent over strapping on her stilettos, plunging her into a pike position.

"You moron! Watch where you're going!" she hollers without looking back. "Oh, it's you." She regroups and stands rubbing the smegma from the carpet off her hands.

"Sorry. Some chick over there gave me the creeps," I start the explanation. "Well, I didn't really see the girl, just her—what are you wearing?" Liza's ruffle-laced pewter halter top with matching Hawaiian shorts stops me cold.

"I got it at a thrift store. Cool, isn't it?"

"No, it's nowhere near cool. Totally geeky! You can't wear that out there." I wasn't going to candy-coat this issue at all. It was horrible; there was no way around it.

"Who cares what we wear. We're taking it off anyway. Besides, you're the one that said to wear hot pants," she said defensively.

"Those are not hot pants. They're cold...very cold pants. Did you bring anything else?" I ask hopefully.

"This outfit was totally cool in the seventies, and the look is back. I'm wearing it. Get over it."

Maybe it was chic back then, but the buried-in-the-archives-of-your-closet-for-thirty-years look was definitely not in now.

"Fine. I hope you make lots of money, Don Ho." She rolls her eyes at me, grabs her backpack full of makeup, and elbows her way through the crowd of smokers at the mirror.

I pull out the polyester bustier and matching slip I brought, examine them closely, and think perhaps they are equally outdated. The only other thing I had was a bikini I packed in case we had time to cop some rays between sessions. Most of the girls wore bikinis or what once may have resembled one, but now looked more like a two-inch by two-inch slab of doll fabric barely covering the areola diameter. I put on my bikini with full brief bottoms, and began my metamorphosis.

An hour later, Liza and I emerge from the locker room ready to launch our Vegas showgirl weekend. We sashay cautiously in our ridiculously high heels, evoking a Mod Squad slow-motion moment as we ease toward the stages. I had teased my thick, dark auburn locks way above my head to invite a more exotic look, then added a little Tammy Faye around the eyes, and lined my lips heavily with MAC's Viva Glam. Liza, usually so well put together, looked like a cross between Catwoman and Magnum PI.

Judging by the stares and snickers from the other girls, we may have been mistaken for transvestites or, at the very least, we slightly overdid it. Oh well, there was no going back now.

We round the corner and cross the marble-floored foyer, both nearly falling on the slick surface so thoughtfully placed where the club's moneymakers are forced to walk in super heels. We heel-toe it back onto the carpet and come to an abrupt halt at the sight of this enormous club in full motion.

"H-o-l-y s-h-i-t!" Liza is stunned at the reality I've dragged her into.

"Don't freak out. We don't have to do what they do." Our eyes shift from one set of boobs to the next, all in various compromising positions. "We're independent contractors. Nobody can tell us what to do, and *we* have complete control over these guys." Who am I convincing, me or her?

"I'm fine. I can handle it. It's just a little…shocking…that they suck on 'em. First, I can't believe the girls let them, and second, don't they care that they're swapping spit with twenty other losers?"

"I think it's best we not overanalyze the situation here. We'll definitely talk ourselves out of it." She agrees, and we decide to hang back and take it all in slowly.

I hadn't gotten a good look at the place when we first arrived, and was pretty much relying on the opinions of the girls from the bikini bar that this was the place to work. It's a classy club, and money was certainly not spared during its construction and creation. There's one main room, another slightly smaller one, and some other dwelling, probably a VIP fake screw room, we thought, back by the locker room.

The decor is trendy with soft lighting strategically positioned to make the dancers' bodies appear flawless…thank God. High vaulted ceilings help disguise the main, smoke-filled room as being open and airy, and other than topless women mounting and grinding unwary tourists, the bar looks like any other high-dollar nightclub at seven p.m.

We mosey over to the long bar at the back of the main room and order a couple shots of nerve and motivation. Just like at the bikini bar, the girls hang out here until pleasantly drunk, then get their workday under way. I'm surprised and excited to see video poker machines along the bar.

"Least we'll have something to do if it's slow or they're not cooperating."

"Don't even go there. We're here to make money, not give it to all the idiot men that run this city." Liza has never fully recovered from the pregnancy and marriage at nineteen, and every year she becomes a bit more cynical. I remind her that I took four thousand dollars from the idiot men at the Tropicana Hotel on St. Patrick's Day in 1989. Royal Flush on a dollar machine. *Cha ching!* She rolls her eyes at me, and downs another shot of incentive.

A few minutes later the DJ calls Sandra and Monica to stages six and seven. I picked Sandra as a stage name since some people think I look like Sandra Bullock, although probably not tonight. Liza went with her favorite *Friends* character. I'm sure the actresses would be proud to be imitated in such a formidable environment.

The seven stages in this club are round platforms about four feet off the ground, with no pole or any other prop to aid in the seduction process. We're required to dance to three songs, and be topless by the last one. Three songs? That's like…ten minutes! An eternity when standing over a group of slobbering misfits from the Midwest anxiously awaiting the removal of the top that's not hiding anything, anyway.

What the hell am I supposed to do up here for ten minutes? I begin walking around in circles, hoping my six-foot Amazon-like frame posing in modeling positions is entertaining enough 'cause I'm all out of ideas. A few blank stares and no money on the stage would indicate it's not. The first year I worked at the law firm, I regularly took a burlesque-style dance class in Hollywood. A 5-6-7-8…step-ball-change…jazz pirouette. A slight roll of the ankle reminds me I'm in five-inch heels, and unless I want my professional dance career to end immediately, I better just sit down, roll around from butt to stomach, and try to look sexy!

I drag out the belly flop seduction for a couple minutes, then notice there are more vacant seats at my stage now than when I got up here. I assume the plank yoga position, and walk my hands back toward my feet, then catch a peek of Liza on stage seven struggling in a backbend. I laugh out loud and realize I'm upside-down with my butt in some guy's face. Laughing is probably not affecting the passionate mood he's hoping to get in.

I stand upright, take notice of the third song beginning, and wonder at what point do I whip off my top during this rendition of "The Cow Cow Boogie." Who requested this? I can't imagine anything more unsexy! On the other stages, girls kneel down in front of the customers, teasing them with their boobs. Gathering their tips. It occurs to me that I forgot I'm supposed to be making money up here.

I kneel down at the padded bar that cushions the edge of the stage, in front of the sole supporter of my debut act. I'm inclined to pay him for staying and sparing me unanimous rejection. Then I spot a twenty in his hand, and he eagerly leans in close to put it in my bikini side. Now this I know. While bartending, I'd seen how the girls playfully collected the stage money in order to provoke more. I sway my hips back and forth teasing him with the idea if he puts a bill on one side, he has to put one on the other lonely side. He does, then boldly attempts to put one in the middle, which I swiftly yet erotically grab with my hand, ending the game in perfect time as the third song finishes and another girl comes on stage. Sixty bucks, ten minutes...maybe I could get used to this.

"Come with me, please."

I'm led from the stage to the back office by the intimidating club security guy. We pass Liza tucking her boobs back in the hideous halter. He gestures for her to follow us without saying a word. She tosses me a panicked look that I identify as, "Were we so bad they're going to put us permanently out of our misery?" I show her the three twenties scrunched up in my hand, and mouth, "How'd you do?" as we hustle in our heels behind security.

She pulls a couple bucks from her cleavage and whispers, "Fuckin' cheap ass losers at my stage."

We reach a caged window harboring a woman making change and selling "funny money" for patrons needing to charge lap dances to their credit cards. The fee for this convenience is anything but funny, and the club also takes a percentage from the girls when the fake money is exchanged for the real stuff. Isn't double taxation illegal?

Security unlocks a door next to the cage and steps aside so we can go in. The short Italian money-taker greets us.

"Fill these out, then go wait in there for Pete." He hands us a pile of paperwork, and indicates we should sit in the small office in the back corner.

The door closes, trapping us in the oxygen-free, bland room that reeks of years of stale cigarette smoke clinging to the walls. It resembles the war room on a much smaller scale. Rows of built-in shelves crammed with employee files, a copy machine, a desk buried under piles of paperwork, and an orange couch that reminds me of one I had in college that we found curbside in a neighborhood with a "free" sign on it.

Liza lays a newspaper out over the couch to shield our butts from any direct contact with the fraying fabric, and we begin filling out the extensive job application. As if where I went to junior high and my computer skills are prerequisites for removing clothes.

"Do you think we should put our real information? It would be nice to not have any legal record of ever being here." Liza again contemplates deceiving the Mafia that dumped us in this room.

"They have our sheriff's cards. It's got social security and license numbers on it. Just coming this far prevents us from marrying any prominent political figures." I'm such a smart ass.

The door opens. Air. Thank God. A forty-something, slender, no-nonsense Italian man enters. I stand, and extend my hand, habitually reliving my corporate days.

"I'm Alex Parker, this is—."

"I don't care. Sit down." He cuts me off. My bathing suit creeps up my butt as I sit back down. I squirm to retrieve the errant fabric while he browses our paperwork.

"Are you all right? Got a problem? Need to go to the bathroom?" He fires all three questions at me at once, sticking his head out from behind the papers, with raised eyebrows.

"No, I'm fine." I yank my suit back in place, and cross my legs uncomfortably.

"I'm Pete. The general manager. I'm gonna give ya' the rules...*once!* You're gonna see them being broken every day. Depending on my mood, I'll either fire ya', or look the other way. Got it?" Seems complicated enough.

"You pay forty bucks to the house if you get here before five. Seventy after. The rest is yours. Dances are twenty a piece." He lectures from memory, and probably doesn't realize how fast he's talking.

"You need to keep both feet on the floor. No touching genitalia. No bending over backwards. No simulated blow jobs. If you get caught with drugs, you're out. And if you get busted doing anything other than dancing, we don't know ya'. Any questions?" We stare blankly for a few seconds, then look at each other.

"I...I...don't have any...uh...questions." I stutter, still trying to absorb the rules. Liza stands and unconsciously cracks her neck.

"When do we work?" she asks.

"Whenever you want." He opens the door, and whisks us out.

We walk briskly toward the locker room without saying a word. Just before entering, we stop, look at each other, and simultaneously ask: "What's a simulated blow job?"

We take a short break from the self-induced humiliation, and get a massage from some guy referred to as the house dad. Seemed strange to us at first that his food, beverage, and body work camp was set up in the girls' locker room. Nobody but us seemed even the slightest bit inhibited about running around him naked. Then he announced that he'd brought his new line of rhinestone-studded T-back underwear for sale, and very neatly displayed them on a pink tablecloth. He had either set himself up with the greatest gig in town, or was as flaming as Las Vegas Boulevard on a full-moon night. Didn't matter to us. He offered a dollar-a-minute massage, had strong hands, and was totally entertaining doing his imitations of Cher, Bette, and Shirley MacLaine. Only in Vegas.

While Liza was getting her rubdown from multiple diva personalities, I'd decided to consult the professionals about the scariest part of the job—the lap dance. I squeeze into a small space at the mirror, sharing a stool with two other butts. The girl closest to me appears to have worked here a long time. She's older, has an indisputable attitude, and knows everyone. The skin texture and deep lines on her face give away a past of drugs and alcohol now replaced with a chronic nicotine addiction. She lights a new cigarette with the old one, takes a long puff, then blows the smoke in my direction. It causes me to cough so violently, my face turns bright red, and I nearly choke.

"Jesus!" She moves her curling iron and makeup away from me. "Take a vitamin or somethin'. Boost your immune system, before ya' spew that shit all over me!" Spoken like a true health nut.

"I'm not sick. I just…I really hate smoke," I say, hoping to prompt her to put it out, or at least move the lethal end so it blows in her direction. It doesn't.

"You're in the wrong business. Everyone smokes here." She holds the cigarette between her lips while rolling the back of her hair onto the iron, then blows the smoke out the side of her mouth, tilting her head up slightly so the stink dissipates over me.

"Thanks." I acknowledge her "courteous" gesture, and discreetly wave the smoke away from my head. "What's your name? I'm Al—Sandra."

"Pebbles."

"That's cute…funny. Where's Bamm Bamm?" I laugh and look around the mirror expecting someone to speak up. No one does.

"So, how long have you worked here?"

"Long enough." A woman of few words. I'm sure I'll regret this.

"Um, could I bother you for some professional advice?" She gives me an *If you have to* look.

"What do you say to these guys to get the lap dance? I mean, do you just ask them if they want one, or is there some trade secret I should know?"

"Are you for real?" She slams the curling iron down. "Just shake your tits in their face, and say whatever the hell you got to say. It's sales! Now leave me alone." She slides her stuff over a few inches and turns her back on me.

I start to get up, and feel someone's breath on my back. Liza swoops in close behind me to reline her cat eyes.

"Makin' friends fast, are ya'?" This is all so amusing to her. I get up and shove my way out from the mirror.

"Let's go!" I say firmly. It's time to get this show on the road.

Out in the club the vibe had changed significantly. The music had gone from soothing R&B to head-banging techno. A long line of anxious, horny men now extends outside the front door, and the number of girls seems to have tripled in the last hour and a half. Dancers jump from lap to lap, strapping twenty dollar bills in garters on their thighs, ankles and wrists, creating an intimidating lap dance hustle that may be a bit hard to imitate.

We do a ready-set-go, split up, and head to opposite sides of the boisterous club. As I search for my first victim, the absurdity of this job hits me. I'm a college graduate with years of professional corporate experience, and I'm parading around in high heels and a bikini seeking to sell three minutes of phony passion designed to arouse a stranger, and then leave him with blue balls and the unanswered question of why he paid for that service.

"Gross. Ugly. Broke. Pervert. Major pervert!" I continue strolling the same corner of the room, and wonder if this is a representative sample of the usual crowd.

A redheaded, red-bearded group from, I'm guessing, Oklahoma or maybe Nebraska, look like they've never seen anything like this in their lives. The foursome gulps down beers with wide eyes, and all nervously tap their feet to the music. Kids in candy stores. Innocent enough and probably a nice place to experiment with my first lap dance. As I get closer and ready to plop down between two of them, all four reach for their Camels at the same time. Ugh! I'll think I'll pass on becoming the lung cancer dancer. Eventually, I suppose I'll have to build a tolerance to the smoke, but seriously hope I never really do.

A waitress delivers a huge tray of blow job shots to a loud group of late-twenty, early-thirty types most likely celebrating somebody's last night of sexual freedom. It's a common shot choice for that occasion. Deciphering who's the bachelor is a crapshoot since all but one have their faces buried deep in Silicone Valley. I guess this is as good a place as any to start, and maybe I can blend into the crowded booth without anyone noticing my novice lap dance techniques. I had practiced at home, and thought I was ready, but my confidence level was vastly depleting as I watched the flawlessly sculpted professional enticers weaken men with their exhibition of the power of the puss. I decide to take my chances, and eagerly approach the dancer-less one.

"Hi, I'm Alex. Shit! I mean Sandra." Maybe I should write it on my arm? "Do you want a dance?"

"No, but I'll take your phone number, sexy lady! Come 'ere!" He pulls me onto his lap, and kisses my neck, following the lead of his buddies. I yank out of his grip and stand, knocking over a few of the BJs.

"Look pinhead! This is not about dating! It's about me entertaining you, taking your money, and walking away! These girls aren't going home with you! Get a clue!" A couple girls shoot me demonic looks as they ingest my taboo remarks, then quickly assess damage control, and return to mulling over their clients.

"Uh! Whatever! I can't play this game!" I step out of the maze of seven-inch heels, broken glass, and hard-ons, then trot away with my dignity, hoping the Baileys/Kahlua stain on my butt is not visible.

I stomp over to the other side of the club, thinking this looked a lot easier from behind the bar. I hate sales. I've never been one to pressure people into getting what I want. Didn't ever have to. My mom sold real estate for twenty-six years and raved about the benefits of a sales job. Freedom to set your own schedule, unlimited income potential, and constantly making new acquaintances. She approached the challenge with honesty, a tactic hardly used by traditional salesmen. Her clients sensed her sincerity, which made others gravitate toward her, and that was her greatest accomplishment on that job. She's always been a social butterfly.

I guess I'm thinking of her now, as I bone up for my next anticipated rejection, wishing I had her gift of gab right about now. I could call her for a few pointers, but somehow I don't think her Honest Abe approach is going to fly in here. Not to mention I left out a few details of my Vegas weekend during our phone conversation last week. She may be a bit disappointed at my new business venture. I'll tackle that later.

"Hello, you...big...sexy...cowboy. Would you like a dance?"

"Well perty lady, 'at depends. What else does it come with?" He flicks his black Stetson up, and reaches for my boob.

"It comes with a stiletto in the chest, moron, back off!" I push him back with my foot. The hairs on my neck perk up, which I attribute to my increased anxiety, and then hear a voice quietly in my ear.

"You're supposed to keep both feet on the floor." I turn sharply, almost losing my balance.

"Quit sneaking up on me!"

Liza laughs at my frustration, and pulls me away from the cowboy.

"You're gonna get us fired! What are you doing?"

"I can't help it. These clowns are totally disrespectful. Nobody wants me. They just want to glob all over me for free and...and my feet hurt!" I plead my case.

"Go try those players over there. I hit 'em for three in a row." She motions to two hotties that could easily double for Brad Pitt and a young Mel Gibson.

"No way am I going to practice on a gorgeous hunk. I'll be working out the lap dance mechanics on some dweeb I'll never see again...like that guy." I point out a loner wearing suspenders, holding up the wall, picking his nose.

"Whatever. It's a numbers game. You got to ask every single guy in here for a dance, and keep going back until they give you one. I've made two hundred bucks already," she brags.

"What! Is there an introductory course I missed, Hooker Shoes 101? How could you make two hundred in less than an hour?"

"Some dipshit over there is handing out hundreds. You just got to sit there for a while and tell him how great he is."

"I don't want to talk to these mutts." I cringe at the thought.

"You have to. There's too many girls that just go up and say, 'Want a dance?' Be funny and lively, and come up with something different."

"Since when did you become an authority? You didn't even want to come."

"Since I made two hundred bucks in forty-five minutes. See ya'...I'm gonna go ride the cowboys in the corner. The rodeo's in town! Yahoo!"

Did she just yelp? I can't believe this. Liza, the minister of man-haters, is having a good time AND making money! I mope back to the bar, plunk down on a seat, and order another dose of enthusiasm. I'm starting to understand why the girls drank so much at the bikini bar. It provides a unique ego shield while one is being shot down all night, and gives one the false sense of bravery necessary to compete in a sales job where all your competitors are in the same room. I feed a twenty in the quarter video poker machine, counting on a more positive response from a computer chip.

An hour later I've built up two hundred and forty credits. Sixty dollars. I've tripled my investment. Maybe I'll make enough money here to justify the time spent off the floor. The word is, if you're not making at least eighty dollars an hour, something is wrong with you. That's only four dances, a total of twelve minutes out of sixty. Doesn't seem like that would be too difficult, but I'd rather try to win it here.

Another hour passes. I'm all out of credits. I reach down in my purse, the garter strapped to my ankle with a rubber band clipped around the money, and pull out a...dollar! What happened to the sixty I made on stage? Those rat finks took my money! Cleverly disguised as credits, the bills disappeared as fast as they came to me. I'm now in the hole twenty dollars from my first day of work, and still owe the club seventy for house dues. So much for my theory of professional gambling.

"You ready?"

"More than ready."

"Let's go eat. I'm starving." I vigorously rub my feet, then give these wretched heels early retirement. "Goodbye. Nice knowing you. It's been real. Don't bother calling." I place them deep into the garbage can, so I won't be tempted to retrieve them. Liza peels off the offensive halter top that apparently was a hit.

"I doubt if I'll ever appreciate a shower as much as my next one. Did you bring any wipes? I think I'm twelve layers deep in makeup."

"No, sorry. You'll have to tough it out until we get to the hotel."

"What time is it?"

"Five," I say in an exhausted monotone.

"I haven't seen five o'clock in the morning since our trip to the Jersey Shore ten years ago." She cracks a smile, and we say simultaneously: "Joey's!" I beam momentarily at the reminiscent thoughts of an easier time in my life.

"Remember Kathy's description of that guy she fell for and couldn't find again?"

"Five-ten, dark hair, mustache…beeper?"

"The entire East Coast in the eighties! That was a fun week." I zip my backpack and throw it over my shoulder, then lean up against the wall and wait for Liza to get dressed.

"How much did you make?" she asks emphatically.

"Five hundred. It all came from that guy you said to ego-stroke. I sat with him and three other girls all night. He was really nice. I think he felt sorry for me…knew it was my first night. I wouldn't have made any money if it weren't for him. How'd you do?" Said in the middle of a yawn.

"Good. But I worked my ass off…literally." She counts her money before putting it in her backpack. "Here." She hands me three hundred dollars.

"What's this?"

"I made thirteen. I only expected to make a grand. Take it."

"I'm not taking your money. You worked for it." I hand it back to her.

"C'mon, I have a job. This was your idea, and I never would have done it if you hadn't made me. And…I'm probably not coming back." She snaps her jeans, and closes the locker.

"Seriously?"

"I go on record for selling my soul for one night…and one night only."

5

The Acceptance

It's Monday morning, late spring in Hollywood. My routine starts with coffee at Kings Road Café on Beverly, where I review the voluminous fax I receive every weekday morning between five and six from an anonymous source that has tapped into the black market of Tinseltown's casting service. All producers for virtually every mainstream TV show and film use the Breakdown Service to cast roles for their project. It's a character-by-character breakdown of what's being cast that day.

The listing is supposed to go only to licensed agents who represent talent that could be considered for those parts. The assistants at agencies don't make much money, and work their butts off. I'm sure they're the ones that first saw the income potential in creating a black market for this information with thousands of unrepresented actors having no other way of knowing what the current casting needs are. Or perhaps it was started by the agents themselves. I mean all they have to do is discreetly re-fax it to their buddy who forwards it to all his "clients" for a fee of about fifty bucks a month.

It usually takes me a couple hours to go through it, find something I might be right for, then prepare my head shots and resume into a proper agent-like submission package, and drop it off at the messenger service specifically designed for hopeful actors. The submission must be received the same day the breakdown came out or it will be too late, and the part will have been cast. This entire costly process is the price you pay for not having an agent. You must deceive the casting assistants into thinking you have one, so that your pics and reses might possibly end up in the hands of someone who'll give a shit.

I filter out the myriad of parts that I have no shot at being considered for, mostly because I'm too old and too tall. You're washed up in Hollywood by age thirty, and the bulk of the roles call for young talent that can play sixteen to twenty-five, and are no taller than five foot four. This height restriction is largely due to most leading men being under five-eight. They don't want the leading lady to tower over her man, or have to spend extra money during the production to tilt the floors so the actors compliment each other. It's much easier to cast tiny little people, and there're plenty of them.

Today's breakdown has four jobs I think I'm right for. Two guest-star parts on a sitcom (my dream job), one drama episodic, and a lame fitness infomercial for yet another piece of cardiovascular home exercise equipment endorsed by a has-been athlete probably still bragging to his family about his achievements.

I've never actually been called for an audition from submitting myself, and it's unlikely it will happen today, but I spend the time and money to do it anyway. How else can I break in? I drop off my envelopes and head to my eleven-thirty dance class to get a second wind on my day.

I've been working Friday and Saturday nights in Vegas for three months, and spending every available dollar and minute of each weekday pursuing my dreams. It's still worth it, the compromise you have to make to do the job, but it is getting to me. Liza was right about selling your soul. These guys will rob you of every ounce of self-worth and dignity you have if you let them.

I used to keep a running count of how many times guys offered me money to go back to their hotel rooms, but I stopped around six hundred and twenty-three. I can't believe the risks they're so eager to take. The majority have wives and kids, and have no thoughts or don't care about what might happen to them if someone found out about their infidelities, not to mention the risk of sharing bodily fluids. There's no doubt in my mind if they ask enough girls someone will go. The guys justify it by the unanimously accepted *When in Vegas* disclaimer: Men don't have to take any responsibility for their actions while in Clark County, and it's expected behavior to drink, gamble, do drugs, and hire a hooker…usually in that order.

At first I thought it was just a few select types of men, but that theory blew up once I'd worked a while. I've met men from one end of the country to the other and everywhere in between. Doctors, teachers, salesmen, lawyers, developers, construction workers, slackers, bikers, professional gamblers, trust-fund babies, casino owners and many a con artist.

They've slobbered on me, told me their life stories, and presented me with opportunities I imagine would be hard to turn down if you were twenty-two and naive. If I were one of these women with no morals, I'd be wealthy and retired after only three months. I thought my opinion of men was low before I started this job, but now I fear I'll never trust a man again. Ignorance really is bliss. Despite having too much information, I get some consolation in knowing I still own my soul.

"A 5-6, a 5-6-7-8." Thirty people in advanced jazz class somehow avoid kicking each other in the head while memorizing the choreography, and trying to watch the instructor's demonstration of it. Thank God they all know what they're doing. I'm the worst one in the class and probably the oldest, but I'm in good shape, and keep going no matter what.

I wish I could find my ideal acting job—a combination of dance and comedy. Unfortunately the musical theater jobs are few and far between, and nobody's gonna hire a dancer in her thirties. Why didn't I start this pursuit earlier in life? I know I have to stop torturing myself for not being assertive with my dreams when I was younger, but sometimes I get so frustrated! Had I studied the arts in college, and skipped the whole corporate route, I'd have ten years behind me already, and be a working actress with a background as a dancer. Instead, I'm an exotic dancer with a background in paper shredding!

My pager beeps loudly from inside my dance bag, totally disrupting the choreographer's speech on toe extension. I slip out of line, reach in my bag, and flick it on vibrate. It fumbles out of my hands and quivers across the floor. I chase it down, joining the group in a series of leaps, and attempting to grab it before each lift off. Got it! I glance at the unrecognizable number with a 911 at the end, and decide I'd better leave class and check it out. It could be someone from one of the jobs I submitted for this morning.

"Hi, this is Alex Parker. Someone paged me?"

"Hold on, please." I sit on the tiny ledge by the pay phone and watch young dancers talk about their summer plans while they balance on one leg and hold the other above their heads. I lift my left leg as high as it will go, and struggle to hold it at shoulder height. The phone slips out from under my ear. I hear a faint voice as it falls.

"Hello? Hello? Ms. Parker?" My leg crashes to the floor.

"Hi, I'm here."

"We'd like you come in and audition for the Tread Climber infomercial. Can you come today at three o'clock?" I dig for my day-timer.

"Uh…yeah. Three o'clock. What should I wear?"

"Fitness wear…shorts. We need to see your legs. And be prepared to work out."

She gives me the address and hangs up quickly. Not the audition I was hoping for, but at least someone actually looked at my submission! If I get the job, I may even break even on expenses this month. Wahoo!

Athletic, competitive posers boasting about their last Nike and Gatorade commercials getting picked up for another thirteen weeks, bitch about this *non-union* infomercial being totally beneath them. The fact that their agents even sent them on this audition merits looking for new representation. I sign in, then sit quietly, and listen to the indispensable gossipers. Most of the girls wear heavy makeup and boast freshly sprayed and curled hair to create that workout-ready look. I can almost hear the advertisement voice-over:

> *"Get the body you always dreamed of. Burn fat and sweat while tinted foundation and mascara pour down your face, staining your matching designer workout bra and bike shorts permanently. Buy the Tread Climber today!"*

"Alex Parker." A friendly female face appears from the secured room and invites me in.

She passes my picture and resume to the group sitting at a long table, then instructs me to mount the apparatus. The three women and two men hover together and whisper excitedly, each glancing at me and nodding. Either they like my look and am hoping I can deliver the fitness level I represent on my resume, or I have remnants of the spinach salad I had for lunch in my teeth.

I step onto the treadmill/stairclimber concoction (what will they think of next?), grab the moving handles, and act like I know what I'm doing. After a few minutes, they tell me to stop, then huddle up again. I gather my belongings and wait uncomfortably next to the machine to hear if I've been bought. Normally, there would be a second audition called a call-back before any final decisions are made, but I get the impression these people are in a hurry and probably don't have the funds to hold another audition.

"Are you available to shoot on Thursday?" Hell yes!

"Um, let me check my book." I pull out my day-timer, turn a few pages back and forth and make a curious "hmmm" noise as if I'm shuffling around my schedule to accommodate them.

"Yes, I think I can make it work. Would it be for the whole day?"

"No, probably five or six hours, but plan on eight," one of the men answers. I nod, indicating that we've inked the deal here.

"Is there a script?" I ask hopefully.

"No. You'll be demonstrating the equipment, and we'll ad-lib lines if we need to." Of course.

They give me all the information, and officially book me for the job. I thank them, then prance proudly through the waiting room, letting the posers know they have one less position to compete for.

"Hey, what are you doing tonight?" I ask my good guy pal Phil.

"Drinking somewhere."

"How about margaritas at El Coyote? My treat."

"Done. See ya' at eight?"

That was easy. One great thing about L.A.—it's never hard to find somebody to celebrate with, and there's always something to celebrate. I met Phil at the bikini bar. He regularly stopped in for a drink after work, and we hit if off really well. As a former Chicagoan and struggling producer, he had a lot in common with me, and we both recognized that finding good friends in L.A. is sparse at best.

As usual, El Coyote is packed. Parking sucks, and the mob outside the front door indicates a long wait. I pull into the valet exit, ignoring the

"Full" sign, and prepare to act like a dumb brunette as the car parker runs to my vehicle in a hostile panic.

"No park here!" he yells loudly in a heavy Spanish accent. "We're full! Back out! Back out!"

"There's nowhere to park…and I've got to get in the line. Can't you find a place for me, please, please, please?" I bat my green eyes, and flash a girly, cute smile, wishing I would have worn a lower-cut shirt.

"We're full! Go down to next block!" He ignores my flirt and waves me out, forcing me to take desperate measures. I step out of my car and hand him ten bucks.

"You sure you're full?"

"Like I said, one space left." Perfect English. He jumps in my car and speeds away.

I walk to the host counter thinking about the absurdity of paying to give my keys to an illegal alien so he can drive erratically. I arrive at the counter and slip the host a twenty without saying a word. He nods to a waiter to lead me to a seat. Good thing the food is cheap.

"Here's to getting your first TV job." *Clank*. Phil slaps my Cadillac margarita with his.

"It's no big deal. Just a stupid infomercial, but thanks." I take a big gulp. "We'll drink Dom when I book a sitcom gig."

"Here, here." He drinks again. "You gotta stick with it. I see so many actors that think they're gonna be the next overnight success—it never happens that way. Five years at least, maybe even ten."

"I know—it's a long road." I dip my chips in the salsa bowl. "Have you seen that documentary on Jim Carrey? He was living in his car, dirt poor, doing standup for years, then finally got a break on that Wayans brothers show. What was it called—with the fly girls?"

"*In Living Color.*"

"Right." Now look at him, ten mil a movie. I bet when he was getting booed off the stage at those hole-in-the-wall comedy clubs, he never thought he'd be where he is now."

"Maybe he did. Probably felt it all along. That's what kept him going…I think it's twenty million a pop." He reaches across the table and wipes salsa off the side of my face. I'm sure it drove him crazy the entire thirty seconds it was there. Another neat freak!

"Yeah, there's no mistaking that nagging voice in the back of your head that convinces you to take risks you logically would never take. I hear it every day." I wave at the waiter for two more drinks.

"Speaking of risks—how's Vegas?"

"Peachy. A new adventure every week. I never know if some clown is gonna steal my top as a keepsake while I'm dancing for his buddy, or if a loser pretends to be a high roller and I waste my whole night dancing for free. It's always exciting." My sarcasm has a hint of anger.

"No way."

"Way."

"Don't they have security to force them to pay?"

"Can't get water from a rock. I'm getting pretty good at spotting the frauds, and for the most part, my nights are idiot-free, but there's always that occasional freak that throws off the whole vibe. Like two weeks ago, I'm sitting with this cop from Seattle. He's on vacation, spending money, and I thought he was cool. After a few dances, he got a little handsy, and it made me uncomfortable, so I figure it's time to leave. I don't like to sit too long with one person. They get too attached, and forget that it's entertainment, not courting."

"I've probably done that." Phil logged many hours at the bikini bar.

"So, I decide to move on, and the guy gets all possessive on me. Says stuff like, *So now you're gonna go rub on somebody else?* I try to calm him down using a humorous tone and the applicable buzzwords reminding him that I'm at *work*, and this is my *job*, and had we met somewhere else maybe things could be different. Then he flashes his gun and handcuffs, and his whole disposition changes. His face—it was like O.J. at the beginning of the trial when the prosecution drilled home the abuse and battery stuff. His appearance physically changed from the football hero to the out-of-control wife beater." Phil tries to follow me.

"Anyway, I had to get security to throw him out. But you know, he's a cop. He could wait for me to leave and follow me or something. It freaked me out a little, and ruined my night. So, now I have to try not to be so nice and just take the money and run, like the rest of 'em do." I take a big swig of my margarita.

"You got to be careful over there. Too many weirdos. If something happened to you no one would know. I don't even know where you work." Phil is the brother I never had. "Can't you find somewhere around here? There's tons of clubs."

"I don't think I can make the money here. It's only two days a week that I risk my life, then I get the other five to be a semi-starving artist." I tilt my head and smile jokingly to lighten the mood. "Maybe you should create a sitcom set in a strip club, and I could be one of the leads? That would solve a lot of my problems right now."

"And we'll just rob a bank to get the thing produced, or maybe I'll come to Vegas with you one night, and we'll roll all your customers in a dark alley."

"Seriously. A stripper sitcom could be a great idea. It's never been done. Lots of opportunities for quirky characters. I bet HBO would go for it or maybe Showtime. They're a little racier." I'm brainstorming here.

"Never sell. Too many conservative bureaucrats. Besides, cable's not doing comedy series yet, and the main networks—definitely too conservative."

We finish our drinks and wind up my celebratory night with a veggie burrito. But I couldn't get the idea of a situation comedy set in a strip club out of my head. Sounded like a winner to me, but I was hardly in a position to do anything about it. For now, I'll put it on my mental to-do list with the rest of my dream jobs.

McCarron Airport is packed. Middle America—so anxious to give their money to the City of Lost Wages. I drag my bag outside and get in the cab line that winds through three lanes of partitions, mimicking a new ride at Disneyland. "What is going on?" I ask out loud. "Why are all these people here?"

"Typical Friday." A man in front of me answers my rhetorical question. "I think there's a big convention in town this weekend." I nod, thanking him for the information, and nip the conversation. I have to save my vocal energy for my all-night sales pitch in the club.

The line inches along slowly, amplifying the soreness in my aching legs. Thirteen hours on the Tread Climber yesterday was a killer. Instead of making millions for Bruce Jenner, I should make my own infomercial: *Quads of Steel.* I certainly earned it, and by the end of tonight I can make another one: *Noodle Legs.* Why didn't I take today off? I could have worked Saturday and Sunday, and not battled this Friday crowd.

"What's going on this weekend?" I ask the cab driver, prepared for an answer I won't understand. Does anyone speak English anymore?

"Pimmers."

"What?"

"Pim—mers!" His tone indicates I'm not the only one that can't understand him today.

He looks in the rearview mirror to see if I got it. I shake my head, then pull the seat belt over my body, and wonder if the bulletproof plastic divider works both ways. He mumbles something in irritated Arabic, then flicks on the radio to drown out the uncomfortable silence. I rack my brain trying to figure out what type of occupation sounds like *pimmers* that would employ enough people to convene in Vegas. Pimps…painters…planners….

We pass UNLV, and my train of thought shifts to eighteen-year-olds from small-town America trying to survive this city. Every known addiction to man is fingertips away and reasonably priced. And I thought my college days were rough.

"Pimmers!" The driver whisks across three lanes of traffic and points to a billboard for Roto-Rooter.

"Plumbers! Of course. I'm so glad we solved that mystery; it would have driven me crazy all night. They have their own convention?" He gives me the same confused look I gave him moments ago. I take advantage of the language barrier. "Guess I better brush up on my toilet humor. I want to be able to plunge through the crowd tonight, and make a butt full of money." I crack myself up.

This place is always the same. Different people, but they're all the same. The routine is getting really old. I say the same thing over and over all night long, and they have all the same responses.

"Hi, my name is Sandra. What's your name? Where are you from? And what's your story?"

"Me? I don't have a story?" Unanimous denial.

"Everyone has a story. Why are you here?" I like to turn the tables and make them think about their lives. Men have this great ability to appear as though no thought goes into any of their actions, and that they have no reason for engaging in spontaneous behavior; therefore, they're not responsible for ending up in a strip club. They somehow aimlessly wandered off and found themselves staring at naked ladies.

"What do you mean? I'm just here." Ok, let's try a different angle.

"Where did you come in from?"

"Texas. Outside Dallas." That explains a lot. I have yet to meet anyone from Texas I like. "Here for the convention," he volunteers.

"So, you're a plumber? I bet you have lots of stories. Going to people's houses, with overflowed toilets…you must have seen some crazy stuff?"

"I'm in sales."

"Me too. What a coincidence! See, I knew if we talked long enough we'd find something in common." I tap him lightly on the shoulder to initiate contact. "What do you sell?" He smiles, and appears to be going for my fake interest in his life.

"Piping mostly, and I have a little side business selling shower curtains, doors, things of that nature. I meet a lot of nice people, repeat business. Lucky for me everyone takes a shower, right?"

"Ideally." I better get to the pivotal question before I start to feel all my aches and pains, or doze off from such stimulating conversation. "Well, from one salesperson to another, would you like me to dance for you?" I'm sure if I weren't so tired I could have come up with a better line.

"Maybe later. I'm gonna wait a little while…have a few drinks, then…"

I get up and leave while he's midsentence. I have no patience tonight. Usually I would have pressured him a little more or forced him to commit to one later, and then returned in five minutes and every five minutes after that. I think I could have taken at least a hundred from him, but it would have cost me another half-hour of bullshit, and I just don't have the energy.

I head back to the locker room, down a Red Bull and change outfits, hoping to lose the dismal mood I'm in. I reapply lipstick and face powder, re-tease, re-spray, and re-perfume. A few girls hanging around the mirror smoking and bitching about today's clientele reinforce that I'm not the only one having a hard time. The room chatter is all about the "butt-crack showing, shit-sucking losers" taking up all the table space.

I don't think the Plumbers Convention has been a real moneymaker in past years. Not a single dancer has walked in saying she's doing well out there, except, of course, Charmene. She's a Pam Anderson look-a-like. Long white-blond wavy hair, twenty-inch waist, perfect tan, and 40-DDD's that probably took three surgeries to obtain. Her body is so distracting, you hardly notice that she has a beautiful face. Not as flawless as her physique, but she looks pretty good for midthirties.

She's a career dancer, but has it together. Married with two teenage kids. She works three days and two nights a week, has all the local patrons as regulars, and is *always* in demand by the visitors. I figure she makes over a hundred grand a year in cash, and seems like she's got her priorities in check. She's always talking to hubby or the kids on the phone, and I've never seen her drink anything other than water. I guess if ever there was to be a role model in a strip club, she would be it.

I watch Charmene through the reflection in the mirror. She counts her stash for the day, peels off her micro-bikini, and packs up to leave. For a quick moment, I think about grabbing her purse, running and never coming back here.

"Alex?" I'm stunned to hear someone call me by my real name.

"Hey…what are you doing here?" I draw a blank on her name, but recognize her from the bikini bar.

"Workin'. Are you dancing now?"

"Yeah, for the last few months. Since the bar closed."

"What a total bummer that was. I made bank in that place. Now I got to come over here twice a month to pick up the slack. It sucks. I hate this place." She squishes in next to me at the mirror.

"Why? I thought you guys came here all the time?"

"Not me. I can't stand 'em globbin' on me. There not supposed to touch us. The laws are the same as California, but nobody enforces shit around here." She grabs my shoulder and whispers in my ear. "The trash that works here regularly…they set the bar for what the guys can get away with, and it's low!"

"Yeah, but you don't have to do what they do," I whisper back.

"You won't make any fuckin' money if you don't!" She intentionally targets the other girls in the room. "Might as well work at Mitzie's and not have to travel."

"Where's Mitzie's?" I ask curiously.

"Orange County. Been there forever, twenty-five years. Total blue-collar place, packed all the time, really low key. Nobody touches. Bouncers are all over them."

"Sounds like a perfect place. What's the catch?"

"Ten dollars a dance. You got to do twice the work, but it's a lot easier to sell dances and they usually get two at a time."

"Isn't it the same money as here if they're getting two at a time?" I ask the logical question.

"Way too much work to make a thou…can't even make five without putting in a ten-hour day and physically—forget it. I slipped a disk last year…can't be on my feet that long. It's so much easier to drag some rich moron in the VIP room, bank five bills in two hours, then do it again with someone else and get the hell outta here."

"I've never made five hundred in two hours, but I haven't been in the VIP room, either. What do they do in there?" I'm afraid to ask.

"Same shit as out here. You just make them think they're gonna get more. Some girls partner up with management. They look the other way while shit goes on under the table, and they throw 'em half the money. I won't go that far. Shit!" She applies a fourth coat of mascara and gets some in her eye.

"Why do you need to make so much money?"

"Mortgage, two kids, deadbeat ex, and nursing school. I'm fuckin' buried, dude." She puts the finishing touches on her face. "C'mon, let's go flush out the losers and get tanked in the VIP room!"

Hey! I'm doing the poop humor here!

I feel like a young protégé prancing around, playing the sister act with Viagra. Even though she's blond, five-two, and considerably younger than I, we haven't encountered one person that didn't buy our sibling charade. I still can't remember her real name or even the stage name she used at the bar, but *Viagra* definitely gets us in the door. The guys laugh and she plays the part with full dedication. Plops down on laps and grinds right from the get-go. Her motto: *Immediate and sustained arousal equals empty wallets and happy women.* Note to self: Put that on a bumper sticker and make millions.

We took a pit stop at the bar for a couple quick shots of control and manipulation. We chug our beer chasers and are approached by two fifty-something, slightly overweight businessmen that tell the bartender they're buying our round. Armani suits, well-coiffed…Scotch drinkers, I suspect.

Years of bartending taught me the ability to predict what someone was going to order by the way they walked toward the bar. Beer drinkers are heavy footed and wobble from side to side from the tire around the waist or thighs rubbing against each other. Cocktail drinkers, such as the vodka cranberries, rum and Cokes, or tequila sunrises, usually hurry to the bar to get the party started as fast as possible. You sense their urgency as they impatiently try to get your attention, and they often order two at a time or doubles. Martini and Scotch drinkers are the quiet, calculating ones. The norm is an after-work professional that moseys slowly toward the bar, looking around to make sure he knows no one. They've usually had three to five drinks somewhere else, and appear to hold their liquor well, although the incessant feeding on bar snacks gives away the need to soak up the booze so the drinking can continue.

One of businessmen reaches across me for the bowl of peanuts and pulls it in front of himself, while the other orders. "Tanqueray martini up, dry, olives…and Glen Livit on the rocks." Nailed it!

The guys start in with some generic small talk about how our night is going and how nice the weather is in Vegas compared to Boston. Viagra and I quickly progress to the "Why are you here?" and "How have the tables been treating you?" conversations. It's always a bonus if your would-be sponsor has just won a bunch of money. He's happy, feeling powerful, and ready to spend.

We decline their offer of another cocktail, and instead suggest we all move into the VIP room, where Viagra promises in her sexiest voice, "privacy in a more intimate environment to do whatever our hearts desire." She slithers her body up and down her guy and nibbles on his ear. My guy puts his arm around my shoulder and pulls me close, hoping I'll say something sexy, too. The best I can do is whisper in my raspy Kathleen Turner tone, "What she said."

The VIP room is truly a rip-off, and most guys that get suckered in there never go back. They pay a hundred dollars to the house just to enter, which includes two drinks. Liquor is very rare in Vegas. Dances are three for a hundred, and they have to commit to getting at least two hundred worth at the time of entry. Of course, this information is passed on to them in front of us so they'll feel extra cheap and stupid if they back out. The guys buy in and are seated in a large, dark corner booth covered in maroon velvet. Viagra excuses us, and leads me through a trapdoor that opens into the locker room.

"We have to wear gowns in the VIP room," she tells me as she undresses while we walk.

"I don't have a gown. Nobody told me I needed one."

"You can wear one of mine or tell Boston Boy he needs to buy you one at the boutique." She opens her locker and pulls out an oversized duffel bag full of stripper clothes.

"I'm not going to make him spend three hundred on a dress I'll have on for five minutes. That's money he could give me. What do you got?" She unzips the bag and unleashes a stench so potent it makes my eyes water.

"Are you kidding me? When is the last time you washed anything in here?" I cover my nose and mouth.

"I don't know…it's my Vegas bag…probably three months or so. We'll douse everything in fake Eternity." She hands me a wrinkled, black, stretch, what's-supposed-to-be-floor-length gown, but is more of a Capri dress on me, and tells me to get dressed.

Minutes later I push through the trapdoor, wearing the flooded dress, and feeling more like Ethel the hamper girl then Sandra the sexy seductress. I'm sticky, sweaty, and reek of multiple scents ranging from Alfred Sung, fake Eternity, and some girl's Obsession that somehow got sprayed on my back during the quick change. Viagra is already on the move, dancing between her guy's legs, with the dress she put on five minutes ago nearly off. I slide into the booth next to my guy, dreading what the following hour will bring to my life.

"You smell good." He pets me on the head, and gets caught in a teased and heavily sprayed mass.

"Thanks. It's…my own special blend."

The next hour and a half goes by quickly, and I conclude this will be my first and last experience in the VIP room. As far as customers go, he isn't the worst, but is far from the best. An ideal client would sit quietly with hands pinned under his legs, not breathe on me, and not force me to listen to mundane stories about his personal life or try to impress me with how much money he has. He would pay double for each dance, and request that I keep my clothes on to create suspense. He would give me all the cash in his pocket, buy a nice bottle of champagne, and then leave happy after two hours, allowing me to get to the airport and go home before midnight.

No such luck with Boston Boy, but at least he's not as gross and disrespectful as his friend. Watching the guy tongue Viagra's whole body and fondle himself three feet away from us makes me want to puke. I suggest to my guy that we move to another booth, ignoring Viagra's facial pleas to stay put. We head to the other side of the small room and pass a young girl, probably nineteen or twenty, straddling a guy in his late fifties, early sixties. Again, I fight the dry heaves. He grabs her hips and rocks her back and forth furiously on his lap. I watch her face while he pinches and bites. Her eyes are closed, and she cringes harder with every stroke. I want to say something to the manager, but he can obviously see the scenario and chooses to look the other way. Why would she let him treat her like that? She's a beautiful girl. Petite, exotic, maybe Brazilian—two years out of high school.

I sit down with Boston Boy, and try to pick up where we left off, which was me doing the same lame dance over and over, teasing him into thinking it will get better the next time. He must just like hanging out with me, 'cause other guys getting a lot more than he's getting are clearly visible to him. I can't get my focus off the young girl and the geriatric who likes it rough, and am curious to see what happens next.

During a dance for BB, I about-face, so I can observe the situation. She sits next to him, and his left hand has disappeared under her dress. There seems to be some kind of negotiation going on. She shakes her head a lot, but he keeps pressuring. He reaches in his pocket with his right hand and pulls out the biggest wad of money I've ever seen. He retracts his left hand, counts out ten hundred-dollar bills, and then aggressively crams them down the cleavage of her dress. She leaves the booth nervously and exits through the trapdoor.

I turn around after a three song session of butt shaking and whatever else I could think to do other than arouse my client, and find him completely passed out and snoring loudly. Luckily, I took Viagra's advice and got my fees up-front before the nine Scotch rocks finally won him over. I close his mouth, reposition his head, and sweep his hair back in place so when management comes to throw him out and videotape his awakening and departure, he'll have a morsel of dignity.

One foot through the trapdoor, and I'm halfway out of the junior dress. Can't get this thing off fast enough. I flick quickly through the combination of the padlock, kick open my locker, and throw the "gown" full of cigar smoke in the corner, wadded up in a ball. I pull on a big T-shirt, sit down against the wall, and knead out the soreness in my thighs.

Oh my God! My legs hurt so bad. I should be glad Viagra cut my night in half by introducing me to the VIP room. Saved me hours of labor I'm sure I wouldn't have stuck out. Unfortunately, the images of what goes on in there now permanently tattooed in my head were hardly worth it. I drag myself to my feet, and think how awesome it will be to jump in the Jacuzzi at the hotel, then order room service before crashing out. Turkey burger and fries maybe, or…pizza! Thin crust, juicy cheese…yeah…pizza.

It's the peak moneymaking time of the night, and the locker room is quiet. It's nice for a change. No gossiping young girls. No complaining commuter strippers, and no belligerent career dancers. I can get dressed in peace.

"Gabrielle, stage three! Last call! Gabrielle, stage three! Move it or pay it." Spoke too soon. The DJ comes through loudly on the PA system.

"Fuck off!" A voice from another row quivers between sniffles. I follow the subtle weeping around the corner, and see the young girl from the VIP room. She changes into her street wear, and packs her bag.

"They charge you a hundred bucks if you miss your stage set, you know." I say gently, not knowing what else to say. She sniffles louder. I move closer and am immediately sickened by the marks on her neck. She's not telling me to get the hell away from her, and I sense if I invited it, she would throw her arms around me and cry on my shoulder.

"You don't have to go with him." I look her straight in the eyes.

"Yes, I do." She wipes her face with her sleeve.

"He already gave you the money. Just leave. You'll never see him again."

"You don't understand. He comes every month. If I don't go, he tells authorities I don't have my papers." Definitely Brazilian. "He takes care of me and my sister." I bet he does. She slams the locker, grabs her stuff, and heads out.

"Be careful," I yell out again, not knowing what else to say. My stomach gurgles and reverses gears. I run for the garbage can. *Bleaaa!* Barfing in the locker room of a Vegas strip club. My parents would be so proud.

That was tough. I'm in my thirties. I can handle pretty much whatever they dish out here. Nobody is gonna get the better of me. I know this is temporary. She's twenty…if that. Not even old enough to drink. Why do they hire them so young? They should have to be at least twenty-five. She'll never get out of this business. How do you take an entry-level job making ten dollars an hour after you've made a thousand in one night? I'm gonna be sick again.

It's a beautiful Saturday along the California coast. The crisp, blue sky soars for miles and miles up the Pacific Coast Highway. I can hear waves crash against the rocks as I cruise in my Camry. Something about the ocean's soothing sounds invites a new perspective. I needed to get away today.

Clear my thoughts. Last night in Vegas was another one of those eye-opening, life-changing moments. That Brazilian girl really got to me.

No matter how hard Vegas' corporate top guns try to change their city's image, it still and always will be the devil's playground. People change there. They do things they would never do in the normal course of their lives. I'm so afraid I could get to a point where all the ugly stuff wouldn't bother me anymore. You'd almost have to in order to tolerate and be productive in your work, whatever the work is. Casino employees see dysfunction every day. Couples fighting over lost money. Women abused trying to get their men off the tables. Kids neglected so parents can continue drinking and gambling. Chronically addicted gamblers pulling all-nighters and losing every last cent they have.

Vegas has the highest suicide rate of any city in the country. Hotels no longer build balconies off the rooms to avoid liability when they end up with a jumper. It's so depleting there. All that electricity in one central location has to have an effect on your body. Nobody sleeps. People do crazy things.

I remember one late night at the club, a distraught, disheveled woman carrying a small child barreled her way past security, rummaged through the club obviously looking for her husband, and found him fondling a topless redhead. She was able to holler a few choice words, and throw a drink on him before security caught up with her, then hauled her out with the crying baby. He acted like he didn't know her, laughed about it, and stayed with the redhead. What a way to spend your vacation. Vegas changes people. I can't go back there.

"…that's what I said, but he ignored me and didn't clean it anyway, hello?"

"Hi, Mom."

"Alex. Hold on a sec. I was talking to my neighbor about our lazy pool boy. Let me close the door."

My mom is always in mid-sentence with someone when she answers the phone. My sisters and I are her usual callers, and she doesn't want to miss our calls, so she answers no matter what she's preoccupied with. It's become kind of a joke for all of us, and we do it back to her when she calls, though she never gets it.

"Hi, what's going on? Haven't heard from you for a few days." Moms always know when something's not right with their kids.

"Uh, nothing. Just taking a drive up the coast today. Thought I'd give you a call."

"You're on a road trip by yourself? Where are you going?"

"It's not a road trip, Mom. I'm just…driving…thinking."

"Is everything Ok? It's not like you to take time to smell the flowers. How was Vegas? Did you win?"

"No. Didn't…really play that much. Can't afford it. The bar closed down and I have to get another job." I haven't exactly been keeping her up to date with what's going on. I didn't want to stress her out too much. She has high blood pressure.

"Oh no. When did that happen?"

"A few…days ago. It's not a big deal. I have a plan. Phil and I have been talking about developing a sitcom, you know for TV?" I'm thinking this up as I talk. "It's a way to take control of my own acting career, and not have to compete with the nineteen-year-olds for parts."

"That business is so competitive, sweetie. I don't know why you won't go to law school. You could still be involved with the theater or do those comedy acts you like, and be around professionals. I always envisioned you with a professional man…" (I'm mouthing her words along with her) "…who would take care of you…buy a nice house…have a few kids. Why make your life so difficult?"

"Mom, no lectures please. You know I have to do things for myself, and I like my manless existence. No burping, farting, hacking in the morning. I'm getting very used to sleeping alone, and I like it. Besides, it took me thirty years to figure out what I wanted to do with my life. I'm gonna make this work. I just have to find the right angle to break in."

"I guess you know what you're doing. You've always been my strong, free-spirited middle child…destined to do something great. I just have to throw in my two cents every once in a while." She's consistently been my biggest fan, no matter what F—d-up choices I've made.

"Thanks, Mom. I'll get there. I promise."

"Tell me about the sitcom show."

"Oh…um…well…it's set in a strip club. The cast will be…a few dancers, a bartender, a waitress, and the club owner." I'm thinking quickly here.

"There's all kinds of possibilities for guest star appearances to be customers, cops, parents of dancers…I don't know. We're in the early development stages."

"Sounds interesting. Are they going to be naked?" I knew she would ask that question first.

"No, Mom. It'll have to be a bikini bar, so we don't limit ourselves to a cable network." Ok, here goes. "I have to do some research, and…I was thinking of getting a job as a dancer at this place in Orange County. I've heard it's pretty low key, heavy security, nobody touches you." All quiet on the other end. I'm hoping I lost reception. "Mom? Are you still there?"

"Yeah, I'm here." Heavy sigh. "I don't know what you want me to say. You know I support my kids one hundred percent. I wasn't worried when you got the bartending job but…I don't know, Alex, dancing? What if these guys follow you home or wait for you after hours? I hear on the news all the time about girls getting raped and killed outside of these clubs."

"Mom, they're teenagers. I'm a grown woman. I got to do what I got to do. The job will give me freedom to keep going, and…I have to be one of them to really find out what's in their heads, and the guys' heads. We have to develop our characters and make them real. This is the best way." I'm almost believing my own words here. "I just wanted to let you know what I was doing, so we can talk freely about this stuff."

"I guess it's not the worst idea I've heard from my girls this week. Did you know Chrissy's joining the army?"

"Yeah, I got wind of that. Our own Combat Barbie. I got to get a letter out to her. Anyway, I got to run, Mom…"

"Alex? You have to put a time limit on this dancing stuff, so you keep focused. Do it for X amount of time, gather your research, then get out of it. And I want you to call me every night you work, so I know you're safe."

"Mom! That's ridiculous. I could get abducted at the grocery store just as easy. Stop worrying. I can take care of myself." Another heavy sigh on the other end.

"Fine. At least keep a diary. Everything people say. Everything you learn. Write it down. You know time will go by, and you'll forget something important."

Mom was always big on writing. When we were kids, if we wanted to do something or go somewhere that called for special consideration, she requested an essay to plead our case. Should have been expected from an English lit. major from Purdue. She kept and framed my summer-between-seventh-and-eighth-grade essay entitled "Why I Should Go To Tommy's Party," and brings it out at every opportune occasion to share with my friends. Even at the tender age of thirteen, I showed a knack for writing, and if memory serves me, it was a rockin' party!

"Ok, Ok, any more rules? I got to go. I'm roaming."

"I love you, and be careful!"

"I will. Love you, too. Talk to ya' in a few days."

I hang up my cell, pull in a driveway, and turn around. I suddenly feel a huge weight lift off my shoulders. I had been dreading telling my mom about the new occupational pursuit for months. I couldn't see the point in telling her about Vegas. It would have only stressed her out, and maybe I was too embarrassed about that choice. Working only on weekends made it easy to forget that it was my job. I hadn't accepted it as a part of my life, even though it was playing a huge role: my income. Now that I've made the decision to stay local and probably have to work five days a week to make the same money, I've got to stop being embarrassed about it. I'm an adult. I've made an educated decision to do this and better my life…pursue my dreams. I'll do it for six months.

6

Kickoff

Dear Diary:

Never kept a diary before. Not sure what to write. Taking Mom's advice to script thoughts. Got hired last night at Mitzie's. Didn't stick around to work. Losers, losers, and more losers. Will make a better effort tomorrow.

It's so dark in here. Much darker than the Vegas club. It takes a half an hour for my eyes to adjust, but, I suppose, that's a small price to pay for the flawless-skin look. I'm assuming I have completely smooth body curves in this sparsely lit room. Everyone else does. Reminds me of Dudley Moore's famous line from *10,* "You look amazing in this light…but then again, you can't always count on the light."

Nice-looking women. Less showy than Vegas. Not everyone has a boob job, although many do. But they're not the obnoxious ones. Well, there is one girl with preposterously large implants. I watch her on stage, and think about how she deals with the ridicule she must attract while going though everyday life. Did she not think about that before going under the knife? I don't get it. She's cute, has a petite body, and a real bubbly personality. No serious signs of insecurity that would merit such a drastic physical alteration. I mean it's one thing to want to feel better about yourself and balance out your body by adding a *little* augmentation, but going from an A-cup to a cup so large it doesn't even have an alphabetized designation is ludicrous.

I imagine the consultation with the plastic surgeon where he must have digitally enhanced her image on a computer to show her what she'd look like after surgery. I envision him hitting the *larger* button over and over until her image no longer has a face, just two perfectly round balloons with arms and legs. Then she says, "Right there! That's what I want."

The two guys that run this place have been here for twenty-four years. They're in their fifties, and I suspect have seen it all and probably done it all. The impression I get is that they have a ton of other business ventures they prefer to focus on, and probably stay clear of any dancer drama. My initial assessment is that the club kind of runs itself, and the owners seem to have figured out the key to a successful strip club is keeping your girls happy. House fees are reasonable. We can come and go as we please. The dressing area is decent, and other than the standard *No illegal conduct*, there are no rules.

It's a small club. Low ceiling with two stages that are hooked together, but face opposite sides of the club. There's a pole on each stage (Thank God, a prop!), and enough space for two girls to be on at the same time. We do one set of two songs on the first stage, then move to the second one for two songs. If you decide to go topless, (and it's not a requirement, but you have to pay more to the house if you don't) you have to stay inside a circle on the stage the farthest point away from any customer. I think the law states that we have to be six feet from anyone, which is awesome! I've been groped by enough Bozos in Vegas to last a lifetime.

The biggest perk about working here? No smoke! Smoking was outlawed in any bar or restaurant in California six months ago, but a lot of the regular bar owners risk the fine and let their patrons puff anyway. I guess strip club owners have too much to lose. They don't ever want to draw legal attention to themselves, since there's always some conservative group lobbying to shut them down one way or the other.

Aesthetically, Mitzie's can't hold a torch to the Vegas club, but they've done enough to keep the place up to date, and it's so damn dark in here you wouldn't see the flaws anyway. I sit in a corner by the DJ and observe, trying to resist the urge to start my workday at the bar. Since I'll be working four or five nights a week here, I've got to break the habit of the two-shot primer before I can utter anything remotely seductive to a prospective buyer. Should be quite an accomplishment to lap dance stone-cold sober. I'm not sure I'm ready for it. Although the clientele is mellow and probably pretty regular given the bar's accessible location, they're still a bunch of misfits that have nothing better to do than hang out, get drunk, and pay girls to talk to them.

The music is soothing R&B. My favorite. I tap my three-inch-high-heeled foot and groove subtly in my seat. A lot of dancing going on here. Almost every girl in the room is moving, suckering somebody. Vegas was so expensive, you really had to convince the guy he needed to buy your dance. It was a lot of physical *and* psychological work. In retrospect, pretty demeaning…and what a nonsensical investment for the idiots. Ok, stop! I'm doing it again. Overanalyzing and…and…hating them all! Time to get up and take a lap.

"Hi, I'm Alex. Mind if I sit?"

"No, please." He moves over, trying not to touch elbows with the guy sitting next to him. I squeeze in.

"What's your name?"

"Ray." He nods uncomfortably, then looks away. Some guys are afraid of us. They invite you to sit down, then avoid talking or making eye contact. If we were anywhere else, I'd think he's a shy guy, but somehow he mustered up the nerve to come in here and is seeking something. Could be one of those quiet pervs.

"So…are you a regular here at Mitzie's?"

"Not really. Haven't been here for years. Used to come once in a while, but my wife would freak out, so I stopped."

"That was nice of you…you know…to respect her feelings. Most guys would come anyway…sneak around and hide it from her. Says a lot about your relationship."

"She's a bitch." He signals for the waitress.

"I take it you're divorced?"

"Going through it." That explains his presence here.

"That must be pretty tough. I can't imagine. How long have you been married?"

"Twenty-seven years." He looks up at the ceiling as if to remember all of them.

"Wow. That's incredible. I have a hard time committing to cellular service for a year." He cracks a faint smile. "You don't look old enough to have been married that long. What up with that, Ray?" Have to lighten things up a bit here.

"Yeah, we hooked up pretty young. She got herself pregnant when we were in high school, got married and…here we are."

"How do you suppose she got herself pregnant? Some government experiment I didn't hear about?" It was the nicest way I could respond to his statement without ruining the potential business arrangement.

"You know what I mean. I guess it was…partly my fault." Uh, yeah! "I was sixteen. Young, dumb, and full of…"

"I got it." Too much information there, bud. I guess it's easier to tell a complete stranger your life story than talk to the person you've spent that lifetime with. I suspect this was the first time he was taking any responsibility for that jointly made decision to have sex almost thirty years ago, and probably has silently tortured his wife about it for as much time.

"Well, that's old news by now. Your…daughter…son?"

"Daughter."

"…she's an adult now, and hopefully you have no regrets…" He tilts his head side to side, questioning that concept. "Twenty-seven years is a long time to stay together, and it all worked out…well…except that you're getting divorced. Can't win 'em all, Ray." I nudge him in the side, trying to be funny.

"You want to dance the next song for me?" Trying to shut me up?

"I was just about to ask."

I stand up and kick open his legs so I have plenty of room. Some guys feel funny with their legs open so wide and constantly fight against me to close them. It trips me up and puts major pressure on my back. I've learned from the on-the-job training program it's much easier to start them out in a wide straddle, thus creating an adequate work space. Saves my aching sciatic and builds my quads.

I feel a bit awkward, kind of like the first few lap dances I did in Vegas. These aren't really *lap* dances. We can't actually touch the lap with any part of our bodies, thus requiring a bigger creative effort to accomplish the seduction. What to do, what to do? Girls dance on both sides of me. We're all sandwiched in on a long vinyl couch. The whole place is mirrored along the wall over the couch, so it makes it easy to watch what they're doing as well as be my own critic when trying out new moves.

The lighter atmosphere merits a permanent wardrobe change. I can see costuming is going to play an important role. My observation in the mirror reflection indicates our outfits function as props during the "personal dance," since we're limited in the arousal technique area. Most girls are wearing baby doll dresses with some kind of shorts and bikini top underneath. Layering appears to be key.

My preoccupation with the particulars here has taken me well into another song. I completely forgot about my client, who may have suffered a slight asphyxiation due to my bodily smothering in order to get a clear perspective in the mirror.

"Ray? You all right?" I pull back to give him a breath.

"Yeah, good. Thanks. Keep going." He's in the zone. Whatever works. Gives me more time to scope the room.

The moneymaking strategy will have to be completely different than Vegas. No hit-'n'-run hustle. I'll see these people again. Girls are friendly with their customers…and each other. Interesting. They're not leaving the guy as soon as the song ends. Makes sense…there're not enough guys in here to jump from one to the next. Got to make it an hour-long session with each guy: socialize, dance, socialize, dance. Should make at least fifty bucks an hour, and why not make it from one guy and cut down the meet-and-greet effort? A barely audible voice mumbles from my midsection.

"You want to take a break?" Back to reality. Who are you again?

"Oh sure, sweetie." I wipe a drop of sweat from my brow and sit down next to Ray. He's a little flushed.

"I need a drink. Want anything?"

Yeah, a Goldschlager, beer chaser, and a hundred dollars. "I'll just have a bottle of water, thanks." I cross my legs all feminine-like, as he signals for the waitress.

"What are you going to have—wait! Let me guess." I recall our conversation, then give him an inquisitive and thorough once-over. "Beer. Imported." He studies my prediction for a second. The waitress arrives.

"What can I get 'cha?"

"A bottle of water and…a Heineken." He gives me curious look. I smile at my accuracy.

"How did you know I was going to order that?"

"Just a little thing I do. I know people, that's all. So let's get back to your marriage."

"I don't want to talk about that. Let's talk about you. You're a good dancer. Worked here long?"

"What time is it?" I ask playfully. He looks at his watch a little confused.

"Nine."

"Two hours."

"It's your first day?" He's really confused now.

"Here. But I've been working in Vegas for a few months. I'm an old pro now."

"My wife and I got married in Vegas. She was seven months pregnant. We took off in my dad's Cadillac in the middle of the night." He laughs subtly to himself. "Crazy. Crazy days." He squirms in his seat. "She was feeling all fat…and self-conscious, you know being pregnant, but she looked beautiful. Preacher was late…Comes limpin' in with a cane…had some kind of cerebral palsy or something." He laughs, remembering the scene. "He talked a mile a minute, and the whole thing was over in about five minutes. We always said we were gonna have a real ceremony, but never got around to it. Time…you know. Oh well, too late now, right?" He catches himself going on and on. "Ahhh, never mind. You probably got other guys to get to."

"I'll get to 'em. What is it about the limpers in Vegas? Everyone's got a leg issue…one longer than the other, hip problem, so fat the thighs are touching. I call them the waddlers. If you get behind them in the casino…forget about it. It's like trying to plow through gridlock on the 405 during rush hour."

"You're pretty funny. Although, I might be one of those waddlers. Carrying a few extra pounds these days." He taps himself on the beer belly.

"Happens to the best of us." I pinch my half-inch love handle. "You ready for a couple more dances?" It's getting to be about that time.

"What the hell." He assumes the wide straddle position on his own, and I jump in between his legs, and put on my sensual face. It's such a peculiar phenomenon…having casual conversation with a stranger, seducing him for a couple minutes, then changing hats again as if no passionate moment was shared. I still don't understand why they pay for this. Maybe I never will.

When the night is finally over, I join the gaggle of girls outside the front door of Mitzie's, waiting for the club van to pick us up and drive us to our cars. It's another way the owners minimize the potential liability should anything happen to one of their girls in the parking lot. We tip the driver a few bucks, and get the door-to-door service. The only annoyance is waiting for him to come back around after he's taken a full carload out. Guys gather out here in the "smoking section." The last thing you want to do at the end of your night is talk to the patrons that saw you in your underwear now that you're out of the metamorphosis and wearing your normal-life hat.

A guy I danced for about an hour ago acknowledges me with a nod. I gesture with the half-smile…pleasant, yet not inviting. He stomps his cigarette out, and I sense he's about to say something to me despite the unapproachable air I'm putting out. I play a little dazed, and whimsically turn my body the other way, brushing shoulders with another girl waiting.

"Oh, sorry. Trying to avoid talking to somebody."

"I hear ya'. Got to keep it in the club." She turns her head and blows cigarette smoke in the other direction. I can't believe how many people still smoke with all the evidence of physical detriment broadcasted through the media these days. This girl is roughly twenty-five, maybe twenty-six. Beautiful skin, great bod…downright gorgeous, except for the cancer stick hanging off her mouth.

"Are you new?" she asks, then tosses the lit cigarette in the parking lot as if she read my mind.

"Yeah."

"I'm Ava. I'd shake, but…" Both our hands are full carrying purses, clothes bag, and the same snack from the vending machine—baked Lay's potato chips.

"That's Ok. I'm Alex. So, how is this place to work…you know, overall?" I hadn't made any attempt to talk to the other girls today. I figure they're not too happy to have another newbie to compete with.

"It's all right. Busy almost every night. That's all I care about. Get in, get out." Sounds like my attitude. The driver pulls up, and we pile in the van with four other girls, then circle out of the parking lot. I notice Ava's designer sandals. Charles David, my favorite shoe store. She's dressed nice. Dark sleeveless turtleneck, black stretch pants flared at the bottom, cool belt. Very sleek. She's sharp. I feel a little frumpy in my sweats and slip-on tennies, but it's not like anyone cares what we arrive to work in. Maybe she has another job.

"You should work Monday nights. When football season starts, it's the best night of the week. That's me right here!" Ava yells to the driver. The van stops and she gathers her stuff.

"Thanks. You workin' tomorrow?" I say, moving my legs to one side so she can climb out.

"Yeah. You?"

"Probably."

"Cool. I'll see ya' then." She exits the van. The driver waits until she gets into her BMW before moving on. The metallic gray 535i suits her.

She pulls away from the curb aggressively. The plate reads: SC FLMBTCH. Interesting.

> *Dear Diary,*
> *Day one at Mitzie's: made $250, kept clothes on, no drama.*
> *Met Ray—midforties, getting divorced but doesn't know why.*
> *Found friend, Ava. Stunning, driven, ball-breaker. Lesbian?*

Summer is the slow time for the entertainment industry. All the block-busters are in theaters already. Film production is halted to nearly half of what it normally is. Most TV shows are on hiatus, which accounts for very little extra work. Phil turned me on to some companies that cast extras and body doubles. When I can, I try to book jobs on fun shows. It's not the most desirable work, but at least it's an opportunity to get on the set.

I had gotten my SAG card a few months back by doing "stand-in" work that a friend of Staci's set me up with. It's a no-brainer job that pays about a hundred a day. As the position indicates, you basically stand in for the actor in-between shots so the lighting crew can reset the lights, and the DP (director of photography) can set up the next shot. You sometimes have to stand there for hours, which is why the actors won't do it.

I got a call early yesterday morning from a background casting company urgently seeking a stand-in for the athletic brunette actress on *Baywatch*. Ideally, the stand-in looks like the actress, or at least has the same general height, weight, and skin color characteristics. They must have really been in a bind, since our similarities are nearly null, but I'm glad I got the gig. I'd hoped my assets would stand out on this particular production, and I especially hoped there'd be a chance I could get asked to do something else.

Everyone knows *Baywatch* is all about the bodies. The entire cast wears bathing suits, and all the girls use stunt doubles. I wouldn't have minded diving into the ocean when Pammy or Tiffany don't want to get their hair wet. I thought maybe Hasselhoff would see how agreeable and non-prima donna I am, and create a character for me. What? I can dream.

The very long day filming on the beach yesterday was slightly less than ideal. Despite my efforts to entertain the crew doing standup while standing under hot lights and the fierce Southern California rays for twelve hours, the only attention I got from producers was indirectly through the second AD regarding the severity of my sunburn and how it might impact their workers' comp. You'd think they'd be doling out the sunscreen on an outdoor set in the middle of summer, but I guess it was my responsibility to bring my own.

The extra bucks made for working overtime, I suppose, will compensate me for taking tonight off from the club. I can't conceive of some needy conversationalist pawing on me after my skin nearly snaps from the bodily distortions necessary to hold his attention. As usual, my entertainment industry gain ends in a financial bust. Will I ever make any money at this career?

"Hey. How goes it?"

"It goes. What's up?"

"Trina's in trouble. She needs money." Liza's tone is one of sincere concern.

"What happened? I thought they were doing really well with Evan's thingamajig?"

"They were. He left. Took off with a younger version, stole all the money, *and* is fighting for the kids."

"What! Oh my God! She must be devastated. What's she gonna do? She's never really worked." I haven't talked to Trina for a while. Her life has been all about kids, and we just don't have as much in common anymore. I miss her.

"I don't know. She wants to talk to you. Hang on, I'm gonna three-way us." She puts me on hold for a few seconds.

"Hello? Everyone here?" Liza leads the convo.

"I'm here. Trina, you on?" I hear a quiet cry. The one where you squint your eyes and open your mouth real big in such a hysterical sob it makes no noise.

"I'm here." She fights to speak, trying to cover the tears.

"Listen, don't worry about a thing. We'll get him. That bastard! Where are the kids?"

"He took 'em!" They both answer.

"Took them where? Did he serve you any papers?" I hurl into legal mode.

"I don't know what it all is." I can hear her fumble with documents. "…temporary custody orders, a restraining order…"

"Restraining order! How did he get that?" I ask, knowing she's not violent.

"When I found out about the girl, I threw a plate at him. I missed, but he picked up the broken glass and cut his hand. I think he did it on purpose. He ran to the ER, then the police station. Seemed like he had it all planned out. He never came home that night, and three days later I got these papers, and he took the kids from school."

"How could you miss with a plate! Should have thrown the whole set." This is the icing on the cake with men for me.

"He locked up all our money, canceled my credit cards, and drained every resource I've got."

"She didn't keep any of her own accounts." Liza is quick to point out the obvious marital flaw.

"I-I-I didn't think…he was really doing it. He made me think I was crazy for accusing him all this time." She's really fighting the tearful outburst. Trina's always been a proud person. Strong, happy, passionate about life. She got a little snobby when she first started hanging in the Beverly Hills circles, but for the most part, she's down to earth and loving when it counts.

"I hate him! That fucker! Eleven years of my life!"

"Ok, take it easy. Calm down. First things first. What do the papers say about visiting the kids?"

"Every other Sunday. Twice a month! I can't be without my kids, Alex. They're my life. What can I do?"

"We got to get you a lawyer."

"I tried. They all want ten thousand dollars up front. I don't even have enough money to live on right now. I'm selling everything I own just to get by."

"What's the deal on the house?"

"You guys, I got to go. They're paging me at work. Trina, call me if you need me." Liza exits the three-way call.

"Evan says I've got sixty days before he'll sell it."

"He can't do that. He's just trying to scare you and control you. Sounds like he's been doing that for a while."

"How could I have let this happen? My kids…I let them down." She starts to cry again.

"Trina, don't do this to yourself. They're old enough to know what's going on. He can't brainwash them now. Be thankful he didn't pull this when they were five or six. They're almost teenagers. They'll survive. Can you call them?"

"Yeah, and they're calling me every day when he's gone."

"Good. Now, let's focus on getting you some money. How about your high society friends? There must be somebody you can go to?"

"I can't, I can't! It's so embarrassing. And they just l-o-v-e Evan. He's been schmoozing all our friends and probably bad-mouthing me for a long time. I think he's been plotting for months, Alex."

"Sounds like it. How did he get the custody orders? Were you notified of a court date?"

"I didn't get anything. Is it legal if he forged my signature or said he couldn't find me?"

"No. And he'll be in a lot of trouble if he did that. Don't panic about anything. I can walk you through the legal process myself. It may take a while to get things undone, but you WILL prevail in the long run. Just don't do anything crazy. Don't go over there. Don't try to take the kids. You got to resist the urge to do what you know is right, and go through the motions of the court stuff. We'll get him, and he won't see it coming. Lay low."

"What am I gonna do about money?"

"Well…you can always do what I'm doing. It's immediate cash." I hate to encourage anyone to do this job, but she's in a pretty tight spot.

"Oh God! I wouldn't be caught dead! I know people. Evan would find out and taunt me every night. I can't. It's way too demeaning!"

"It's whatever you make of it." I have to defend myself a little. "You could always telemarket. Those jobs are easy to get."

"Bothersome phone solicitors? I don't think so."

"What about car sales?"

"Cars! Don't get me started. He took my Benz! I'm driving my nephew's station wagon. It's from 1973!"

"A true Griswold wagon."

"Can you imagine me in this thing? Is it self-defense if I kill him during an emotional outburst that *he* caused?"

"Take it easy. How about cocktailing? I could probably get you a job at Mitzie's."

"Alex, I haven't done that for years. I don't even remember how. My life has been so different than the old days. I belong to the Beverly Hills Wives' Club, for crying out loud! Fifty grand a year! I can't sling cocktails for a hundred dollars a night!"

"Did you say sling? I heard sling. The ol' bar slang rears its ugly head. Sling slang, sling slang...say that five times fast..."

"Cut it out! Come on, be serious. I have to figure this out."

"Listen, I know you don't want to take a job that's *beneath* you, but your options are slim at the moment. You have two choices: borrow from the Rodeo Drive Snobbery, or join the Orange County Man-Haters Association and come work with me." She lets out an annoyed sigh.

"We got to get your kids back, and he's not getting off scot-free. He owes you a lot of money, Trina."

"I don't remember one thing about cocktailing. They're not going to give me a job."

"You drink a lot! It's the same thing...no-brainer. It'll all come back to you, I promise. Don't forget about what I said about laying low. I know it's gonna be hard, but he has resources that you don't, and if you freak out and do something stupid, it will be a very long road to getting them back. Call me when you've made your decision." With that we hang up.

I know I was a little harsh with Trina, but sometimes people need a push when going through life's transitional stages. Especially when that change was forced on you by someone you once loved and trusted, and has now violated your most basic human rights.

A woman in my office at the firm had gone through a bitter divorce and custody battle. I watched her deteriorate as she went from a smart, sophisticated, dedicated worker and mother, to a complete basket case. Her ex was relentless—mental abuse and constant harassment. She ultimately resorted to kidnaping her children and went into seclusion somewhere on the West Coast. Her lawyer, a products liability attorney from our firm and a good friend of hers, advised her to surrender the kids and face the felony parental abduction she was being charged with. We all figured that her ex had mentally depleted her so badly that her brain couldn't possibly have been functioning in full capacity when she made the decision to hang herself. The control freak had won.

In my opinion, Evan had always been a controlling personality. He made sure Trina didn't have much of a life of her own. When the kids were young, she used to tell Liza and me not to come to the house. He was afraid of germs and airborne bacteria breaking down the twins' immune system, and preferred that no one came in. The first time I saw them was through the window out in the yard, and he still insisted we wear protective masks. I'm sure it was his way of pushing us out of her life, so he could maintain complete control over her.

The sudden money they came into launched them into a totally different lifestyle. They dined in expensive restaurants almost every night, traveled a lot, and had many toys. I assumed she was happy. She never let on to any major problems, which I did think was strange since my personal views were that he's a scumbag. It's all in the eyes. The passageway to the soul. His are black. Piercing. When he looks at you, it's as if the wheels are turning so fast, he can't keep up with his thoughts of how he could manipulate you into getting something he wants.

I remember at one of their anniversary parties, I caught Trina's mom saying in jest, "It's hard to kill a bad thing." I assumed she was referring to her husband, who had run off with a foreign exchange college student that they housed that year, but now I wonder if she had the same feeling about Evan that I did, and didn't know how to tell her daughter what she was in for. Why is it that deviant significant others are so transparent to everyone other than the person closest to them?

7

First Down

Dear Diary,

Sorry I haven't been writing every night after work…too exhausted. Back, neck, quads, calves, feet, and ego all hurt. Had no idea it was going to be so hard on my body to work every day…and the rejection! It's as bad as in entertainment. Am finally starting to generate regular customers. Ed: forties, bald, lonely, computer geek, chronic gingivitis. Diagnosis: eternally single. Marty: thirties, divorced with money (DWM), deep, internally tortured, married a cheerleader who took him for a ride. Diagnosis: quietly bitter, will probably repeat dumb-blond adventure. Jim: late-twenties, obnoxious, arrogant, narcissistic, drinks too much, marital status unknown (he lies), likely single, never been in a meaningful relationship. Diagnosis: will date dancer after dancer after dancer. Bob: fifties, happily married, successful, generous, good guy. Diagnosis: searching for something…hmmm.

It's Monday night. The first pre-season game of the NFL is almost underway. The club is filling up fast. And so is the locker room. Girls that I've never seen before flock in here like they own the place. Not that I know everyone that works here, but in the past few weeks, I've seen the same faces every night, and it seems strange to see so many new ones tonight. Ava and I metamorphose in the back corner, claiming our mirror space and lockers.

"What's with all the new girls?"

"They're Monday-nighters. Seasonal strippers. Bring in their own guys, and just come in to party. Don't worry, they won't tap into your regular scene." Ava knows the lowdown.

"How can they not? There're so many of them." I need to make money tonight. I haven't quite gotten up to quota here yet.

"They're not hard-core hustlers. Most of them have other jobs, and they come here for extra money. Hey. How's it going?" She nods at a black girl across the room, who nods back. "She's a teacher…eighth grade at Inglewood, I think."

"If her math class only knew what she does for recreational cash."

"Yeah, they'd be model students…at least the boys, anyway." We share a laugh.

"So, do you go to SC? I saw your plate."

"Yeah. My last semester. Can't wait to get out." Ava scoots toward me to give another girl room at the long mirror. She's upside down, putting makeup on her butt. I lean across and address the girl quietly.

"I get that same rash from the vinyl seats. You need a cream?" The girl stands upright and looks at me like I'm crazy.

"Nooo, I'm just covering a scar, but thanks for the tip. Gross!" So much for trying to be helpful.

"Anyway…so you're in the homestretch? I remember my last year of college. Brutal."

"Where'd you go?"

"Arizona State."

"Top-ten party school."

"Number six this year." I'm so proud.

"What are you going to do when you get out?" I ask, prodding for more insight into my new friend.

"Make movies." She squirms into a very tight, fluorescent, Lycra mini-dress.

"Cool. I'm an actress…sort of…trying to be. Maybe we can do something together after you graduate."

"Maybe. My final project is to make a short. I'm not sure what I'm gonna do yet, but I'll keep you in mind for something."

"Great. Thanks." She shuts her locker and fluffs her hair, then heads out the door tapping a little Mexican girl on the butt on her way. The girl smiles and winks at Ava.

I'm pretty neutral on the whole gay thing. To each their own, as long as they respect the normal physical contact boundaries that we all adhere to. No one wants to see anybody, same-sex or hetero, slobbering on each other in public. I'll never understand why the sex part of being gay is the most emphasized characteristic of that relationship. It's not like every time you see a hetero couple walk down the street, all you can think of is them having sex. (If you're doing that, you might want to talk to a professional about it.) Most of them probably aren't having sex anymore at all, and yet the relationship still exists. I wonder how many gay couples love each other, share their lives, grow together, but hardly have sex anymore.

Ava is likely a trendy lesbian. She's sexy, strong-yet-feminine, and probably had lots of boyfriends through high school and college. Maybe she's had a few too many letdowns from men, and is at a point where she prefers the companionship of someone else sexy and feminine. This business could do it to you, too. I mean, all you see are men behaving badly, and attractive, seductive women luring them into a trance-like state where they will willfully do anything you want them to do. The more powerful the woman, the weaker the man.

The concept intrigues me, but I don't think I'll ever resort to lesbianism. I'm too fond of the penis. Women just don't do it for me. The best of all worlds may be to use guys for sex, and stop thinking they're worthy of anything else. God, am I really at that point?

"People, people! Clear a path. Coming through! The V is here!" A familiar voice enters the locker room, dragging a large duffel bag behind her.

Viagra makes her way to the back corner, high-fiveing girls along the way. I find myself analyzing the unusually strong sense of camaraderie. There must be a bonding process that takes place after putting in so much time in this business. A unanimous understanding that the job sucks, but we do it since the benefits outweigh the disadvantages.

Viagra plows through the welcoming committee, and takes possession of a locker near mine, not yet noticing me. I haven't seen her since that night in the VIP room in Vegas, and I never did figure out her real name. I feel stupid calling her Viagra.

"Hey…you." She looks up.

"Hey! We got to stop meetin' like this," she jokes. "What's going on? I knew you weren't gonna last long in the City of Doom."

"You called it. I reached my point of no return. Are you still going?"

"Here and there. Only when I absolutely have to. How long you been here?"

"A couple weeks. It's going Ok. Thanks for turning me on to this place."

"No worries, dude. It's way easier, right?" She opens the dreaded bag full of dancer clothes that have never seen the inside of a washing machine.

"Yeah, I guess." I pull my head back to avoid getting hit in the face with the escaping stench.

"Dude...check it out." She spreads the bag fully open, and exhibits piles of what appear to be clean and folded exotic dancewear.

"No way! You washed everything? Doesn't that violate your rule of not doing anything courteous for your sponsors?"

"Semiannual laundering I do for myself. Kept getting some kind of sweat rash. Figured it was time."

"I got a good cream for that. So, what's your plan? You gonna work here for a while? I could use the support."

"Yeah, at least through football season. Monday nights rock."

"That's what I keep hearing. I guess I'll find out tonight." I put the final touches on my makeup, adjust my boobs to a more flattering position, and decide I'm ready to tackle the crowd. Viagra reaches in her bag, pulls out a tiny yellow handkerchief, and hands it to me.

"Here. You're gonna need this."

"What's this for?"

"Penalties."

"What am I supposed to do with it?"

"Just tuck it in your side. You'll know when to bring it out."

"You're the pro." I do what she says, and tuck it in my side, trying not to create a bulge. I start to head down the stairs, then hesitate, and feel compelled to use this moment to resolve the great mystery.

"Ok, I feel like a big idiot...but I've got to ask. What is your real name?"

"I knew you didn't know. No worries, dude. Everyone here calls me V."

"So you're not going to tell me?"

"Just call me V."

"Ok. See ya' down there…V." What is the big deal? I guess some people just don't like their names. It's funny how those with the same name tend to have similar personality characteristics. You'd never see a Tiffany or a Heather that is anything other than blond, soft and feminine, with a tendency to be timid and/or needy. I like guys' names on girls. Randy, Sidney, Jo, Andy, Reece—all good inner-strength-building names. Too bad it doesn't go the other way. A boy named Sue just doesn't cut it.

Whoa! I can barely push open the locker door to get out! Standing room only. They weren't kidding about Mitzie's being the place to be on Monday nights. There's not an empty seat in the house. I groove over to the DJ to sign in and make my music request for the stage. Most of the girls have pretty good musical taste. Each girl gets to pick her first song only, then dance to other girls' picks for the next three. It sucks if you get a sappy, weepy, chick harmony tune to have to be sexy to. I think I'll go with a little old-school funk tonight—*zap*.

The football game is on, and most of the beer-drinking faces are staring upward at the wall-mounted screens. I catch some guy peeking his head out from Ava's midriff to check the score. She doinks him upside the head.

I'm feeling good, wearing a new outfit, and ready to make bank tonight. I scan through the crowd looking for anyone I know. The problem with this many people in the room is figuring out where to start. I always avoided large groups of guys in Vegas. You know what they say—power in numbers. It's much easier to make some kind of connection with one single guy who might yield a hundred bucks, than jump into a party group that wants to try every girl in the house once, or wait until their buddies get one to decide if she's worthy. I spot Marty in the back corner rocking back and forth.

"Hi, Marty. How are you?"

"Fine." His bodily twitching indicates otherwise.

"Can I sit?" I ask.

The unwritten rule in strip clubs is if you invite the girl to sit down, you're agreeing to buy at least one dance or pay her for the time she spends with you.

"Ok."

I slide in next to him. He stops rocking, then bites his nails nervously.

"So what's going on? Haven't seen you the last couple days."

"My father has Alzheimer's. He's running our family business into bank-ruptcy."

"Bummer."

"He can't remember any decisions he makes, including the one where I'm in charge. Every day he fires me, that is, if he remembers who I am."

"Wow. Talk about negative work space."

"My mom tried to commit suicide, and is institutionalized up north. She thinks she's at Sears." And they say the dancers are messed up.

"One big happy family, huh?"

"What?" he yells over the noise.

"I said, probably used to be a happy family?"

"No, not really." He looks at the floor as he talks. "My ex-wife moved to Tahoe with my son. I won't be able to see him for months."

"Marty, this is really depressing. I wish I could help you, but I'm not the person you should be..." He breaks down, and grabs my shoulder, sobbing. "Oh, for crying out loud. Are you Ok? You're drizzling on my bustier." I hand him a napkin.

"Sorry. I didn't mean to lay all this on you. But it's just that...I...I don't have anyone to talk to." He pulls a wad of cash out of his front pocket. "Here. Take this. Will you please just talk to me. I don't want you to dance. Just talk." He hands me a hundred dollar bill.

I nestle back into my seat and realize how lonely life must be when there's no one to talk to. I've always had people around. Never at a loss for friends, boyfriends, or family. If anything, I was the one trying to be alone. Someone was always in my space. Even if I never have another relation-ship, and all my friends and family move away, I don't think I'll ever know the true meaning of being lonely. Someone like Marty has probably had a lifetime of tormented loneliness, all the while surrounded by people.

I let Marty talk non-stop for over an hour. I got the impression he'd never done that before. He gave me more details than I cared to know about his family, marriage, sex life (or lack thereof), business, and the only interesting part, his five-year-old's incredible athletic skills. I felt bad for him, but what could I really do to help him? I'm practically in my under-wear with boobs seeping out of a saliva-drenched bustier. I'm not dressed for counseling. I do have an unused psychology degree, though...hmmm ...maybe I should dust off some old books and brush up on my Freud and Jung?

I see Viagra across the room hurriedly coming my way. She bullies her way through the shoulder-to-shoulder crowd, smacking one guy for copping a free feel. Three others block her path just as she's about to thrust onto my scene. They solicit her services for a group dance. She's not one to be intimidated, but she is petite, and could easily be overpowered. The three take her by the arm and begin leading her to a booth. It's obvious this is not what she wants to do. She shakes loose, and throws her yellow hanky at them, then yells.

"I don't think so, boys. Too many men on the field!" She hustles toward me.

"Come here. I want you to meet someone." Viagra yanks me out of my seat.

"Marty, I'll see you next time," I yell to him as V drags me away. "The good thing about being down…there's only one way to go. Keep your chin up." Cliched advice, but it was the best I could do at the moment.

"Where are we going?" I ask V as she parades me through the maze of drunken gropers.

"Just follow me. Some guys I haven't seen for a long time are here. They're really cute *and* have money."

"I don't like dancing for cute guys. It makes me nervous, and I don't know what to do."

"That's ridiculous! Do the same thing you always do." We pit-stop in the bathroom and continue our conversation through adjacent stalls.

"It's different with the derelicts. I'm usually making up my grocery list during the dance. The whole thing is fake, you know, and…they're easily entertained. Cute, normal guys are a way tougher crowd to please. I freeze up." I hear V's toilet flush, and she exits the stall.

"You got to get away from the fat, bald slobs. There's no future there! These guys are cool. They like to party, and maybe we can hook up."

"I don't want to hook up with anybody! Especially someone I meet here. They all have issues…and…and…I'm in a bad place with men."

"You're overanalyzing. Fuckin' chill out and have some fun, will ya'?" She shoves me out the door. A feisty little thing, isn't she?

We weave through the crowd, and arrive at her friends' table. There're three of them. A short, Italian loudmouth who probably spends five hours a day in the gym, taking breaks only to admire his physique in the mirror. A tall, skinny, surfer type with big blue eyes, who's proud to be three-fisted with drinks. And the rugged, baby-faced, quiet observer, taking it all in slowly.

"Bobby, Fish, Jode…this is my sister…" I shoot Viagra an abrupt look and shake my head. "I mean, my friend, Alex."

"Hey. How's it going?" I'm thrilled.

"Well, well, well. What do we have here! Bobby Terrelli at your service, ma'am." The short Italian takes my hand and kisses it. I see his eyes shift to a huge rack that belongs to a blond walking by. I pull my hand back, and grab a glass of champagne V pours for us.

"Alex used to bartend at the bikini bar." V initiates conversation. "These guys were regulars there for a long time."

"Yeah, we made our rounds. Those chicks would call us…beg us to come in. We were like royalty in there." Bobby is his own greatest fan.

"I don't remember seeing you. Did you ever come to the bar?" I ask.

"Baby, we were VIP-ers all the way. They came to us. Drinks, girls—shit, the managers set us up with whatever we wanted, right, Fish?" He clanks the surfer dude's glass with his.

"No doubt, bro." Well said, well spoken, BG.

"What the hell happened to that place?" Bobby asks as his eyes wander back and forth between the TV, various sets of boobs (including mine), and V's butt as she begins a dance for Fish. I test his listening skills.

"Health department closed them down. There was an epidemic of syphilis and herpes going around. Got in the food and everything."

"Bullshit!" he screams at the TV. "These refs are blind! Did you see that?"

"No, no…I was talking." I catch eye contact with the quiet one, Jode, who caught my little anecdote about the bar. We share a smirk.

"Fuck, this game's over! I can't watch this shit anymore!" Bobby gives me a twenty. "Dance for my friend. I got to piss."

V winks at me as she continues dancing for Fish. I watch her technique. She nibbles on his ear, and does the occasional forbidden bump and grind. Surfer Dude appears to have been blessed in the most masculine of ways. Things are growing around here.

I stand up and prepare to go through the motions of my usual blasé routine for Jode. He is really cute. Thirty-two, maybe. That perfect amount of scruff on his face. Green eyes, sandy brown hair, nice build. Ok! Snap out of it! No liking the customers!

"You know, I'm not really into the whole dance thing. Doesn't do it for me. If you just want to hang and have a drink, we can call it even." He closes his legs politely.

Fine with me. I didn't want to risk looking stupid anyway. I seem to lose my sex appeal when I need it most.

"Oh, thanks." I sit down next to him. "I could use a break, anyway. Been pretty busy the last couple hours."

"Yeah, I bet you're in high demand in here."

"Why do you say that?"

"Well, you're far from ugly." I guess that's a compliment.

"Thanks, but I would probably be a little closer to ugly if it weren't for the exceptional talents of the club designers that installed the ever-so-flattering soft yellow lighting."

"Here's to the crew." He raises his glass. "You really are beautiful in this light…" We simultaneously finish the perfect setup. *"But you can't always count on the light."* We surprise each other being on the same wavelength. Seems to scare him a bit. It's been somewhat of a hobby of mine for years…quoting movie lines from old comedies. Trina and I used to do it all the time. Drove our friends crazy.

"So…Jode. What's your story?"

"Don't have one. Just a normal guy, hanging out, watching the entertainment." He clams up, and adjusts his attention to the TV.

V is marathon dancing for Fish. She hasn't taken a break since we got here. Not much help with the conversation lull. I'm not usually at such a loss for words, but something about Jode intimidates me.

"They say the quiet ones are the most dangerous." I try again.

"Who says that?"

"You know…they."

"You're just looking for a reason to find something wrong with me so you can put me in one of the categories here."

"Very intuitive…for a guy with a girl's name. How do you spell that, by the way?"

"J-O-D-E. And it's not a girl's name. It's unisex…kind of like Alex. *No! You idiot!*"

I spill my champagne and nearly fall off the seat as he jumps up and yells at the TV. Somebody dropped something, I guess. I'll never understand men's obsession with football. It's not like their kid is playing, or anyone they know. Imagine if women were as emotional while watching their favorite cooking show. *Moron! You forgot to grease the pan! Pass the spray! Just pass it already! Forget it! It's all over!*

"Well, I think I'll go mosey around. It was nice meeting you, and I'm sure I'll see you again." He looks a little disappointed that I'm leaving, but he's not fighting for me to stay, so I follow through with my threatened exit.

"Hey! Where you going, babe?" Bobby spins me around, wraps his arms around my waist, and rubs his pelvis against mine to the beat of the music. "We're just gettin' started. C'mon, let's party." I whip out my yellow flag and stuff it in his mouth.

"That is a foul! A flagrant personal foul!" I picked up a little football lingo in my day. I peel his hands off my body, and push him back. Jode intercepts and leads Bobby to his seat.

"Sorry about him. Can't take him anywhere."

"Par for the course, I guess."

"Listen, I was a little distracted before. Takes me a while to unwind after work. Are you always here on Mondays...'cause I'd really like to talk to you some more."

"I'll make that decision at the end of the night." Not the best moment to ask me.

"Well, I hope so. I definitely want to see you again...and maybe next time, I'll let you dance for me." He smiles boyishly.

"You'll *let* me? Are you sure you can get through it? Tough guy...with a girl's name?" I punch him in the arm playfully. "See ya' around. *I'll be back.*"

Dear Diary,

Don't know about this stripper thing. Money's decent. Trying hard to apply myself to career goals, but am so damn distracted by club activity. Can't do what other girls do. It's becoming a real problem for me. They play games with customers. Lead them on and make them think they really like them. It's a dangerous game. Some of these guys teeter on a paper-thin line of sanity. I wouldn't be surprised if one snapped and lashed out in an unspeakable fashion. Every day something happens that takes a little piece of me. Some idiot says something stupid or grabs me offensively. Why do they think they have power over us in there? We're providing a service that apparently is in great desire, yet none of them have an ounce of respect for what we're doing. Why does it have to be so negative? Need to gain something more than $$ or can't keep doing it. I'm giving up too much to play this role. One of my regulars got mad when he asked to have lunch with me. I told him I don't socialize with customers outside the club. He threw money he owed me on the floor, and left in a huff. I hear other girls respond to similar requests making endless excuses. Their guys keep coming back. What do they all want?

P.S. Trina got hired. Looking forward to laughing with my old friend again.

8

Second Down

September has been a busy month. I've been working a lot at the club and, in my spare time, studying up on family law and psychotherapy. Trina and I got through the first phase of paperwork to get the ball rolling on her court case, and I've decided that lap dancing is the cheapest form of therapy for the Mitzie's misfits, so I should milk it for all it's worth.

The entertainment industry is finally heating up, and I'm auditioning more regularly. Last week I went on one for a Reebok commercial. I had to do a standing backflip on a wood floor in the ad agent's office. They kindly gave me an area about four feet by three feet in which to do it. The theme was going to be a black screen with this figure wearing a string of little fluorescent round balls flipping through the air. It was going to be so cool, and could have yielded anywhere from $10,000 to $50,000. They booked me for the job and said someone would call me for a fitting the next day. No one called, and by the third day I called them.

"I'm sorry, Alex, but we decided to go with a man. We fear that your breasts would pose a problem for the sleek look we're going for."

"These little things? They're no problem, trust me. I can flatten out easily with a sports bra." Nobody has ever accused my 34-Bs of being too big.

"I'm sorry. We already booked him. But we'll keep your pictures on file and if anything else—"

"Was anybody going to call me? You did officially book me for the job!" Now I'm irritated.

"Actually, we were just about to call you when you called. And again, Alex, we're really sorry things didn't work out. We have a lot of this kind of work coming up, so we will definitely keep you in mind. Good luck with your pursuits."

I can't believe how producers and ad agents take advantage of talent. Do they think we're stupid? Or don't know our rights? I went home and read through all the union stuff I have, then marched straight into SAG's office and filed a grievance report. They won't be able to air their commercial until I get paid for the work I was rightfully hired for. These companies gamble that starving artists won't risk compromising the possibility of future work with the ad agencies, and most probably don't. I wasn't about to let them get away with that. All they had to do was call, and maybe I wouldn't have been so pissed, but to just blow me off like I have nothing better to do than wait by the phone was not going to be tolerated!

I've read about actors that go through this kind of stuff over and over for years and by the time they get their break, they're so cynical about the business that no one wants to work with them. I can't let that happen to me. I have to learn to shake it off, but the rejection is so hard. My acting teacher says not to dwell on all the disappointment, and have adequate balance of work, family, and social activities in order to combat it. It's been a while since I've done anything fun. The last thing I feel like doing after selling my personality and dancing in high heels for six hours is go to a bar and make small talk. Maybe the girls and I will take a trip when I get the money from the commercial. Note: Check into Cabo, South Beach, Palm Springs, and various spas.

Thursday nights are the slowest night of the week. I like them. It's mellow. Not too many girls…not too many guys. I can spend more time with my regulars, and not feel like I'm missing opportunities to meet new ones. We get to be a bit more creative on stage when it's slow. There's only one girl at a time, and we can dance to our own music. It's taken me this long to get comfortable up there. I didn't go on the stage very often in Vegas. It was easier to pay to stay off and not have to worry about missing my name being called, since I usually had a different one every time I was there.

The stage is a scary thing. You can always spot a newbie dancer. Legs shaking, awkward movements, trying too hard to be sexy, utterly petrified inside. We all went through it—complicated outfits that won't come off, shoes that blister immediately, drinking too much so you can't keep your balance…typical work hazards.

I've always loved to dance, and when the elements are right, the time on stage can be most empowering. I've had a few instances where I forget where I'm at, let myself become mesmerized by the music, and slip into my own passionate moment. I think, deep down, most women secretly want to be seductresses. It's part of being a woman. One of my favorites for this performance is Madonna's "Justify My Love." Does it to me every time.

I exit the stage smiling at the eager applause I induced, and head for the bar. It's Trina's first night, and my afterthought of the day is that I forgot to warn her about the bartender.

"All right…I need a…draft beer…a vodka tonic, another draft beer…two whiskey sours, a Scotch and water…and another draft beer." Trina wears a black, floor-length sequined dress, and heavy jewelry. She fumbles with the bar tickets, and sends the bartender, Kelly, running back and forth to the beer tap. Kelly stops cold in her tracks after the second trip.

"Anything else?" she says, patronizing Trina. "We have a call order here. Do you know what a call order is?" She doesn't give her an opportunity to answer. "It's used to make my job easier, so I don't have to spend time with you lame waitresses. I'm here to make money, aren't you?" Trina looks at me like she's gonna kill her. This is a woman with a restraining order, so I better jump in.

"Hi, Kelly. This is my very dear friend Trina. It's her first night. Can you cut her a little slack? It's been a while since she's waitressed."

"Really! I couldn't tell!" She plops the drinks on Trina's tray and walks away.

"I knew there was a reason I haven't worked for twelve years." She sucks down the Scotch and water in record time. "I'm in way too fragile a state of mind to be insulted by a skinny bitch bar troll every time I need an order! You gotta do something, Alex, or this is not going to work out." She reaches for the whiskey sour. I snatch the tray from her. "You can't drink all your orders! Get the guys to buy you drinks. You're here to make money, remember? Your own money! Imagine the possibilities."

"I know, I know. I phased out for a second. I should drink the beers…they're cheaper." She grabs one off the tray. I swoop it out of her hands and hold the tray high above my head.

"Listen, we have a lot of work to do to if we want to bury Evan. You need this job. Kelly only works a couple nights a week. I'll talk to her, but in the meantime, stay semi-sober, get off your high horse, and go serve people." I hand her back the tray. She scoffs at me.

"I have a staff that waits on me hand and foot. *This* is despicable that I have to serve men that are all cheating on their wives!"

"You *had* a staff, and *this*, my friend, is our reality. But the good news is it's not forever. Remember that motivational speaker you like…Suze Mormon?"

"Orman."

"Right. Temporary problem toward a permanent solution. We got to get the kids, then we'll work on getting a life, Ok?"

"Fine." She pouts and tugs on her gown, then reluctantly delivers her drink order.

"Hey…Ginger?" I call out to her. "You're supposed to wear black, not black tie." Couldn't resist. She smiles sarcastically at me while collecting money from her customer. Twelve years of pompous attitude won't undo overnight, but little by little, we'll get the old Trina back.

I take a lap around the room and spot three of my regulars. It's so much easier when they're here. I know I can make at least sixty bucks from each of them. I'll wrap up my whole workday in a couple hours. Let's see…who to counsel first. Marty is doing his usual rocking back and forth. Ray is sitting with someone else. Ed gets dances from a lot of girls. He's alone right now. That's a good place to start. His bad breath is so potent it tears up my eyes. Time must be limited. I stroll over to the DJ booth, pick up some mints, arrange to be called on stage in exactly twenty minutes, and then put on my happy face and head toward Halitosis Man.

"Hi, sweetie…how are you?"

"Hey, Alex, have a seat." I sit down close to him trying to disguise the involuntary gag that occurs immediately after he opens his mouth as a yawn.

"So…what's new in the software business? Come up with your million-dollar program yet?"

"Oh no, I don't have time to research anything new. Busy, busy, busy with other people's computer problems."

"Seems like they're always breaking down. Call me crazy, but I think life was simpler without them."

"Well, I don't know about that. If everyone went back to a manual system of business, I'd be out of a job."

"Bite your tongue! We can't have that, then you wouldn't be able to come in here and sponsor all our activities. Don't tell anybody I told you, but...you're one of our favorites." I stroke his ego, and pet the few hairs on his head. "Mint?"

"No, thanks." He declines my hint that his permeating gum-disease odor is killing me. Too subtle, perhaps.

"So...you get benefits over there at IBM...medical, dental...you know, all that stuff?"

"Oh yeah, they're really good. It's the biggest reason I don't go out on my own. It would cost me a fortune to have the same benefits."

"I hear ya'. We're all independent contractors here. Don't get paid by the club, so there's no benes. If I had insurance, I sure would be using it. Got to stay on top of that stuff. If you let things go, you can really end up with a big problem." Hint, hint.

"Yeah. I guess I should make some appointments. So...you ready to dance?" The gingivitis conversation not sexy enough for you?

"I was born ready, baby."

I get on my feet and assume the dance position, staying a measurable distance away from the reason he's not in a relationship. I had to lead him in the right direction without completely insulting him. Other than the repugnant mouth, he's really not that bad. He can pull off the balding, and is only slightly overweight. He's very smart, and could be appealing to someone who likes the simpler things in life. I don't get pervert vibes from him, and doubt he would be hanging out in strip clubs if he had a reason to go home.

"Hi Marty. Good to see you again."

"You, too. Want to sit down?"

"Yes, I do."

He looks exactly the same as the last time he was here. A wrinkled, frumpy, black T-shirt and black jean ensemble. Both too big for his thin frame and hardly indicative of a person who makes a six-figure income.

His body language reeks of low self-esteem—disheveled hair, shoulder hunching, and the disturbing rocking while staring at the floor.

"Sooo…what's the latest on the family drama channel?"

"Got fired again today…in front of all my employees."

"Sorry to hear that. I was hoping things calmed down a bit."

"Nope. Gettin' worse. Tax guy came in. Rummaged through the files. Seems Dad's 'forgotten' to file company taxes the last few years."

"Not good. Did you get a bottom line?"

"No. Dad thought he was a burglar, hit him over the head with a flashlight, then fired me for leaving the door unlocked during business hours. The guy called the cops, and it was a big, ugly scene. They took him away." He buries his face in his hands. "I can't take all this. My family is gone. The business may go under. I have to watch my dad disintegrate every day. I don't know what I've done to deserve this."

I put my arm around his back, and try to steady his nervous rocking.

"Nothing, Marty, nothing. I hardly know you, but I can tell you're a good person. Sometimes bad things happen to good people, and they just can't be explained."

"I am a good person. I only ever wanted to have a good life. That's it. Why can't I have a good life?"

"Having a good life starts with having a good day. One day at a time. There must have been something good about your day today?" He shakes his head.

"C'mon…think." He stops rocking, shrugs his shoulders.

"Nothing."

"Little things…anything."

"My son called. He said he made a picture of me, and told his class I was number one Dad."

"That's great! See, I knew there would be something. Maybe you should shift your focus onto the one good thing that happens to you every day, no matter how trivial it might be. Even if it's just the Starbucks girl giving you the good, flavored coffee for the same price as the blah coffee." He smiles.

"I drink a lot of coffee."

"I know. No one wants to watch their parents go from healthy, influential super-beings to old, ornery annoyances, but we're all going to get old. Your dad needs you to stay strong for him right now. You should embrace whatever time you have with him. Just remember to duck when he's swinging flashlights."

Marty laughs, and sits up a little bit straighter. I'd not seen him laugh before. He has nice teeth. I hear my name called to the stage. Just in time, as my work here is done.

"I got to go. You take care, Ok?" He reaches in his pocket as I start to walk away.

"Alex, wait! Here." He waves a C-note at me. "Take some money."

"Don't worry about it. Just start smiling, will ya'?" I couldn't take his money for such a short visit, and figured I'd pass by later and deliver a few more words of wisdom.

Those few moments made me realize just how easy it is to impact somebody's life by really listening to them. I'm not usually paying attention to what anyone says in here. Words generally go in one ear and out the other, while I secretly gauge when the right time is to ask for a dance. Any other day, it's all about the money.

I walked away from Marty feeling for the first time like I gave somebody something real. He listened to me. I made a difference. All I had to do was take his mind off the bad stuff for a few moments, and it was like he became a new person. I know the therapy approach isn't going to work for every guy, but perhaps it was some insight as to what they were all searching for here…an escape.

Sunday afternoons on Sunset had been a regular lunchtime outing for Trina and me when I first moved to L.A. Great shopping, star sightings, and swanky café-style eateries made for the perfect weekend girl gettogethers while Evan was on monthly kid duty. We hadn't caroused on the boulevard for the last couple years, so when Ava suggested we check out this new hip and trendy health food joint, I rallied Trina to join us just in case I was getting looped into a lesbian singles event. It *is* West Hollywood.

My apartment is less than two miles from Sunset, but the route getting up there crosses three of the most congested intersections in L.A. County. It can take a half an hour to get through one traffic light, so I don't make the effort too often. I haven't kept up on the latest happening bars and restaurants in the area since I never go out, due to the fact that I'm in a bar five nights a week. Today should be fun, and I'm looking forward to getting to know Ava better and bringing Trina into the mix.

"It's weird in here. People are staring at us." Trina fidgets as we enter the funky, dark, seventies-ish vegan restaurant.

"It's Hollywood. Everyone stares at everyone. What does vegan mean?"

"It's some kind of no-meat, no cooking, no real-food food."

"Great. I knew I should have grabbed a slice at Serento's before we left." My favorite pizza joint is walking distance from my place.

We move through the semi-crowded small room, brushing bodies with some interesting characters. I'm relieved to see males, females, and couples, regardless of creative piercings and multicolored hair.

Trina predictably makes her way to the bar, as I inspect the room searching for Ava. She could be one of the heavily pierced ones, metamorphosed completely different than in the club. We've never seen each other outside of Mitzie's, and really know very little about each other. I recall the first night I met her when being taken to our cars, and she was dressed nicely and rather normally. I'm gambling she's not the one with bright magenta hair and green striped jumpsuit gazing intensely at the wall-projected video of a bug flying through a forest. The round, blue-screen video curiously draws me to it, and I find myself standing next to Crayola Girl.

"How do ya' think they got the camera to stay on him?" She shifts her eyes toward me without moving her head, then moves closer as if to locate the camera. The computer-generated video switches from seeing the bug flying to the bug's point of view as he's flying.

"I bet it's one of those tiny chips they implanted between his eyes." I have a little fun with the dazed and confused one. She looks at me, then back at the bug.

"That's what I was thinking."

I get back to the bar just in time to mediate the riot Trina ignites over the lack of alcohol in the establishment. It appears one washes down the non-food food dishes with elixir drinks. I've heard of those, but never ventured out and actually tried one. They're herbal concoctions of natural ingredients designed for different types of mood enhancement. Energy, mental awareness, stress relief, and male sexual longevity are among the menu options. Trina's near fistfight with the barkeep prompts an order of two large Extreme Relaxations.

"Are you Alex?"

"Yesss." Who wants to know?

"Come this way, please." The hostess leads us into a curtained room where a few people lay back in velvet chaise lounges drinking elixirs while inhaling oxygen through miniature hoses placed in their noses.

"Hey…we're over here." Ava lifts her head, being careful to not lose her hose. She puts her drink on the table next to three empties between her and V.

"V? Cool." We low-five. "I didn't know you guys knew each other."

"Totally, dude. We go back to the Houston days when everyone who's anyone in the stripper world was on the circuit."

"What's the circuit?" I ask, as the hostess sets Trina and I up with our hoses and we settle in next to our friends.

"It was like the jackpot trail of clubs between SoCal, Reno, Dallas, and Houston."

"A couple of us banded together to split costs, and we'd pop from one event to another. There was always something big going on, and we were the new blood cruising in for the weekend. Made a ton of money." Ava remembers the days.

"No shit! Wish I still had some of it." V signals the waitress for another round.

"What happened to the trail?" Trina asks.

"Too many fuckin' dancers got the same idea and most were screwing their clients. Clubs got shut down…conventions all moved to Vegas."

"Yeah, it was short, sweet, and extremely profitable for the time it lasted." Ava chugs her drink.

"Fuckin' good ol' days…when the business was easy. Guys treated ya' like royalty. None of this crap we get now." V takes a deep breath through her nose hose.

"Why is it so different? What changed?" I ask curiously.

"Evolution, that's all." Ava gives us the textbook explanation. "The invention of the lap dance ruined the mystery. Created too much competition between girls, and gave the guys control. It should have been left as a stage show…you know…vaudeville, burlesque, cabaret. I bet those days were so cool."

"Yeah, but we don't make squat on the stage. It's the lap dance that generates the big income, thus attracting a higher-quality woman." Present company included. "Imagine how disrespectful the clowns would be if all the girls were skanks?" I point out the Catch-22 of the biz.

"True, but if their *only* option to see perfect, sexy bodies was on stage, they'd pay for it."

"That's right!" V concurs. "The fuckers would cough it up big time! We'd just have to be more creative with our act."

"And talented." Trina speaks out. "Real dancers could put together something sexy and entertaining that might attract a better crowd than a bunch of drunken losers with nowhere to go." Ava and V look curiously at Trina.

"Have you guys met Trina?" It hits me that I forgot the introductions. "She's an old friend of mine. Just started cocktailing." They exchange nods. "So, why aren't there any of these new-age burlesque bars?" My wheels are turning.

"Because the fuckin' owners are small-dicked, greedy bastards!"

"The club won't make all the money if there's no lap dance. We pay them, remember? If the girls are employees, they got to pay us, give us insurance, carry more workers' comp…all that shit. They'd never do it."

"And they'd have to limit the amount of girls workin' there."

"Yeah, and why would they do that when they make millions off as many dancers as they can cram in there?"

We shake our heads and all agree about the flawed business sense of our chosen occupation. Nobody ever plans on working in it very long, so thoughts of infiltrating and causing any type of real change never occurs. We're all there for the same reasons—*money* and *freedom*.

We finish our oxygen rejuvenation therapy hashing and rehashing how much we despise the fact that the sleazy club owners, who do virtually nothing to contribute to the success of their clubs, make all the money. Trina seemed most interested in the idea of women owning a strip club. That a club could be effectively run without any men at all, other than security, piqued a business side of her I'd never seen before.

She had it all mapped out—cover charge and drinks would be expensive in order to cut the girls in on what the house makes per night. A limited number of dancers would do cabaret-style burlesque acts on the stage, then mingle into the crowd and socialize with patrons. They could still play the teasing game, and work the guys into contributing to their cause without having to do lap dances. The entertainment would be top-shelf, and the music, a draw on its own. It would be like an updated version of the bar in *Flashdance*.

The other debated option was opening a male strip club. Turning the tables entirely, where gorgeous hunks paid us for the opportunity to work there. We laughed about the possibility of some of our regulars auditioning for the show. The mental picture of any of them in a G-string or even baggy boxers was one I never want to envision again. Except, of course, the film noir image I created of Jode sauntering toward me in his Calvins, backing me into a corner, and insisting on giving me a full-body dance for free. That one I'll keep to myself.

The mountain of empty elixir glasses and full plates of bizarre raw food on our table illustrate the progression from girls' afternoon gossip session to early evening Male Analysis Talk Show:

"Why do men go to strip clubs? What are they searching for? V, you have the floor. Thirty seconds." I'm playing the host.

"Two words: mama-fucking-drama! Their mamas messed 'em up. No lovin' from mama. Total inferiority complex. So, they come to a place where they can feel powerful over women, even if it's just for a few hours, and convince themselves…Everyoneelseisfuckeduptoo." She swigs the backwash from her sixth relaxation drink.

"Interesting. Ava…your thoughts?"

"Escape. Avoidance. Illusion. Bad day at work. Don't want to go home. Believe the bullshit we tell them, and take the minuscule shot in hell that they might get a date."

"Ok. I might buy that. Trina? Your observations from the few nights you've been there?"

"Immature, lonely…midlife crisis…I don't know…haven't had sex with their wives for…" She counts mentally, "Three years. Think they're better than everyone else, and…just want to behave like they're twenty again! How's that?"

"Good…good. Very personally related." Only I know how closely related.

V grabs the asparagus chunk doubling as a microphone from me, and takes the host job.

"Ok, Dr. Laura, what's your *professional* opinion on why every man in America beats off in a strip club?"

"First of all, I'd like to say to my audience, thank you for being here, and if your man is beating off in strip clubs, get a new man!" V clunks me over the head with the asparagus.

"C'mon, speak! Seriously, I want to hear your assessment."

Ava leans into the asparagus mike and commentates quietly:

"That was a very big word, and it was noted that she did not say *fucking assessment*. Continue."

"Thank you. Now as I was saying—I believe you are all correct in coming up with different reasons why they come to our blessed place of business. However, no one answered the question, *What are they searching for*? Today, I am prepared to solve that mystery—oh!…It seems we are out of time, and will have to spend yet another week wondering how men even get themselves dressed in the morning with the pea brains they have. Thanks again, and see you all next week."

"C'mon! You totally dodged the question!"

"I don't have the answer. I'm still in the early stages of my research. Patience, my dear Ms. V, who won't tell us her real name."

"I know what her name is," Ava proudly butts in. "It's @#% !"

"NANANANANANANA!" V chants over Ava's voice.

"Oh, for God's sake, this is ridiculous. How bad can it be?" My curiosity takes over. "Edweena? Myrtle? Bertha? Come on V…give it up!"

"It's not…bad, really. I just don't want to give my parents the satisfaction of using the name they gave me. I'm estranged from them."

"Officially? Like, they don't know where you are?" Trina is mortified at the thought.

"They know where I'm at. We just don't talk. They don't get me."

"Her parental units are loaded. Big time!" Ava gives us the unauthorized dirt. "Pompous socialite assholes, right?" V nods.

"They wanted to set me up with a trust fund, but it comes with too many rules, you know. Like I'm fuckin' ten-years-old. Fuck them! I don't want to talk about it anymore. It'll ruin the all-natural buzz I got going on here. Trina, you remind me of Martha Stewart. What's your story? Why are you working at Mitzie's?"

"Ex-pompous socialite. Got shafted for a younger version. No marketable skills." She lowers her head.

"You forgot drama queen!" I egg on my old friend. "She's been a rich mom for the last twelve years, and is going through a divorce. And you have plenty of marketable skills. We just need a little development time to sharpen them."

"Hey, I know how it is with kids. You fuckin' can't catch a break. They take all your time, and if your deadbeat isn't of any help…you know…what the fuck!" Eloquent words from the would-be trust-fund baby.

"I should do a documentary on rich kids that dance in strip clubs for my grad project." Ava seeks to profit from V's situation. "There's probably a bunch of them working in Vegas. 'The Ultimate Retaliation'?" She tries out a title.

"Maybe, but it would be the same story over and over. Parents want to control everything, but not be involved. Kid gets pissed, quits school, moves out. Parents cut them off. They take their clothes off for money. Textbook revenge. It's been done too many times. If you want to single yourself out from your class of future filmmakers, you got to come up with something original." I've talked to a lot of actors at auditions that are putting together their own gigs, and it seems like they're all the same.

"I know. I've been racking my brain for weeks. The best I've come up with is medical marijuana use in the gay community."

"I don't get it? What does one thing have to do with another?"

"I don't know. That's what I was going to investigate." Ava shrugs blankly.

Trina eats an entire soy loaf, and notices us staring at her.

"What? I broke down. I'm hungry." She wipes her mouth daintily. "I think you should present some kind of funny perception of the strip club world in general. The concept of guys paying to get turned on, and being left to take care of it themselves later, is so absurd. The lame brains that keep coming back for that are such idiots…it's hilarious. There's got to be women out there that want to know why their men hang out in strip clubs." Quiet speechlessness overcomes our table. We all take in the possibilities.

"Trina, you're brilliant!" Ava has that excited, confident look on her face. "I'll do a mockumentary on why guys go there, and how to keep them home."

"Yeah, maybe we can teach housewives how to lap dance too. It'd be a hysterical scene." I'm finding a part for myself in this project somewhere.

"Ok, producers? Hello? If we teach housewives how to lap dance, we won't have fucking jobs!"

"Don't worry V, if everything goes the way it should on this project, it'll open doors traditionally cemented shut, and we won't need this job."

On the cusp of Ava's powerfully spoken words of hope, a waiter magically appears at our table offering a plate of something unidentifiable.

"Hemp?"

I lean across the table, and address Ava square in the eyes. "What *is* this place?"

9

Field Goal

Outside the superior courthouse, Trina and I wait in a long line surrounded by a group of mostly ethnic young males with a few attorney-likes
interspersed. The offenders are dirty, heavily tattooed, and wear baggy jeans
around the hips, forcing a two-foot crotch line to hang parallel to their
knees. Courtroom attire that will be most appreciated by His Honor, I'm
sure.

In any other situation, this crowd might instill fear of a mugging or
perhaps even a more severe attack. However, sharing the common goal of
removing one's name next to the coveted title of *defendant* has initiated
unexpected bonding for Trina and the others preparing to face the judge.
She shares a few tokes off a cigarette with a juvenile delinquent, careful not
to get ash on her Jessica McClintock patterned pantsuit with matching
fedora.

"Since when do you smoke?" I cannot cope with smokers, and if my
best friend becomes one, I may have to invest in a gas mask to make my
point.

"Since I have to take my children from their maniac father, and not be
able to tell them what a fucking slime he is." She's been spending a lot of
time with V. "I can't hold it all in, Alex. I have to have a vice."

"Ohhh, so the martinis in the morning, and the Valium at night
are...therapy?"

"Look, I'm scared, stressed out, and I don't know what he's going to do. He could say things, and they might believe him. Everyone else does." I grab the cig out of her mouth, and stomp it into the pavement.

"Listen, you're too blessed to be stressed." My new motto. "He's not going to do anything. He's a big bully who enjoys railroading people for sport. If he encountered any resistance at all, he'd probably give in without a fight. He doesn't want to take care of two kids. He's just trying to punish you to make you think you've done something wrong so he can justify his actions. Mental abusers are cowards. They use subliminal messaging, deceit, manipulation…whatever verbal assaults they can to force people to destroy themselves. You've got to stay strong. The badgering and intimidating days are gone! You're free. Now let's go in there, and free your kids."

We touch the top of our heads together, and share a quick empowering moment. Trina composes herself, takes a deep breath, grips her Italian leather briefcase tightly, and follows me through the glass doors.

I know Trina is a good mom. She's done everything for those kids. Evan was never home, and hardly participated in family events at all. I remember when he blew off the twins' eighth birthday party. There was a yard full of kids anxiously awaiting the cake that he was supposed to pick up. We waited and waited, but he never showed. I put together a good stall act teaching tumbling routines in a makeshift clown outfit, while Trina whipped together in record time a cake big enough for twenty people.

Evan cruised in well after the party was over, and offered no explanation at all. He could have made up a story to make the kids feel better, but he didn't even do that. Instead, he scolded Trina in front of me and the kids, insisting that his whereabouts were none of her business, and suggesting she "go clean up the confetti shit in the yard." Father of the Year.

Soon after that episode, Trina started drinking heavily. Evan enjoyed the Beverly Hills party scene, and encouraged her to overdo it. Probably so she wouldn't be aware of his womanizing. Their socialite friends thought he was a perfect gentleman…life of the party.

She tells me she never drinks around the kids, and I believe her. After we get past a few of the bigger obstacles here, we'll work on drying her out. One thing at a time.

We find our courtroom and take a seat in a back row. I want to be able to scope Evan without him seeing us. I spot him sitting on the opposite side, next to a woman who's either his scantily clad attorney risking being disbarred for getting involved with a client, or the new girlfriend. Trina hasn't seen them yet. She's taking my advice to stare straight ahead confidently, and not give him any opportunity to intimidate her. I study his pathetic display of, "Look at me, I'm a victim."

He sniffles and wipes his eyes methodically, giving away his strategy for the day. I had figured him for an aggressive approach. Coming in with a sophisticated legal team that would surely overpower Trina and throw the incompetent-mother card. I've seen those types of lawyers browbeat the opposition who is not represented. Judges don't like when one side has counsel and the other doesn't. It's not a fair fight, and they tend to give the unrepresented one a lot of room to screw up legally. If they can at all logically articulate their case, they have just as good a chance of winning. I was banking on Evan's egotistical disposition rubbing the court wrong, and exposing his abusive nature, but it seems I underestimated the chameleon, requiring us to get a bit more creative…quickly.

"All rise. The Honorable Judge Mason is entering the courtroom." The female judge takes her position at her throne.

"In the matter of Willis versus Willis, would the parties please come forward?"

Trina gets up, head held high, hands shaking, and walks toward her table. Evan gives the girlfriend a sloppy kiss, then he proceeds to his table. Trina stops short, and throws me the expected look of anger, panic, and…*help!* I quickly jump up and join her at the *barre.*

"I hate him, I hate him, I hate him!" she whispers in my ear. "How could he bring her here? I'm way too sober for a meltdown right now!"

"Keep it together, keep it together." I sense the judge's irritation with our powwow. "Your Honor, could we have a few moments?"

"Make it quick, counselor. We have a calender to get through."

"Thank you, Your Honor…and I'm not Ms. Willis' attorney. I'm just here for moral support." The judge waves us off, and begins familiarizing herself with the paperwork. Trina and I step outside the courtroom.

"How could he? I'm gonna kill him! He's probably got her around my kids!" I resist the urge to smack her across the face, and instead recite the movie line that goes with the slap.

"Snap out of it! Focus! It's a good thing that he brought her. She's a bimbo! They're not going to buy his *Poor me, my wife is a drunken cheater* routine." She gasps at the harsh words.

"You think he's going to say that?"

"Most likely…if he's smart. What else is he gonna say, *I'm the mental abusing adulterer who kidnaped our kids and falsified court documents?* You keep cool in there. I'll sit behind you, and write what you should say on a piece of paper. I'm allowed to pass you notes. Don't worry. He's going down."

I wasn't sure what was going to happen or even how to explain to the court what he's done and what Trina is seeking. My family law research indicates judges really don't care about the he-said, she-said crap, and if there's no documented evidence of criminal behavior, substance abuse, or child abuse, it's likely the court will give them a temporary joint custody order until everything else is litigated. The kids are old enough to go back and forth between residences, and even though it's not the most desirable arrangement for Trina, it's better than what she's got now.

I convince Trina to check her ego at the door, go back in the courtroom, and calmly fight for what's right. I can only imagine the pain of spending twelve years with someone who in the end turns out to be a person you never would have given the time of day to. The closest thing to this level of disrespect that I've ever had to cope with was my old boy toy's blatant cheating event. Without the commitment of love and kids, it's hardly a comparison, but I remember how awful I felt when I saw him so easily give away our sacred passion to a stranger. That event has caused me to be so guarded emotionally, and to truly believe my life is easier without men. I hope Trina can recover from her life's defining moment, and ultimately find happiness. She deserves it.

Evan played the game as I anticipated, and tried to make a case for saving the children from their neglectful, drug-addicted mother…sniffle, sniffle. He went down a long laundry list of legally viable reasons that a parent can take children from the other parent. Trina tried to cut him off a few times in her own defense, and I quickly and discreetly reminded her that we'd get our turn, and we actually wanted him to go on and on with accusations he can't support. We'd prove him wrong, the blatant perjuries would demonstrate the deviant level he's willing to go to, and his whole strategy would backfire.

At one point, Evan informed the court that his children were being cared for after school by his "longtime, reliable female friend who came today to provide support." He made a point to tell a story in which the kids referred to her as, "Mom."

I thought Trina would dive across the table and slit his throat with her freshly manicured acrylics. No one would have blamed her, but luckily I had prepared her for the possibility he would say something like that. She didn't even flinch at his intentional Freudian slip, which he tried to cover up to appear sensitive to the court. Fortunately, it didn't work. My observation of the judge noting the subtle enjoyment he got out of saying it indicated it was yet another strategic backfire for him.

When all was said and done during the twenty minutes of the court's time so generously granted to decide the fate of two children, the judge ordered temporary joint custody. The kids would alternate weeks between parents, and she granted a continuance on the money issues so both parents could support their claim of needing spousal *and* child support from each other! Yes, that's right. Not only did Evan steal all their money, he had apparently hidden it so well, he's the invisible man on paper. And he claimed he was so broke, he couldn't even afford an attorney. He insisted Trina spent all the money, and they'd been forced to file for bankruptcy. I'll say it again: Father of the Year.

Trina left the courthouse with an array of mixed emotions. Happy she's got more time with the kids; worried about how she'll support them. Jealousy, anger, and hurt, as Evan walked arm-in-arm with the replacement, pinching her butt as they strutted by us.

"Don't say anything!" I stop her just as she opens her mouth.

"What a piece of shit he is! I feel so stupid to have not seen any of this coming! He ruined our lives over some *bimbo!"* she screams out. "Wish I never would have met him!"

"You can't say that. You have beautiful kids from this…person. You got to think about the good stuff. If you dwell on the bad, you'll empower him—fuel him with all your anger and fear. It's part of Universal energy." She sighs heavily. I don't think she wants a lesson in metaphysics right now, so I'll cut to the condensed version.

"Look, I learned the hard way about karma. He's gonna get his…eventually. And we just might give the Universe a little help to speed things up." *Wink, wink.* "I have a plan."

I arrive at Mitzie's a little late for the Monday night hustle. It's good to get here before the game starts, and not be propelled into the ruckus. It's much easier to slip into the seductive aura all women possess when properly motivated, not be thrust into it harshly. I guess I'll have to snap out of my post-audition blues, and make the appropriate attitude adjustment quickly. This may be a night I violate my working rules and start at the bar.

"Hey." Ava enters the locker room sweaty.

"Hey. Busy down there?"

"Yeah, it's pretty good tonight. I've been bopping all over the place gettin' two at a time from everybody." She does the quick wipe-and-change.

"That's good." I rifle through my stripper clothes bag, bored with my outfits. Some have proven better than others, and the big moneymakers are always the ones I like the least. I lean up against the locker and yawn.

"What's wrong? Tired?"

"Yeah, of the same old industry crap. I had two bummer auditions today. One for a T&A cable series. We had to show our boobs to the director. I guess they got burned once when they hired this girl who looked like she had a great rack, you know push-up bra and everything. They get to shooting the topless scene, and find out she's got grandma titties. Had to pay her anyway and hire someone else. So now they make you show 'em at the audition. Real classy gig, right?"

"Did you get it?"

"No. Rumor was one of the producer's girlfriends had already locked in the job. They were holding auditions to humor the union."

"Typical. What was the other one?"

"Some real-life mystery-solving show. They improv everything. I got excited 'cause I fit the breakdown perfectly." I pull the breakdown out of my back pocket and read. "5'7", dark hair, olive skin, lean athletic build." I toss it in the trash. "I walk in the audition room, and there's fifty girls that look exactly like me. It was like a bad episode of *The Twilight Zone...Performing Clones.*"

"It's so hard to get your foot in the door, but once you do...it's gonna be totally worth all the lame shit you have to go through," Ava consoles me.

"I can't even get my toe in the door. My new, novice agent sends me on stuff that's all wrong for me. It's a waste of my time. How's the prep for the mockumentary going?"

"Good, but I got to find a way to raise some money. I can do most of the post-production work at school, but I got to cover film costs, location fees, and a bunch of little stuff to get it shot first. *And* they won't let me shoot here."

"Don't tell them. Wear a hidden camera. Get footage of your regulars. You can record actual conversations with guys, and no one will know." I'm scheming here.

"That's a good idea, but there's still costs involved. We need more money. I'll figure it out. Hurry up, it's good down there." She runs out the door.

The locker room is empty except for one girl I never talk to. Not because I don't like her. I don't even know her. It's just that there are certain girls you never seem to cross paths with. Then when you do, there's weirdness 'cause we've seen each other naked a hundred times and never said anything. I apply my makeup and see her clip on a long, brown hairpiece in the mirror.

"That looks totally real. Where did you get it?" I initiate the conversation.

"I make 'em. I'm a hairdresser…mostly weaves." She combs it out to blend in with her own shoulder-length crop. "I have some of these clip-ons with me if you want one."

"How much?"

"Twenty-five. You can pay me after work." She hands me one that matches my brassy auburn perfectly.

"Cool. Thanks." I try to clip it in, but don't really know where it goes. She notices me fumbling with it.

"Girlfriend, let me help you." She clips it on and styles my now very long hair into a voluptuously playful do.

"I'm Alex."

"I know. Ed talks about you all the time."

"Oh, you're one of Ed's girls, too? How 'bout that breath?"

"Naaasty! Whew! Knocks me out. Can't sit with him very long!"

"I know exactly what you're talking about. It's too bad, 'cause he's a nice guy."

"It's always something, right?" She tops off my new look with a little spray. "There. What do you think?"

"I like it. Just what I needed tonight…a little change."

"I got to warn ya', don't let the jokers pull on it. It's not a strong clip."

"Got it."

I head downstairs and plunge into the Monday night madness. I do my usual quick scan of the room, and prance toward the bar, swinging the new hair from side to side. Stares, whistles, and a "Look at *that*" tell me it's probably going to be a good money night.

Prior to starting this job, I would have been offended to be referred to as a "that." I've learned to brush it off, and silently treat men with equal disrespect while in the dark fantasy world. I stop and chat briefly with a couple guys I've seen before, then excuse myself and "accidentally" whip my new long locks across the face that belongs to the mouth that called me a "that."

Trina is in the waitress station at the bar ordering drinks from her favorite bartender. It seems Kelly's lesson on call order and ticket arrangement actually made a difference. She's organized, prompt, and only taking small sips from customers' drinks in lieu of guzzling their entirety. I guess she's found a way to maintain a constant state of buzzed without paying for it.

"Hey, how's it going?"

"It's going." Trina piles her drink order onto her tray. "I'm in the zone tonight. Making good money. I got to keep movin'.'"

"Ok, I just wanted to say hi. Can you get me a shot of tequila?" She utters an annoyed sigh, and whips out her pen.

"Real or fake?"

"Real. I'm ordering it. It's only a fake shot when the guys order for us."

"I knew that," she snaps, then writes it on a ticket and waits impatiently for Kelly to acknowledge the order.

Fake tequila shots are easy to make: 7-Up with a splash of coke. Used mostly when guys are trying to get you drunk and keep ordering one after the other.

V is at the DJ booth jamming out to an old AC/DC track. Not my kind of dance music, but it makes me want to try something different tonight. I love Pearl Jam. Can't understand a word he says, but Eddie Vedder sings with so much passion, you gotta love it.

"Hey Scottie, you have 'Yellow Ledbetter'?" I shout over the bellowing "Highway to Hell." He gives me the just-a-minute finger, then puts on his headphones and blends in the next song. V dances over to me.

"Cool hair, dude! You look ten years younger!"

"What are you saying…I'm old?"

"No, you know, you just look like you're in your twenties."

"Thanks. I think."

"Hey, you got your penalty flags? You're gonna need 'em. It's a real touchy-feely crowd." She reaches in her mini-purse, and pulls one out.

"Uhhh, no…no, no…no thanks. I don't have anywhere to put it." She stuffs it in my side.

"Guess who's here?" I raise an eyebrow blankly. "Jode."

"So? Who cares?"

"You should. He likes you. Fish told me."

"Big deal. What am I going to do, date him? Then have to see him in here watching me seduce other men? Pointless."

"You think too much. Why don't you just have some fuckin' fun. He's totally hot!"

"I got other things to think about—like my tequila waiting at the bar. Seeeya." She yells out at me as I head toward the bar.

"Meet me at their table in an hour!"

Yeah, yeah. I wave at her. That brush-off wave you do without looking back. I'm secretly having my own little affair with Jode in my head. I really don't want to ruin it by acting on it. Plus, they're all the same, and…I hate men right now. That's my position and I'm sticking to it.

"Ray! Long time. How goes it?" My first victim of the night hasn't been in for a couple weeks.

"Hey Alex, Pretty good, I guess." I sit down close to him.

"Where you been? I thought the soon-to-be ex-wife pulled a Jimmy Hoffa on ya'."

"No, not yet. She's pretty pissed off, though. We're still going through it, ya' know, screaming at each other every day. Trying to divvy up all our stuff. It's tough."

"You guys aren't still under the same roof, are ya'?"

"Yeah. Nobody wants to leave the house. I don't think it should be me. My brother and I built that house. She says she made it a home, and she's not going anywhere."

"Why don't you sell it, then you'll both have to move, and the problem takes care of itself?"

"Yeah, we're thinking about that. It's a lot to take in at once. What about you? What's going on with your movie stuff?"

"The usual. Spend all my money getting a bunch of bullshit auditions where no one recognizes my talents. The good news is that Ava—do you know Ava?" He shakes his head.

"She's over there." I point her out as she dances for two women across the room. It's weird dancing for girls. I don't know what to do for them. You can't grind on their laps or discreetly rub your knee on their balls. I'm at a total loss.

"She's a film student at SC, and I'm helping her put together her grad project. We're doing kind of a comedy documentary on the stripper business."

"A comedy, huh? What's funny about it? Us?" Uh-oh, I forgot who my audience was.

"No, well…sort of. Not you, of course, but there's some guys here that are really…funny."

"Funny looking? I don't get what you mean?"

"Some are funny looking, yes, but it's more…I mean…it's just that…well, put it this way, it's important to know your limitations in life, and most guys, not you, uh…don't. And it could be perceived as humorous to a specific audience, if done correctly." I'm great at not answering the question. I should have been a lawyer.

"I see. Just keep my name out of it, Ok? The last thing I need is for my wife to find out I spend money in here. I'd never hear the end of it."

"Deal. Speaking of spending money…"

"Yes, you can dance."

I like Ray 'cause he gets it. He knows we're trying to make a living here, and even if the personal dance thing isn't what he's ultimately seeking, he understands that time is money, and is always willing to make a contribution.

I assume the dance position, and begin with my standard, emotionally distant routine. As the superbly sexy and soulful music of the band Morcheeba echoes through the club, I suddenly feel overcome by my own movements, swaying in perfect sync to the delicate beats. Maybe it's the tequila, but for the first time I can feel myself slipping into my own passionate moment while dancing for a client.

I delicately stroke the back of Ray's neck, brush my body close to his, and faintly pass my lips by his ear, blowing softly as I arch through the movement. I close my eyes and allow myself to experience the intense power of seduction. Ray seems to be in the same trance. I never touch him or say anything, just authentically feel the music involving every inch of my body in its rhythm. How freeing it is to dance like nobody's watching when everyone is.

By the time Ray snaps out of the trance, thirty minutes have gone by, and even I didn't realize I had danced nine songs in a row. It was the best set of music I'd ever heard in here, and I truly was lost in it. Halfway through I became very aware of the effect it was having on Ray. He was melancholy and excited at the same time. I felt him breathe heavily, almost letting out something bottled deeply within.

Maybe because I was so open to the energies around me, I could honestly feel some of his pain. He seems like a decent guy, and never does anything weird or tries to ask me out. I believe he still has a genuine love for his wife, just doesn't know how to tell her, and is more willing to let twenty-seven years go out the window than swallow a little pride and tell her how he feels. I don't know why I care. Maybe I'm justifying my own existence here by providing some other service than the expected one, but I can't help but pass on a piece of information that may be helpful to someone if I have it.

"Ray, do you want to get divorced?"

"I don't know. Sometimes. Not really."

"Do you love your wife?"

"Of course. She raised my daughter…she keeps a clean house—" I cut him off.

"No, do you *love* your wife? Are you going to miss her? Do you want to live the rest of your life without her?" He looks away for a few moments, as if he's never asked himself these questions. His eyes squint, and he tilts his head a little, then smiles with his revelation.

"No," he says confidently. "I don't."

"Well, then I guess you're the doing the right—"

"—I don't want to live without her. She's the best friend I've ever had." He gets up, pays me, and waddles out of the club faster than I've ever seen him move.

A-mazing! Women will analyze a relationship to death. Every word that was said weighed against every action taken. Every happy, sad, sexual, angry, jealous, disappointing, exciting minute, dissected second by second. Men don't even consider for one single flashing instant what their true emotions may be for the person most influential in their life until they're about to lose them. I just don't get it!

I sit for a few minutes after Ray leaves, laughing to myself about how silly it is that I'm helping these men repair their relationships. If V knew I was counseling them right out of the club, she'd have a vocabulary melt-down:

"Are you fucking crazy! You're supposed to fucking keep them here, and take their fucking money, not send them home to their fucking wives! What are you fucking thinking? Are you fucking listening to me? I am seriously fucking worried about you! Fuckin'-A, dude!"

I stand up and start to head toward the Bobby/Jode/Fish table. Jode and I catch eyes. I do the nod-and-smile, then exercise my most confident, sexy walk on the way over. On final approach, my head is yanked back unexpectedly, and I turn sharply to see Jim, the obnoxious narcissist, holding my new hair in his hand.

"*You idiot!* You don't grab somebody by the hair!" I scold.

"Well, I didn't expect it to come off." He laughs and puts it on his head singing "Davy Crockett was a…"

"What, did you think my hair grew three feet in the last week since you've been here, pinhead?" I snatch it off his big bald head.

"Like I pay attention to any of that stuff. Get over here and put your God-given talents to work. I'll make it up to you…as long as you can get my dick hard."

I hate this guy. He's condescending, confrontational, and disguises with humor his deep-seated hatred for women. I try to avoid him, but he always catches me when I need money, so I end up biting it, and toughing it out long enough to take a few bucks from him.

"Fine, but can you…not talk while I dance? It ruins my mental aban-donment of reality." He plops his six-foot, three-inch large-framed body into a booth, wraps his arms around me, and pulls me onto him by my butt. I push back.

"Look! You can't touch! I'm not going to spend a half an hour of my day peeling you off me! You're gonna get me in trouble!"

"All right, all right! Keep your pantyhose on. I won't touch. Scout's honor." He holds up four fingers.

"You? Honorable? Don't make me laugh."

"What? I have honor. Get on her, and stay on her. Don't get off her 'til you get a better offer."

"Ughhh! You need so much work!"

After escaping the hip-lock and death grip Jim had on me for forty-five minutes straight, I spot my favorite customer, Bob, at the bar. He's a businessman that lives in Northern California. One of his companies is down here, close to the club. He breezes in every few weeks on his way to the airport. He's funny, intelligent, happily married, and has always treated me with respect. He says the last time he was in a strip club before stopping in at Mitzie's was fifteen years ago for a bachelor party. I believe him. He's a little novice with the routine.

He willfully pays double for each dance and tips me on top of it. My dances for him have always been structured differently than for others. I like him as a person, and feel compelled to give him what I think he needs. A dose of genuine, mysterious sensuality. From what I can tell, it's the only thing missing from his happy home life. I apply the newfound approach I experienced earlier with Ray, and it seems to go over well. He gives me three hundred dollars for the hour he was here, then leaves respectfully to go catch his flight.

"Hey guys." I finally make it over to the Jode clan, happy that I've earned well over my daily cash quota in only a couple hours, and can now blow off some time socializing with my virtual-reality hunk.

I squeeze into the booth next to V, who sits on Fish's lap stroking his ego…amongst other things. Bobby and Jode are engrossed in the football game and haven't noticed my arrival.

"Dude, what's up?" V says.

"The tent in Fish's jeans…Oh, you mean with me? Nothing, just that I'm done with my night."

"Somebody gave you a load?"

"Yeah, three bills from my Northern Cal guy. In and out, just like I like 'em."

"Sweet!" She high-fives me. "Now you can hang with us, and get to know *him*."

She nods in Jode's direction. His eyes come unglued from the TV, as if he sensed we were talking about him. He does a double take when he sees me.

"Hi."

"Hi."

"Haven't seen you in here lately. Where you been?" he asks.

"I've been here. Five days a week. Where've you been?"

"I was here last Wednesday. Looked for ya'."

"I take Sundays and Wednesdays off. Breaks up the week. I thought you said you only come in on Mondays, anyway?"

"Yeah, usually, but lately I can't get away on Mondays. Been workin' long hours." I scoot closer to him, so we don't have to yell over the music. His eyes look blue tonight. I thought they were green. Hard to tell in the dark.

"So, what do you do?" I ask.

"Camera work. Mostly for commercials. I'm trying to book a show for pilot season. You know, more regular schedule."

There's an assumption in L.A. that everyone knows how Hollywood works. Pilot season starts at the end of January. It's the time when networks buy up the new shows they're going to begin airing in September. It's the beginning of the busy time for the industry after they come off a slow holiday schedule. TV shows tend to be more desirable work for crew members than films. Their union forces a twelve-hour turnaround time, which means they get twelve hours between wrapping one day and starting the other. Producers try to be done everyday by six p.m., so they can get started by six a.m. the next day.

"I don't know anything about that stuff. What do you mean, a more regular schedule?" I play stupid so he'll keep talking. I need to mentally make out with those luscious lips of his. Pass the tequila, please.

Jode loves his job, and is eager to talk about it. I can already tell he's a passionate person. He's refreshingly animated as he recites information I already know, then gives me a bit of education on the physical requirements of steady-cam operators. The camera weighs fifty pounds, and is harnessed on his body. He has to look through the tiny lens and run to keep up with whatever action is taking place. It requires great strength, balance, and concentration. His job description prompts a perfect opening for me to ask to see his biceps…and abs, while you're at it.

Trina arrives with a tray full of shots, compliments of Kelly's extended bathroom break. She's just in time to join the heated debate Bobby has ignited with Ava, voicing his unsupported opinion of how the dancers swindle men out of their money.

"…all these girls are whores! They parade around in their little clothes, and get us so horny we offer everything we've got to get laid!"

"Let me get this straight. Because you guys are weak, we're whores?" Ava is on the verge of rallying a mutiny.

"We're not the weak ones! We have all the power in here, right, Fish?" Bobby solicits support from Fish, who is unaware a debate is going on.

Only a small portion of his head is visible as V smothers him for yet another hundred-dollar fifteen minutes.

"Oh, yeah, somebody help her…she's being overpowered! Please!" Ava's tone changes from sarcastic to seductive. She leans in inches from Bobby's face. "All we have to do is make you *think* you'll see us naked, and you boys are like putty in our hands!" She grabs a handful of his "putty." Trina joins in on the double team against Bobby.

"So you think just because these girls are dancers they have no other marketable qualities or anything positive to offer society?"

"I…I…I didn't say that…I was just…" He's sweating, and looks to Jode for support. "Jode dude, back me up here."

"Yes, I'd like to hear your thoughts on this issue," I ask him innocently.

"I think the women in here are beautiful, intelligent, ambitious beings with the tenacious drive to be self-employed and make a good living." What else was he going to say while observing the crotch-lock Ava had on Bobby?

"Thanks, buddy, appreciate it." Bobby squirms in pain. Trina moves in close, and in a sophisticated, motherly tone whispers in his ear.

"These women are great entertainers. Trained dancers, educated professionals. Women with goals." She reaches in his back pocket and grabs his wallet. "Don't ever insult my girls." Ava tightens the grip. "You will *not* refer to women as *bush* anymore. You will *not* grab, pinch, or otherwise inflict pain or compromise their personal space. You *will* pay for their time, and support their cause! Have I made myself clear?" She takes a hundred from the wallet.

"Crystal. Crystal." He clenches his jaw. His eyes water. "Take what you want. Seriously…just take it. I wasn't even talking about you guys! Please, please, please…let go!"

Ava releases the grip. Bobby takes a deep breath, shakes out his leg, and walks around in small circles.

"Evil! Evil strippers—" Trina goes for the jugular. "Dancers! I meant dancers." He backs away from arm's reach, and wipes sweat from his forehead. "Can you please bring me another drink? A double?" He respectfully gives Trina another hundred.

"You are the weakest gender…goodbye." She snatches it out of his hand and prances off, laughing with Ava.

"Dude. She's brutal!" Bobby blows his nose into a napkin. "I think I like her." And off to the bar he goes.

Jode and I sit quietly stunned, like the parents of fighting siblings after a huge brawl has just finished. No one knows what to say. There's a slightly uneasy air between us. V and Fish never seemed to hear or notice anything, and continue in their own private fantasy world.

"Well…as I said the first time I met you, can't take him anywhere."

"Yeah, I see that. You guys been friends a long time?"

"A few years. We do a lot of work together. He's a set decorator, and we have the same management company."

"Bobby does interior design for movies? I would have never pegged that. I thought most of those guys were gay?"

"They are."

"Maybe that's why he feels the need to overcompensate, and act like a macho asshole."

"He's totally different when he's not around women. Really, he's a good guy," Jode sticks up for his friend.

"If you say so. So, did you mean what you said about dancers, or was that just to keep your privates out of the vice?"

"I'm pretty neutral. To each their own, you know. But I got to admit, Ava is pretty scary. Beautiful, but scary."

"Yeah, she's tough. I think she may actually have more issues with men than I do."

"You don't seem like you have man issues. I thought you had it all figured out?"

"You don't know me very well, but I am actively working on the figuring-out part. I may write a book. Men are interesting creatures. They intrigue me. Primitive beings in desperate need of evolution."

"Maybe I could be one of your case studies? You could analyze me for hours."

"*Analyze,* huh? Maybe I'm already doing that." I love flirting with him. "I could be *analyzing* you right now."

"Well, then you have an unfair advantage. You're getting useful information, and I'm just trying to get a date."

Fish has sprawled his body out across the booth to accommodate his fully aroused physique, and is embarking on our space. V, in an effort to reach his slouching form, slips off her heels and rams her butt into my head. I throw my flag.

"Offsides! Or clipping…or something. Move over!" I shove her back to their area. "Now, where were we? Ahhh, right, the date. I don't date my customers."

"I'm not one of your customers. You've never danced for me."

"Good point, but you are a customer of the bar."

"I'll stop coming here. There's plenty of places to have a drink."

"Look, seriously, it's cute that you would be willing to do that…but I just don't see anything good coming out of me dating someone I met in here."

"Harsh…but I respect that. What if we were to coincidentally be at the same place at the same time. Such as the Classic Comedy Film Festival at the Directors Guild this Sunday? Wouldn't really be a date?"

"Captivating that you remember my interest in old comedies, and you do score points for that. However, there are no coincidences in life. So, you'll either have to rely on fate, or recite movie lines and laugh your butt off solo." I wink at him, then stand up and walk away.

"Is that a yes?" he yells out.

I like playing with him. He's so cute, and I totally would have fallen for his approach had it not had been delivered in here, and if I were in a more responsive frame of mind toward men. In the old days, I would have already had sex with him, and be reaping the problems that would have arisen from doing that. At least now, as I near my midthirties, I take the time to glimpse the aftermath of stupid, female, hormone-driven, logic-defying urges. I could actually be growing up.

> *Dear Diary,*
>
> *To date or not to date? I know I said I was done with men, but that was before I met HIM. There's a lot to be said for instant attraction. On the surface, it's all wrong, but something about him feels very right. A lot of successful relationships start off under worse circumstances, right?? I don't know…I'm not going to lose sleep over the issue, and I guess I have to recognize my limitations at this time, but it doesn't mean I can't think about future possibilities.*
>
> *I'm beginning to understand what the common denominator is for all men who come to the club…and probably all men, period. Tapping into the psyche of the aroused male has given me an invaluable tool that I look forward to using in all areas of my*

life. On a career note: the girls and I have decided to take Trina's suggestion and put on a cabaret-style show to raise money for the mockumentary. Should be interesting, as we've promised the full monty to lure them in, and justify the costly cover charge. Of course, we won't be delivering on the false advertisement. Not sure how we'll get around it yet, but am confident our combined creative minds will figure out something. Final thoughts on Jode: not to date.

10

Halftime

The girls and I decide to take a Saturday off and spend a day doing good for our skin and bodies. Most of the girls at the club regularly get massages, facials, body scrubs. and all the other pampering menu items L.A.'s famous spas offer. I hadn't wanted to spend the money or time consulting the professionals for these services and was getting quite good at the homemade beauty treatment applications. Still, since it's a prerequisite for the job that we look good, I figured it was time I make more of an investment.

I had gone a few times to one of these bathhouses in Koreatown. For the money, it's the best quick fix out there. But being in hot eucalyptus steam rooms, herbal soaking tubs, and sauna-like oxygen rooms touching shoulders with a bunch of aged naked Oriental women gabbing loudly in Korean was, unfortunately, anything but relaxing. Not to be racially insensitive, but the Koreans, at least the women, have some pretty gross habits. And the language—totally annoying while trying to meditate. Perhaps they were all in on it, meaning to drive us crazy so they could have their culture all to themselves. The gall!

We arrive at the prestigious Burke Williams Spa in Santa Monica prepared for a full day of spoiling. Facials, nails, massage, lunch…the whole nine yards. V had accumulated four gift certificates from one of her customers, who didn't seem to notice she had six birthdays last year. Since most of our treatments were already paid for, we decide to upgrade to the

145

private champagne room for our manicure/pedicures in order to hold a business meeting regarding the particulars of our money-raising efforts. Of course, we would find a way to make our beauty maintenance day tax-deductible.

"Let's throw the lap dance party first, so we know how much money we're going need from the cabaret." Trina's raring to go.

"Well, first we need to know what the fuckin' thing's gonna cost us, right?"

"V! Tone it down. We don't want to offend the nipps." Ava's logic needs work.

I cup my hand over the side of my mouth and whisper to Ava, "I'm sure they speak English. Can you not insult them while their razor-sharp instruments are under our toenails?" I mouth, "I'm sorry" to my manicurist. She smiles unknowingly.

"I've already drawn up a budget. I figure we need roughly ten to fifteen grand to do it right, and that's keeping it pretty thin. If we can limit locations, we can keep it closer to ten."

"Do you need help with the script? I'm a decent writer, and could probably help out with characters and stuff." I volunteer to create my own part.

"Don't worry, I got you in there. I'm not going to use a script. I have a format that I'll follow, and everything else is gonna be improvised. I'll shoot stuff in the club and locker room while we're working, and bring in some of my guys for private interviews. I want to get in their heads."

"Ok, so back to the money. I'm going to call my old assembly from the Beverly Hills Wives Club, the less conservative ones, and invite them for tea." V scoffs at Trina's strategy. "Once they're there, I'll confess everything that's going on with Evan, and hopefully they'll feel sorry for me and support my new venture."

"That's your plan? Trick them into donating to our cause? It's never going to work, Martha." V calls it like it is. "These are snob-nose sophisticates, right?"

"Most of them, but they're my friends! They'll help me."

"You didn't want to go to them before for money, why do you think they'll give it to you now?" I remind Trina of our earlier conversation regarding this group of women.

"I've changed. Is that Ok with you? *And*, it's not just loan money so I can live. We're doing something, and I believe in it. These are people that live extremely bland lives. They'll jump at the impromptu chance to be wild. I'm sure of it."

"Look, I've dealt with snobby assholes my whole fuckin' life. They're not stupid and you can't just spring something like, *Hi, we're all outta tea, but we've got T&A instead.*"

"V's right. You got to approach the cool ones with a proposal about empowering themselves in their relationships, and taking control of their men. If they're that bored, it'll pique their interests."

"What if they don't like their men anymore and could care less about seducing them, let alone controlling them? They probably want them out of the house as much as possible." I point out the obvious female trend…or is it just me?

"Don't go to the blue hairs. You got to talk to the young ones that married for money, and the thirty-somethings that still like their guys, but are concerned about them cheating." Thank God Ava has a plan. "They might really want to learn the tricks of the trade."

"Don't discount the blue hairs. Sexy comes in a lot of different packages, you know." Trina is defensive on this issue.

"Why not just *ask* them for a donation for the mockumentary? Avoid the whole lap dance thing? I'm sure they'd be happy to invest in something exciting."

"I don't want investors! Let's get that straight." Ava nearly knocks out her manicurist at the thought. "They would own some of it, and have their big snobby noses in it. It's better if we just have fundraisers. We don't have to pay anybody back." It *is* her project.

"Ok, just so everyone is clear. Trina will set up the party…get lots of booze. Alex, you and V will demonstrate and teach technique. I'm gonna tape interviews with them and record their progress. Should be interesting. Moving on to the cabaret."

As the meeting advanced through green cucumber masks and aromatherapy massages, the fundraisers began to take shape. Both the lap dance party and the cabaret would take place at Trina's house. It was the only locale big enough and discreet enough to pull this off. Her spacious living room had little furniture in it these days, which would give us plenty of room to move about freely as we produced sexy snobs.

The game room in the basement could easily be transformed into a club atmosphere for the cabaret, and we could probably stuff fifty guys in there. They're used to rubbing body parts with each other, since most of the guys we're targeting are Monday night regulars. At a hundred dollars a piece, a fraction of what they usually spend on any given night at Mitzie's, it would be a bargain for creating the ultimate visual for them, even if we had no real intentions of doing so.

We didn't exactly figure out how to get around the full nudity issue. In fact, we decided we weren't going to show any nudity at all, despite that being the sole motivation for the guys to show up. Trina suggested if the acts were put together right, our talents alone would "woo" them, and they wouldn't even notice we never took any clothes off. I wasn't so sure about that, but it definitely didn't make sense to show our muffs to raise money for a documentary about how women can be sexy without being naked.

Ava concluded she wanted *that* to be the theme of the film. If we could pull off the cabaret without any nudity, we would have proved the theory that sex or the hope of sex was not why men frequent strip clubs. As I was developing my own hypothesis that all men are chasing passion, the idea of promising nudity and not delivering it became more and more challenging. Could we keep their attention, get their blood boiling, and make them feel as though they got their money's worth without revealing any skin?

The next few days, the girls and I swapped ideas about what kinds of acts we would put on. None of us could hold a tune except Trina, who used to be a great singer. I had some concerns about casting her in a solo, since I knew that with Evan slowly depleting her self-esteem, she had picked up the microphone less and less over the years. We bought a karaoke machine and forced her to sing along with the funky 70's CD, but after a few hours, it became apparent he had done permanent damage. She was nervous, scratchy, and way off key.

With no time to waste, Ava made the executive decision that Trina would remain the prime coordinator of the event, and would possibly participate in a chorus dance number. Trina was relieved that she wouldn't have to perform alone, and seemed to really shine in the authoritative position of Director of Operations, so we left the issue alone. We could always lip-sync our way through some great old vaudevillian numbers, but frankly, the men were not coming to hear us sing.

A standup bit, a couple performance-art solos, a girl-girl number, and the traditional top-hat, long-cigarette, fishnet, group-burlesque gig, and we had a show. We needed funding from the lap dance party to facilitate the cabaret, and plenty of rehearsal time, so we decided to schedule the cabaret for the third week in November, giving us a little more than three weeks to choreograph and perfect it.

Trina went to Kinko's and put together a mini-brochure for her snooty association, using the empowering and motivational theories of Suze Orman, her idol. It was titled: "Want To Keep Your Man Wanting More And Getting Less? Take Control Of Your Bedroom." She planned to meet the group for lunch, and get the party on the books for the weekend before Halloween. We were all taking Halloween off from the club, since the owners issued a memo requiring us to dress as cats. Must be their favorite musical or something. To me, every day in there is Halloween. We put on disguises, go from lap to lap, beg for loot, and fiddle with our costumes all night. The only difference: There're tricks AND treats.

While I was drawing up the flyers for the cabaret, I brainstormed an idea about getting Evan into the club. After that day in court and seeing his new girlfriend, who could easily have been a dancer herself, I was thinking he must go to strip clubs. If we could somehow lure him into Mitzie's, we could get one of the girls to sit with him and siphon out the information needed regarding the whereabouts of his money. Trina still had to prove he hid it somewhere if she wanted to secure what was rightfully owed to her.

I had some of Mitzie's advertisements with me, so I made a few alterations adding an offer no man could pass up, and printed off a dozen of them. We would send them every day to his house and office, then wait for him to show. It was a long shot, and somewhat risky if he waltzed in unnoticed and saw Trina or me before we could hide, but she was desperate to find out this information and couldn't afford a private investigator. There really wasn't much to lose.

The kids knew she was working as a waitress, and if word got out it was a strip club, I'm sure they'd understand. There was nothing Evan could do to her for working there. It's legal, and it looks good to the court that she's making an effort to support the kids.

"Ladies! Ladies! Let's take our drinks and move into the living room. The exhibition is about to begin." Trina sashays around the kitchen with a shaker full of ice-cold Kettle One martinis, graciously hosting five budding seductresses and making sure they are well on their way to sheer drunkenness.

The turnout was significantly less than predicted. Trina had initially approached thirty of the younger, hipper women in the association, and we were counting on at least twenty of them desiring to spruce up their love lives. Most were offended that she would even associate herself with such "lowlifes," let alone solicit their involvement in "the despicable underground world of pornography."

I guess our business proposal needed work, and something was obviously conveyed incorrectly. But when you think of it, Ava was going to record the event, and although there would be no disrobing of any kind (we didn't really want to see *any* part of them naked), the negative comment wasn't all that far off.

Luckily, there were still a few open-minded, faintly perverted, Beverly Hills middle-aged women that were in dire need of seduction instruction, and we got our students. Because of the limited class size not bringing in the money we had hoped for, we were now committed to ongoing weekly training for the next month.

We draped black sheets around the windows and the doorway into the living room, darkening it so that the low-lit room mimicked a club-like atmosphere, and gave V and I a mysterious way to enter. Seduction is all about presentation, and we were going for full effect here. Fish set us up with some essential lighting tools. Strobes, revolving disco balls, and real movie-set lights with colored filters so we could change the vibe to illustrate different techniques needed for different personalities. To make things more perfect, he and V are officially dating, and we didn't have to pay for a thing.

When Ava and V went to Fox Studios to pick up the lights, Bobby saw them coming and locked himself in the prop room. He came out moments later wearing an ironclad "cup" strapped on the outside of his jeans. Ava laughed, admired his noble sportsmanship, and ostensibly a truce was made. Bobby asked her to come back later that night when everyone was gone, took her to the prop warehouse, and showed her an eight-by-ten stripper stage equipped with a pole that was once used for an episode of NYPD Blue.

In exchange for us borrowing the stage for a month, Ava agreed to get him ten free lap dances from the dancer of his choice the next time he was in Mitzie's. She also had to make a valiant effort at getting Trina to go out with him—his real motivation for helping us aspiring filmmakers, I'm sure. We're waiting for the right time to mention that to Trina.

"Lesson number one: Know your audience," Trina begins. "Communication is key. Know his true desires. What he likes, what he dislikes, what he fantasizes about. What totally turns him off, and most importantly, what turns him on. Everyone is different. Studies show that Good and Plenty candy acts as an aphrodisiac…" She passes a bowl around the group, "…and that men generally react positively to the smell of cinnamon." She lights a cinnamon incense stick. "Instead of incense, on your chosen night of passion, you might want to bake cinnamon rolls, so the smell permeates throughout the house. Vanilla body spray has also been known to have the same effect. You should have plenty of these items on hand at all times, as the spontaneous seduction can sometimes be the best."

V and I compiled the course synopsis for Beginning Lap Dancing. We combined various information found in *Cosmo* and *Playboy* magazines, books by Masters and Johnson, and lots of our own experiences in the club. It's kind of scary that we've become authorities on this issue, and are now passing on information to some not-so-young protégés.

Trina told her students to wear comfortable clothing that they might wear on a night out with their husbands. We're trying to get to the root of the relationship's sexual problems, and wardrobe plays a big role. Two of them are wearing conservative Jones New York skirt suits and low pumps. Another wears a restrictive pair of black pants that couldn't appear any more tight if they were sprayed on, and the other two sport pantsuits that match, making it obvious they either went shopping together or hung out a lot in the eighties. No wonder nobody's getting laid!

Trina had the women write down what in particular, if anything, their men have requested they do for them. We wanted to make sure we weren't dealing with any serial perverts. Other than one request to shave the upper inner thigh of his wife's leg with a straight razor blade, which incidentally landed him in sex therapy for six months, most desires were standard passion-seeking erotic foreplay.

She then invited V and I to demonstrate the difference between the amateur and professional lap dance, which led us to the meat of lesson one: Getting Past Your Fears Of Looking Stupid While Dancing For Your Man.

I've learned from working in the clubs that sexuality is largely about confidence. No matter what you look like, if you walk with self-assurance and poise, you will attract attention from the opposite sex. It might not always be the attention you want from the targeted person you want, but with time and continued self-reliance, you will eventually pique the interest of someone desirable.

"Nothing says, *I feel fat and unattractive* more than big, baggy clothes, hunched-over posture, staring at the floor, picking your face, and avoiding eye contact. Be proud of who you are and how you look. Walk tall, and own what God gave you." My words of wisdom for the day.

V takes the stage and illustrates the absolute *Don'ts* of exotic dancing, while Trina commentates.

1) *"Don't move too fast.* The key to drawing them into your moment is long, slow, swaying movements that float with the music."

2) *"Don't smile.* No giggling. It's supposed to be a fantasy for him. Slightly pouty lips, and a mysterious cheshire-cat smirk works wonders."

3) *"No complicated ensembles.* Don't wear an outfit that will get caught on your shoe as you take it off, and cause you to trip, ruining the entire moment. Should that be unavoidable, fall into his lap and abruptly segue into the bump and grind, creating adequate distraction from your clumsiness."

4) *"Don't attempt difficult dance maneuvers.* This performance will not win you a Tony award. Stick to the basics, and no twirling unless you seriously know what you're doing. He'll be much more impressed with your confident hip swaying, lightly grazing his body, than you Fosseing around the room ten feet away from him."

5) *"Don't touch your body aggressively.* You're not masturbating for him. Accent your best qualities by subtly brushing your hands by them, allowing him to imagine that he's doing it."

Last but not least:

6) *"Don't give in too easily.* Dodge his masculine urge to pull you onto his body and strip you naked as soon as you start. The longer the tease, the better the sex. Plus, the forced restraint teaches those *premies* out there some much needed self-control."

After V finished with the no-no rules, she gave the ladies a hands-on demonstration of how to touch themselves seductively without appearing uncomfortable or perverted. We may need to repeat that lesson.

The ladies left their first tutorial seemingly content. They'd picked up a few new tools, yet we left them wanting more, like any good salesperson would do. They paid their hundred dollars, and all noted next week's session in their date books. We must have done something right.

The best part of the day happened when one of the wives, who's married to a powerful Hollywood producer, invited us to her Halloween party. She said she admired our tenacity as aspiring artists, and wanted to help us make necessary industry contacts. It was a nice gesture, but I really don't think passing our mockumentary proposal around a room full of Draculas and Frankensteins chasing Playboy bunnies and supermodels dressed as themselves, would prove to be all that helpful. My opinion however, was outvoted, and the girls talked me into going anyway. I guess you never know who'll be there.

A horn honks loudly outside my apartment. I peek out the bathroom window to see a limo driver get kicked in the head as V struggles to squeeze through the tiny window divider into the back of the stretch Lincoln. She had flung herself up front over the shoulder of the driver in order to lay on the horn, and must have slipped through the window into his lap. All blows to the head aside, he didn't seem to mind helping the scarcely clad Miss V back into her seat.

Before I became a dancer, I never understood the need for women to take their clothes off on Halloween. Bunnies, superheroes in thong leotards, trashy witches, slutty brides—they all had one thing in common—scant costumes! It's as if women are making the statement that one day a year they're allowed to unleash their true fantasies, get wild, maybe have sex with a stranger in a Zorro costume, then huddle back into their stifling turtlenecks and long skirts, and wait for next year to come out of their shells again.

Having talked extensively with female patrons that frequent strip clubs, I've concluded that all women want to be successful at being sexy, and would willfully dress promiscuously if they had more confidence in their bodies. I guess unveiling on Halloween offers a mask and holiday punch laden with Everclear to hide behind in case everyone else looks really good in their skimpy attire, or no Zorros want to show you the haunted closet upstairs.

Trina was evolving into a more powerful woman these days, and was noticeably enjoying being the *leader* of her seductresses. As such, she decided our theme for the night would be pimps and hookers. Quite a stretch from our daily realities! She wanted to be the pimp and instructed us to go way over the top with our getups.

From the looks of the near hole she put in the limo driver's face, V had pulled out the black, thigh-high leather boots equipped with a staggering stiletto no stripper would even attempt to work in. She bought them when she first started dancing, wore them one night, then retired them to the pile of unwearable ensembles purchased purely as a result of amateur misinformation. Note for any aspiring exotic dancers out there: Seek wardrobe advice from the professionals before spending a bundle at Frederick's. No returns on shoes or underwear.

Seeking comfort over attention, I exit my apartment wearing my favorite sweat outfit, then slide into the limo next to the persuasive hooker, her pimp, and Ava making yet another compelling proclamation dressed as Billy Jean King.

"Where is your costume?" the three of them recite in sync.

"This is it." I put on a black pointed hat. "I'm a lazy witch. You know, like…on a rainy Sunday. You think they're always in flowing capes, wearing fake eyelashes, flying around on brooms? I don't think so!"

"That's great, Alex. Now we look like the idiots." V acknowledges her costume overkill. "We're supposed to be a fucking posse! We got dyko tennis pro over here, and you…making no effort whatsoever!"

"That's not true. This was dirty, *and* it had a big coffee stain that I worked on for an hour." She rolls her heavily mascara'd eyes at me. "Who cares, anyway. Half the people aren't even going to dress up, and we don't know anybody. Just chill out over there, Divine Brown, you'll still be able to steal the show." V needs a lot of attention. Childhood neglect always surfaces in adulthood.

"The whole point of going is to meet people." Billy Jean speaks. "You're isolating us by not wearing a costume. They're gonna think you think you're too cool to dress up."

I take off my hat. "Fine. Now I'm a professional athlete, just like you." They scoff simultaneously. "Why would I want to dress up, especially as a hooker? We wear that stuff five days a week!"

"All right, all right!" Trina interrupts. "Let's just forget it already! It's a party remember? Can we have fun, *please?*"

After twenty minutes of weaving through the narrow roads of the famous Hollywood Hills, we arrive at an extravagant house behind four other limos. As expected, dapper-looking men wearing tuxedos, capes, fangs, and a dollop of fake blood, escort hopeful starlets bearing not much more than fishnets and glittery halters. The yard is meticulously decorated, sparing no expense. Good to know one of our clients has so much disposable income. We probably could have financed the mockumentary for half of what she spent on the outside decor alone.

At the entrance, a midget troll directs us through an intricate maze of spider webs, bats, and creepy flying objects that line the hallway into the main "haunted house." It's pitch black. If not for a few strobing lights and glowing ghouls, we'd be domino-ing into each other as we made our way to the bar. Most everyone has some kind of costume on. Certainly within a room full of entertainers and producers, there's bound to be a few outstanding scarers. I put on my hat as we belly up to the bar.

"Ok, so I feel a little stupid about not dressing up. You guys were right, almost everyone wore costumes."

"Almost? No! *Everyone's* wearing one!" V snaps at me.

"Not that guy." I point to a dweeby character in checkered pants, suspenders, and a beret holding a CAA script, talking to one of the models.

"Dude! C'mon, he's got toilet paper hanging out his pants. It's a costume!"

"What is he, Hollywood nerd? Ten bucks says he's a writer."

"He's probably somebody important. Go talk to him." Ava pushes me toward him.

"I'm not mingling. *You're* the producer. You do it." The four of us huddle around the bar trying to figure out who's famous and who's not, never noticing our client right next to us. The Queen of England recognizes Trina.

"Trina, darling…how cute you look as Heidi Fleiss. Huh! The irony." She laughs. "And here are your girls! I'm so glad you all could come. There's a zillion people I want you to meet, but mum's the word on our arrangement. I don't want Mitchell to know I've been *training*, you understand?"

"Don't worry, Mrs. Clinefeld, it's not like we want to broadcast the whole stripper thing either." I nudge V in the side and mouth, *dancer*!

"Mrs. Clinefeld, we totally appreciate your invitation. Your house is amazing, and no worries about the classes." I zip V's mouth. "Our little secret."

"Speaking of secrets." She huddles up with us. "It's good to have a sense of humor about it all, but I think my husband may have been on that list…" She pats Trina's costume prop—the infamous little black book. "…along with most of the men in this room. Go. Mingle. Have fun. We'll catch up later." She skates off like royalty.

"Great! You in no costume, *and* we've got the Hollywood Madam everyone wants to avoid! I guess I'll be networking alone!" Ava throws her racket over her shoulder, adjusts her wig, and stomps off.

"Well, since we're here, might as well get drunk." I grab two champagne flutes off a passing waiter's tray and separate from V and Trina.

I decide to give myself the house tour, and mosey upstairs. A few giggly young girls and their phantasmal escorts come out of bedrooms on the second floor. I suppose they were paying their dues for the invitation to hang with the in-crowd, or participating in the ever-ramped Hollywood drug scene. So much ugliness in this town so cleverly disguised as glittery hopes and dreams.

The third floor of this spectacular mansion opens into a bathroom that most people couldn't conceive of. Just looking through the entryway, I can see it's bigger than my whole apartment. I push through the half-open door, and walk slowly on the marbled floor. This bathroom is utterly amazing. Everything styled with precise elegance. I round the corner, passing by a shower that could easily fit ten people in it, and am startled by a man snorting cocaine off the tank lid of one of the two toilets in the room.

"Oh! Sorry. Didn't know anyone was in here." I turn to leave.

"Wait! Don't go." He comes at me. I instinctively search out my escape options. "You can't tell anyone you saw me in here." He's nervous, wide-eyed, full of drugs.

"Ok. 'Bye." Again I turn, and head for the door. He grabs my arm.

"Listen, seriously I'm in rehab. It's my last chance. Nobody can know…or my career—it'll be…it'll be gone. Poof! Gone." He talks fast, still holding on to my hand.

"I'm not going to tell anybody. Can I have my hand back?"

"Sorry. I'm just a little strung out. You know, withdrawals. I was doing good, really good for a while, but things just, you know…my work…it's…it's…it's just so hard…'cause it's everywhere—" He's bouncing off the walls, walking in circles. "—the pressure to come up with good ideas, brilliant ideas…is so intense! I can't think of stuff without it." He plops down in a velvet chair, then stands up quickly.

"What do you do?" I ask, hoping to talk my way out of whatever he has planned for me.

"I'm in development at HBO. So much pressure! I have to come up with something…something…something brilliant! Praiseworthy! I need that. I need it!"

"Ok…and good luck with that, really. I hope you figure it out. I'm…I'm gonna go now." I inch away from him slowly.

"Don't open the door!" He screams out. "Please! Don't go. I can't go out there, yet. I can't let them see me like this. I just…I just…I just…need to talk to somebody for a little while, until I can get it under control. Please?"

No matter where I go, I can't seem to escape the counseling calling I may have missed in my life. I certainly never envisioned my first visit to such a sumptuous privy would be admonishing a drug addict of the physical perils of crack cocaine. He talked unremittingly for an hour and a half, telling me how it got started and why it continues.

He recounted the entertainment industry pressure to stay at the top of the creative ladder while the new, young originators were taking over. Despite the on-again, off-again drug problem, he managed to maintain a powerful position where his ideas could at least be heard.

He asked what I did, and instead of lying, I blurted out, "I'm a stripper." I had never said those words before, but figured: A) He'd never remember this conversation, B) I'd never see him again, and C) He's a drug addict—like he's going to judge me!

I told him about my past work experience at the law firm, and how I decided to change careers to follow my dream. He commended me for doing that, and told his dream-chasing story of always wanting to be a writer. When he was younger, he wrote a few screenplays that never made it anywhere, then took a job as a script reader at HBO to help move them along.

Nobody ever took any interest in his work, so he gave up writing and worked his way into developing other people's projects for the network. He isn't a bigwig over there, but is part of a team that could get ideas onto the screen. I took the opportunity to pitch my idea of a stripper comedy series. I based the characters on me and the girls, adding a bartender, club manager, and plenty of room for star power on each episode. He acted as though he really liked it, but I'm sure he was just humoring me. Wannabes pitch their ideas to guys like him a hundred times a day. The odds that someone gets a development deal from a bathtub meeting? Better than the golf course, but still slim!

We decided it was time to exit when the crowd outside the door issued a few heated threats. He was still in no shape to be seen by work colleagues, so I dug through some linens and found him the perfect costume. I led the ghostly druggie down the stairs and out the door. He thanked me for my help, gave me a business card, and wished me luck with my career.

I went back into the party laughing to myself about the crazy encounters I've had these past few months. I thought about all those boring nights in the war room sorting documents for hours, not having desirable human contact for months at a time. As fatuous as my life has gotten since I left the firm, I wouldn't change a thing, and am happier than I ever was there.

"Hey, you guys, you wouldn't believe who I met in the bathroom." I catch up with V and Trina. "This guy—"

"You're not going to believe who's here!" V turns my body to face the opposite direction. I see a Chippendale dancer, a sexy fireman, and I'm not sure what the other guy is—a bum having a bad hair day? "It's Jode."

"Yeah, I can see that. And how did they know about this party?"

"Fuckin' fate, dude."

"You told Fish!"

"I didn't. Swear."

"What on earth is your man wearing?"

"He's windblown." She laughs. "Isn't it cool? His hair is blown back, and all that garbage is stuck to his pants. Totally brilliant!" She winks at her man, and waves them over.

Of course my figmented romantic has to be dressed as a hunky fireman. Why couldn't he be Big Bird?

"Hey you."

"Hi. Fancy running into you here," I say, suspiciously.

"Strange coincidence?" He knows my next line.

"There are no coincidences."

"Nice costume, Alex. Real sexy," Bobby butts in. "Spend all day on that one?"

"Ha, ha. You're hilarious. I see you wore your work uniform." The group cracks up.

"You're just jealous 'cause Trina's gonna get all my lap dances tonight. Right, babe?" He puts his arm around Trina. She squirms out of his grip.

"Only if you're paying *me* for them…babe!"

"Is that all it'll take? I gotcha covered."

V and Fish make out like they haven't seen each other for a year. They swap spit like teenagers, and as usual, could not care less who they offend.

"Are we gonna have to hose you two off?"

"Yeah, get a room. Preferably one not in this house."

They unlock lips for a split second.

"Great fuckin' idea, dude!" She takes Fish by the hand. "Let's do it in every room in the house, baby." She leads him up the stairs. I stop her.

"No, no, no, no. You can't have sex in Clinefeld's house. She's our client!"

"Oh please! What do you think everyone's doing up there?" The stairwell is full of ghouls and goblins coming up and down...smiling. She whispers in my ear. "This is what you do at Hollywood parties, Alex. And if you were smart, you'd snag *him* right now, before somebody else does. C'mon, let's go." She drags Fish up the stairs.

"I should have been windblown. It was *my* idea," Bobby pouts. "Who wants a lap dance? On me." He pulls out a bankroll of dollar bills.

"This I got to see," I say.

All indications are that Trina will play no part in Bobby's removal of clothes. For entertainment's sake, I must convince her otherwise. I lean in close to her, and in my most serious of tones plead, "Trina, we've been friends a long time. Sometimes, you just gotta take one for the team. *Everyone upstairs!*"

Jode and I sit on a couch, keeping our distance from the strip show. Bobby sets up his music, of course he brought his own, and prepares his big entrance. Trina guzzled two cosmopolitans on the way up the long staircase. She's a little more receptive now.

"I will now proceed to entangle the entire area." David Crosby's preamble to Crosby, Stills, Nash & Young's famous 1973 track "Almost Cut My Hair." Classic choice. But can he dance?

Bobby enters the room with a long, dark mane of hair over his own, and dances his routine, dramatically hitting the pivotal beats of the song. Jode and I laugh so hard, we're both in tears, as Bobby acts through this rehearsed piece of performance art. He rips off his velcroed chaps and thrusts his tighty-whities in Trina's face. She buries her face in her hands, trying not to get hit with the gyrating penis.

He grabs her hand, yanks her off the couch, and engages her in a tango. Where's my camera? Bobby in his underwear dipping our own Heidi Fleiss in a complete backbend, then pulling her up with precision maneuvering.

"He is strong. I'll give him that!" I yell over the music to Jode.

Trina laughs at him, but tries to keep up with the tango. The closer they get to us, the farther we move away.

"This is the funniest thing I've ever seen in my life!"

"You should see him at work!" Jode yells back.

At the end of the song, Bobby dips Trina back for the big finale, and plants a dramatic, theatrical smooch on her lips. She doesn't fight it, and in true tango style, allows him to drag her out of the room into one across the hall.

"Well! He has talents I would have never…ever imagined." I wipe my eyes.

"He's pretty crazy. Bobby Crazy—his nickname at work."

"Has a nice ring to it. What's your nickname?"

"Don't have one. I told you, I stay out of the limelight. I like to sit back and people-watch."

"Thus the cameraman job?"

"You're catching on. I see everything through a lens. Getting rid of exterior influences creates a very clear picture. I like to see people for who they really are."

"Tough to do in a world full of exterior influences."

"Not really. Just got to block out all the bullshit. Dig out the gritty personality traits."

"Look who's analyzing now." I give him a noogie on the head. "You're so thought-out. Mr. Controlled. Don't you ever do anything crazy?"

"Occasionally. I'm not all that comfortable taking center stage. Other people are far more entertaining than I am."

"That's a matter of opinion. I bet you could be wildly entertaining. Why don't you give it a try?"

"And do what?" He laughs at the prospect.

"Dance for me."

"I don't think so."

Bobby's head appears from the side of the doorway. "Dude, got a condom?"

Jode gets up hesitantly, reaches in his back pocket, and gives him one.

"You da man!" His naked butt runs across the hall. He stops short, turns back, and yells, "Would you two get it over with! Screw already!" He disappears into another room.

"Not much on subtlety, is he?" He looks at me, and we say simultaneously: "Can't take him anywhere!"

Jode refills our wine glasses with a bottle he snatched from the bar. I get up and flick on the intercom system so we can hear the music downstairs. I'm so comfortable with him, yet so conflicted.

"I'm not going to have sex with you. In case…you were wondering," I blurt out boldly. He raises an eyebrow, betraying a hint of disappointment.

"I was wondering, but not expecting. Probably best, since I gave away my only condom."

"Yeah, that wasn't very smart. Ahhh! I love this!" My favorite Morcheeba track comes through the intercom. Uh-oh, we're in trouble. I can't not dance to this song. It moves me.

"Turn it up," he says with anxious anticipation.

He relaxes his enticing body on the couch, sips the California Cabernet, and shrewdly watches me get taken over by the music. The artist's voice is deliciously sexy. The lyrics, plush and feminine. No passionate person could resist such a mood. Jode closes his eyes. I hear him breathe deeply. I kick off my shoes, and become further engulfed in the Now. An abrupt thought of how I must look in my T-shirt and sweatpants dancing around in an alluring fashion enters my head, but quickly leaves when we lock eyes, and I glide my trance-like posture closer to him.

Skillfully, I part his legs with mine, then lean over him, commanding a tantalizing stance. I let my eyes pass his for a brief moment, penetrating them deeply, then close them as I allow the music to carry me into an arched-back head roll. He casually slips the fireman's suspenders off his bare shoulders, igniting an uncontrollable urge to lift my shirt and rub my chest on his. I resist, but tug on the shirt, teasing him enough to convey my desire of wanting him to see, but not letting him. He shifts his weight, then extends one leg out longer than the other. I'm completely aware of his aroused body language, yet losing myself in this impulsive, forbidden juncture.

"I know you're not really into the whole lap dance thing, but maybe you could just humor me while I have an internal sultry moment?" I say seductively, not really caring what his response will be. This is my hour.

"I do like to help out wherever I can." His equally seductive, so-cool response.

My T-shirt falls off my shoulder. I shrug girlishly, and continue the rhythmic journey up and down his body. I'm in control, yet totally lost. I've always loved passionate music, in all its different styles—funk, rock, blues, country. In the past, I never permitted myself to really hear it, or let go of life's inhibitions enough to truly feel it. This man, this beautiful inspirational man, is doing so much more for me than he'll ever know.

Why can't I be with him? Why can't I trust them again? Why can't I just take a risk like everyone else does? I kiss him softly on his upper lip as the song ends. He fervently takes control of the embrace, and for one second I give in to my thirst for passion, then pull back abruptly, snapping us both back to my reality.

"Sorry. I can't."

"Why?" he asks in-between heart-pounding breaths.

"I don't know." I fan myself with my hand, and step back away from him.

"I got to get some air." His frustration leads him out to the balcony.

Ok, now I feel stupid. Did I really think my sweatpant dance wasn't going to make him want more? For someone who methodically analyzes men, I didn't plot that out very well. But it wasn't really for him. I was having my own moment! Maybe I should just give him a chance? *I'm so confused!*

Jode leans against the rail, staring into the brisk darkness distantly lit by the Hollywood sign. I gather my thoughts, refill our wine glasses, and join him on the balcony.

"Are you a neat-freak? Smoker? Martini drinker?" I fire at him.

"No, no, and no." He takes his glass, then gulps a sip.

"How 'bout beer?" Without hesitation, his frustrated disposition turns comedic, and he jumps in on my movie line lead-in.

"It's seven o'clock in the morning."

"Scotch?" I finish the quote, then we share a brief laugh for being on the same wavelength.

"See how well we work together? We should be together."

"That's real cute. Throw off my interrogation with a classic from *Mr. Mom*. There's got to be something wrong with you. I know it. I'm gonna find it," I say humorously.

"I guess you will if you keep looking. Can I ask you something?" I give him a hesitant go-ahead look. "What are you so afraid of? I just want to know you."

"Why?"

"What do mean *why?* I can't believe how hard I have to work for this date!" He shakes his head, momentarily looks off in another direction, then back at me. "You're beautiful, smart, unbelieeevably passionate, and…occasionally funny…when you're not interrogating me. That's why."

"What about the stripper stuff? It doesn't bother you?"

"Not at this point. We haven't even had a first date! But, in all fairness, if you were my girlfriend, would I want a bunch of guys slobbering all over you? Probably not."

"Well, see…that's a problem." I defend myself here. "I've made a choice, an educated choice, to take this job so I can facilitate other things in my life—"

"And I can appreciate that. I would never stand in the way of someone chasing their dreams, but—"

"Look what we're doing," I cut him off. "We've haven't even gone out, and we're already fighting about it. I hear other dancers talk about their boyfriends. They're either total losers, or constantly badgering them to quit!" He opens his mouth to interrupt. I delicately put my hand over it, and keep talking.

"Why even have a first date, when that's as far as it can go? I can't let myself be romantically vulnerable. It's a setup for another huge man disappointment, and I just don't think I could handle it. It's easier to keep you on the pedestal I've put you on, and not know what could have happened, than risk a potential heartbreak."

I take my hand off his mouth. He stares off into the crisp night, and shakes his head.

"I…I don't get it, but obviously I've been reading the wrong signals here." He downs the rest of his wine. "I got to go."

He bolts out of the room, bangs on the door where Bobby and Trina are, announces he's leaving the party, and hurries down the stairs. I'm such an *idiot!*

11

Does time seem to increase in speed with every passing week, or is just me? One of my greatest fears is that Mondays and Fridays will soon become the same day, and I'll be fifty, adapting the word *menopausal* as a daily part of my vocabulary. It's been three weeks since that dreadful Halloween party, but it seems like just yesterday I ruined a perfectly good opportunity for passionate sex and a possible boyfriend. I haven't seen him since that night, and the word from V is he may have gotten back with an old girlfriend. My loss, someone else's gain.

I'm trying hard not to have a bittersweet attitude about anything these days, and truly rely on the Universal slogan that *You are where you're supposed to be at any given time.* Thus leaving it up to fate to decide if we're meant to be. But I can't get that kiss out of my mind, and could kick myself for not getting another one.

The girls and I have been training hard for the cabaret. My dance studio lets us rehearse there for free as long as we agree to give some of their top dancers extra parts in the mockumentary. It wasn't a problem since there's plenty of room for background dancers, but we insisted on a clause that none of them are allowed to show us up. *We're the stars!*

The show is only days away, and we still haven't mapped out Plan B: *What to do if/when a riot breaks out over our non-nudity.* Ava keeps telling us not to worry about it. "We'll keep the booze flowing and tease them long enough to call it a show, and if they're still not satisfied? We make an anonymous call to Beverly Hills PD and the party gets busted before we can get naked." Her saving grace is that, "We'll never see most of these guys again once we get the project off the ground, so who really cares?"

She's probably right, but I'm still going to come up with a backup plan.

Yesterday, we gave the last lap dance lesson of our four-week course, and had an intimate graduation party for our five sirens, who have all turned into borderline nymphomaniacs. In order to receive their official *I'm a qualified stripper* see-through mesh negligee with matching thong, which we gave as class certifications, they each had to perform one stage routine with requirements of pole work, floor work, some degree of flexibility, an intentional screw-up with recovery moment, an edgy comeback line for a shouting heckler, and a bring-them-to-their-knees final pose.

Additionally, each had to lap dance for the others, exhibiting something unique for each person. After the first two had gone, we realized we needed more clarification on that phrase since they were flashing their privates to satisfy the requirement. We reminded them all that great seductresses withhold the goods until the last possible moment, if at all. Surprisingly, all five pronounced-temptresses passed with flying colors, received their negligees, and inquired when the next semester would be starting. We told them they'd be notified discreetly by mail.

Clinefeld was so excited she could now compete with the black-book professionals, she gave us a $1,000 bonus check, and took a pile of flyers for the cabaret to distribute to her friends in the industry. There were undeniably a few tears as our apprentices left stumbling through the yard in their stilettos, yanking Victoria's Secret lace underwear out of their butts.

"Hi Mom."

"How did you know it was me?"

"Caller ID. It's a new feature on my cell. Gives me the number that's calling, so I can decide who not to talk to."

"That's nice, honey, are you driving? You know fifty percent of accident-related deaths are caused by driver distractions. They're going to ban cell phones in cars soon. Mark my words."

"Thanks Mom. Is that why you called me—the driving-while-distracted lecture? 'Cause I think I have that one memorized, and only have a few minutes to talk. I'm on my way to work."

"No, and don't be a smart butt. Are you coming for Thanksgiving? You know it's next week." She uses her stern, motherly tone.

"Oooooh crap! I did know it was next week, but…kind of forgot to make arrangements. I don't think I can get a flight, and really don't want to battle the traffic into Phoenix. Do I have to?"

"Well, Alex, you're an adult. You don't have to do anything you don't want to do—"

"Ok good, 'cause I really don't want to come—"

"But your sisters are coming…from farther away, and of course we'd like you to be there."

"Mommmm," I whine. "Remember last year? Cousin Joanie? The bone over my eyebrow is still tender where she coldcocked me."

"Oh, you're making such a big deal out of it. You know she was drinking, and that she had a problem. I think your aunt got her into a one of those expensive treatment places, and apparently she's all better now."

"Yeah, yeah, I heard she went to rehab, but I'm pretty sure there's a city ordinance in Scottsdale that says getting punched in the face at the Thanksgiving dinner table relieves one of obligation to attend future family gatherings at holidays. I might get a citation or something."

"Ok, now you're just being funny." You think? "I'm going to let you sleep on it, and tell the girls you might be coming."

"Mom, I'm not. Seriously, I can't. We're doing this cabaret thing on Friday, and I just don't have time to get it together." I could do it, but why travel four hundred miles to stuff my body with food, yak about nothing with my family, and then get back on a crowded plane. I'd rather get drunk with Phil and share turkey jerky with my Pomeranian.

"So you'll sleep on it?"

"Fine. I'll sleep on it. But I'm not coming."

"'Bye sweetie. Hope you gather lots of *research* at work. Love you."

"'Bye Mom. You too." I think she's on to me.

The last few years at family gatherings have been trying for me. I haven't really wanted to go, but forced myself anyway. Maybe it's a biological clock thing. I should have my own family by now, and my psyche is rebelling. Last Thanksgiving, my distant cousin Joanie showed up drunk at nine o'clock in the morning with a hitchhiker she picked up on the way to my mom's house. Mom had decided to wait until everyone had arrived before she shopped for the day's menu. I knew my procrastination was inherited!

We all have different tastes, and dinner at the table wasn't something we made a priority growing up. Each one of us was involved in various after-school activities that always seemed to cross the dinner hour. McDonald's and Wendy's were supper hosts more often than not.

So there we were Thanksgiving morning with no food, nothing set up, and a disturbingly drunk relative that no one could definitively place on the family tree. Not to mention the filthy degenerate she dragged in with her. Mom always supported an open house policy.

I ended up shopping, cooking, *and* cleaning for the group, who humored our transient guests by letting them spike the eggnog with bourbon *and* rum, two liquors that should never be in the same highball.

The crème de la crème was having to clean up someone's puke prints that drizzled their way from the living room to the bathroom, leading to the full load which was left in the toilet for all to see. By the time we sat down for dinner, I hated everyone in the room, and had bit my tongue for so many hours it was swollen. I finally blew when my thirty-four-year-old cousin announced that as of that moment she was a vegetarian, and I should get off my lazy butt and make pasta for her. My directed profanity sobered everyone up at the table, and ultimately provided my sisters with abundant storytelling comedy for many months after.

Joanie staggered out of her seat and approached my side of the table holding a fork. I laughed at her and commented to my youngest sister how *scared* I was that she might stab me with the fork. My sarcasm fueled Joanie's anger, causing her to bump her hip on the corner of the table, spilling wine into the mashed potatoes. Thankfully, she dropped the fork and decided to take a different vengeful approach. The unexpected hard right to my upper eye probably saved me from a partial loss of sight, or possibly a stress-induced lethal aneurysm, as it gave me an excuse to leave the table and go home.

I graze by the full parking lot at Mitzie's en route to the lot designated for the entertainers. Another Monday night. Only two months left in football season. Two months to make something happen with my career. Time is moving way too fast. I wonder if *he'll* be here tonight.

"Did you see who's here?" I rush Trina at the waitress station.

"Jode and the clown crew?"

"You can't keep calling Bobby names…now that you've had sex with him."

"Why not? It didn't change anything. Great sex doesn't make him any less of an idiot!"

"Fine, forget about that. Evan's here!"

"What! Where?" She ducks down behind the wood barrier in the station.

"Over there. Talking to Adrianna."

"Oh shit! I've got to get out of here! He can't see me…or you! He'll know we sent the bait!"

"Will you calm down! He's not going to see us. It's pitch black in here. But you can't be walking around. Go fake a stomachache and hang out upstairs for a while. I'll do the blond librarian thing for a couple hours, and stay close to him. If all goes well, Evan will wish he never came in here!"

"But what if—" Evan and Adrianna head our way.

"Go, go, go! He's coming!" We hurry through the locker room door.

Within fifteen minutes, I had metamorphosed into a totally different person. I borrowed one of those short, plaid Catholic school-girl skirts and a tight white blouse from a girl who always wears this look. I put on a blond curly wig, and a pair of black-rimmed glasses I pulled out of the lost and found bin, and was now ready to put the disguise through its first test.

I approach two of my regulars and ask if they want a dance. They both decline, but neither seems to recognize me. I don't say too much, as I've been told my signature raspy voice is unmistakable, and I do sense they seem a bit confused when they first hear me. I'll have to change that. With preliminary testing out of the way, it was time to put the Ivana Trump divorce mantra into full motion: *Don't get even. Get everything!*

Trina and I had talked about the day Evan might eventually come in, and had sort of schemed out a plan. But I think both of us deep down never really thought we'd see the day. We certainly didn't expect him to come in so fast. Mitzie's offers a VIP, all-inclusive rate of two hundred dollars to spend an hour with the entertainer of your choice, unlimited dances, and two free drinks. The club takes fifty bucks, and the rest is for the girl.

No one ever buys this package, since it's not a deal at all. Even if the girl danced nonstop for the entire hour, which would leave her sweaty, smelly, and exhausted, it might add up to twenty dances, costing the client two hundred dollars anyway.

In reality, the client would get maybe ten dances during that hour, fewer if the girl is educated and can carry a conversation, which she would do to take up all the time. The drink savings might tally twelve to fifteen dollars, so if anyone was so stupid as to buy this package, he would actually be losing about eighty-five dollars.

I had altered Mitzie's flyer to give newcomers that deal for free, as long as they agreed to pay the girl a hundred for the next hour. Its works out to be pretty much our basic rate of fifty dollars an hour. I knew Evan would take the bait, since Trina always complained about how cheap he was. No matter how much money they had, he consistently tried to get everything for free. They'd dine at five-star restaurants, eat their entire meal, and when Trina would go to the bathroom, he'd tell the waiter she got food poisoning, and that he owned the local newspaper. The restaurant would, of course, comp the meal and usually gave him a gift certificate for another one.

Trina never knew what was going on. Evan convincingly made her think he had a lot of "friends" that just liked doing things for him. She finally clued in when she overheard him telling the kids how to look sick at the all-you-can-eat shrimp festival, and how fun it is to make people do what you want them to do. He's such a shyster! And for the record, I bet he orders two Jack Daniels shots with a Coke back. Classic small-penis over-compensation mix.

Judging by the shaking of Adrianna's head, and her meticulous scrutiny of the flyer, I have about two seconds to perfect my Swedish accent, and put my disguise to the ultimate challenge. I sneak up behind Adrianna and whisper in her ear, "Let me have this one. I owe ya'," then grab the flyer from Evan, and nod and smile, saying "Yah" a lot.

Adrianna looks at me weird and walks off. I take Evan by the hand and lead him to a seat. I catch him indiscreetly check out my body, as any true male chauvinist would do, then he pats me on the butt and says:

"Nice stems...for a foreigner."

I giggle and in my best Swenglish respond, "In my country, men don't like women with strong legs. Too...how you say...inteem-idating? They afraid of me. Afraid where I might *keek* them." He flinches when I show him where. "Yah, Yah...see...you afraid, too!" I laugh, then assertively sit him down and mount him like an animal.

I run my fingers through his hair, put his nose in my cleavage, and massage the back of his neck aggressively.

"No be afraid of Helga! Helga here to make you feel better." I nibble on his ear. Puke! "You tell Helga deep, dark fantasies...secrets...and I make you feel like a man!" Bump. Grind. "Helga love secrets! Make me very, very frisky!" More bump. More grind. Growl. Nibble. Yuck!

I dismount, scanning the room to see if the bouncers have eyed my blatant disregard for club rules. I then delicately lay my legs across his lap, pout my lips, and let him stroke my *stems*, while he spews on and on about his horrible soon-to-be-ex-wife who refused to satisfy his insatiable sexual needs and spent all their money on drugs chasing younger men, forcing him to open Swiss bank accounts to secure enough money to support his twins.

After six rounds of JD shots with beer chasers, mine quenching the thirsty fern next to me, I convinced him I was as drunk as he was, and he could trust me with anything. Helga can be *very, very* persuasive! He spoke loud and clear into the microphone buried in my Wonderbra and attached to my old, reliable office dictaphone, as he bragged about his million dollars offshore, and his plan to take the kids to Europe so they could escape the horrendous maternal influence they would surely be susceptible to.

When our time was up, he reluctantly paid me under the promise I meet him in Paris at his newly bought villa that overlooks the city's spectacular sights. He gave me the address and all the information I would need to find him there.

As I led him to the door full of booze, eager to get behind the wheel of Trina's Mercedes, I put the final touches on what will ultimately and forever be referred to as *Le Coup Du Siecle* (The Plan of the Century). I emphatically let the retired LAPD officer, who stands guard in our parking lot, know we'd be doing everyone on the streets a favor tonight by making sure the guy in the white Benz got a DUI. Can you say *sole custody?*

I was so excited about my performance as Helga, the information-swindling femme fatale, and so eager to play the tape for Trina, I didn't even notice Jode and the guys sitting in their usual spot, until I had run right past them. It's doubtful he recognized me. I tripped over V's seven-inch moon-boots tangled between Fish's long, lanky legs, said a quick "sorry" and kept moving. I didn't look back, but I heard her yell, "Watch where you're goin', fuckin' clumsy newbie!"

I raced up the stairs, ditched Helga in the garbage, and dragged Trina to the small window in the bathroom where we bore witness to Evan being carted away in handcuffs. She was a little bummed out about how the kids would feel if they found out he got arrested, and felt like maybe we did the wrong thing. Then, I played the tape. She *freaked!* I had to physically restrain her from climbing out the window and lunging at him. I reminded her she hadn't won yet, and still had to get the tape in the hands of the right lawyer, who she won't have trouble retaining now that she's got evidence of the money.

As three cop cars, called as backup to calm the belligerent Evan (who insisted he wasn't drunk and threatened to sue the city) pulled out of the parking lot, Trina hugged and kissed me, then appropriately went home to cuddle with her kids.

The night was still early, and I was on a huge high from my certified Golden Globe-winning accomplishment. That was my first real acting job, and would probably yield more money than I may ever make from the industry. I didn't even know I could do a Swedish accent. Although my audience was undeniably under the influence of a controlled substance, I still deserve kudos, and just might accept my award in the form of an evening of hot, steamy sex.

"Hi," I say, all peppy-like.

"Hey." He barely looks at me.

"How've you been?" I ask.

"Good. Real good." He looks away again.

Something's going on here. The vibe is off. He's not talking, not looking, acting like he's watching the game. I must have really bruised his ego at the party. Damage control...think...think...how can I undo this?

"Sooo, you been working a lot? I haven't seen you around for a while."

"Yep. Keepin' busy." He doesn't take his eyes off the TV.

"Yeah, me too." Ok, the stupid small talk isn't going to fly. I may actually have to step up to the plate. I put my hand on his shoulder. "Listen, I know this is an important game and all, but if I could have your undivided attention for about a minute, I think that...maybe...I could explain some things, which could hopefully lead to a more meaningful conversation...like we used to have?"

"You don't need to explain anything. I got the message loud and clear, and not to be mean or anything, but I'm over it." He looked at me when he said that, then back to the TV.

"O-k. Well, then I guess I'll just have to talk to myself, so at least I can feel better knowing I said my piece."

He shrugs.

Do I deserve this snub? I mean all I did was decide not to follow through with a passionate moment I started. Don't we still have that right? Couldn't have been the first time. Why is he so pissed? Maybe he really likes me...*or*...maybe I was the only woman to reject him. Ugh! The male ego is so fragile! What if he knows I never had any intentions of acting on my urge, thus feeling like I played him? But did I really know I wasn't going to do anything? Could I have used him to develop my own inner passion without any thought of how it might affect him? Is it possible I've become so mechanical about the seduction that I didn't even care about the effect on him? But I did care, and...and...it wasn't mechanical. *I'm so confused!*

"*Fumble!* Sweet!" Jode shouts and gets in Bobby's face. "Five hundred bucks dude! Pay up!"

"Don't be gloatin' on me! It's not over yet." Bobby acknowledges me. "Hey, where's Katerina? We need shots."

"Her name's Katrina. We call her Trina. Sound familiar?" I patronize him. "A piece of advice? Letting her best friend know you forgot her name...probably not going get you a second date." I roll my eyes at him.

"I already got a second date, and a third. High five!" He waits for one from Fish. "For the record...there...uhhh...sweet eyes, I didn't forget her name. I just misspoke." He turns his back on me with a childlike *ha ha ha* smirk on his face.

"Hey Bobby! What's *my* name?" He thinks for a second, opens his mouth as if he knows, then turns to Jode.

"Help me out here, dude. Wait! Don't tell me. I got it. A-A-A-Alm-A—*Alex! Ha!*" He pats himself on his back, then proudly leans on me, and puts both hands on my knees and says softly, "Never forget a green-eyed thoroughbred like you." He winks at me, then stands up. "So, where is she?"

"Right behind you." He turns fast with a look of panic.

"Funny. Real funny." He hustles to the bar, slithering between a lingerie-clad set of twins. "Ladies, ladies, drinks on me."

"Can't take him anywhere." I mumble loud enough for Jode to hear. He cracks a faint smile. "Oh, careful. That subtle movement around your mouth might be interpreted as a smile, which could indirectly compromise your sour attitude toward me, thus leading to the inference that this snub session is all an act." He laughs, takes a deep breath, and sits down next to me.

"You're analyzing me again."

"Sorry. Habit." I smile girlishly.

"Look, I'm not...snubbing you. I just...you know...it's just easier to..." He sighs trying to gather his thoughts. "After the party, I thought about what I was doing, and came to the conclusion that you were right. I would never be able to handle this...dancing situation, and there's really no point in pursuing it any further." Ouch.

"Well, I guess I can respect that, since it was my argument to begin with." I try to hide my disappointment. "But just so you know, I did some thinking after the party, too, and realized that my trust and...various other issues with men are stopping me from...you know...basically...letting anybody know me." He raises his brows, concurring with my analysis. "And I'd probably kick myself later if I didn't say...that I really do want you to know me, and...I'd like to get to know you." There. I said it.

"Alex, stage one! Second call."

"Crap! I gotta go...to the—"

"Yeah." Jode looks relieved that his response to my vulnerability got saved by the DJ's unprecedented timing.

"I'll talk to ya' later?" I say hopefully.

"Actually we're leaving right after the game. I got an early call tomorrow." We stare at each other uncomfortably for a few seconds. His silence confirms my realization. The opportunity has passed.

"Alrighty then. I guess I'll just...see ya' when I see ya'."

"Take care of yourself," he says genuinely.

"Always." I hold back a frustrated tear, change hats quickly, and parade to the stage to perform for the room full of squawking, perverted misfits. All the while wishing I would have kissed him a second time when I had the chance.

I finish my stage set, and decide my current mood would severely impair the profitability of the night, so I may as well drown my sorrows. I throw on a sarong to shield my butt from the vinyl seats, and belly up to the bar, joining the ranks of the girls that can't sell dances, and the voyeurs that either can't afford them or prefer to watch from a distance.

I'm tempted to request one of my own bartending creations, which would require our perpetually irritated mixologist to make a significant effort in its preparation. However, the precise measuring of top-shelf vodka, beer, sweet and sour, and orange juice combined with a flash mix in the blender, and a layer of grenadine poured slowly over a cherry to produce accurate floatability would unequivocally send her digging in her apron for yet another dose of Zoloft, proving the prescription's insubordination.

I decide to resist the craving for my invented Sex After Dinner cocktail, and instead offer to help dig Kelly out from the four-customer-deep, post-fourth-quarter happy hour that has embarked upon her. She scoffs at me for wasting her valuable time with such a ludicrous proposition, since I'm just a dancer and would have no idea what to do behind the very complicated bar she thinks she owns.

Kelly then abruptly turns away from me, igniting a forced communication with the sophisticated, well-dressed man to my left in order to quench my palate with the club's elegant house Chardonnay dispensed from a box.

"Excuse me, could you do me a favor?" I ask.

"That depends," he says boldly. "I'm not going to give you any money."

Great. A denial type. My first thought is to lecture him on coming out of the closet. He's already taken the first step by walking in here. It's only a matter of time before he decides to sample the product and donate to the cause. There's no way around spending money in strip clubs, bud. On second thought, I think it's best if I let it go. He's definitely big money, high society. Probably wouldn't be receptive to my thoughts anyway.

"Of course not. I wouldn't think of it." I class up my dialect. "I'm just having a bit of trouble getting the barkeep's attention, and I thought perhaps you could order me a Chardonnay alongside of your order?" I unstrap a five from my ankle and hand it to him. "It would be much appreciated." He doesn't take my money, and seems perplexed by my worldly tone.

"Madam, I would be most content to buy you a glass of wine if you in turn could assist me with something?"

Here it comes, pervert request. "Well, that depends. What would you like me to do?"

He pulls a picture from his wallet. "I'm looking for a young lady." He passes it to me. "Her name's Vivian. Have you seen her?"

I look closely at the picture of the blond girl standing in front of the Eiffel Tower at the Paris Hotel in Vegas.

"How funny, she looks a little like my friend—" I stop short. "Oooooh…Vivian, you say?"

"Yes. Do you know her?"

"Maybe."

He pulls out a twenty, hands it to me, and repeats firmly, "Do you know her?"

I give it back to him. "Are you a cop?"

"Hardly. I just want to talk to her."

"What do you drink?" I'm going for whatever information I can get. This guy is a little baffling.

"Club soda. You're wasting my time. Does she work here or not? I have three other clubs to get to."

"Wait here. I'll go ask the manager." I get up from my chair, and head for the locker room, then yell back to him. "And I'll take that Chardonnay! The good kind!"

I run up the stairs, chuckling to myself that I now know the big secret. I burst into the locker room. No one. I run back down the stairs, into the bathroom.

"Oh Vivian! Vivian, dahling, you in here?"

"Fuckin' Ava, the big mouth!" A voice from the stall.

"It wasn't her. There's a guy out here asking about you. And what's the big deal about Vivian?" I stand on the toilet, and peek my head into V's stall. "It's a bee-yoo-tiful name. Vivian, dear, report to the atrium for gardening lessons," I mock.

She looks up at me. "You got a tampon? I just started my fuckin' period!"

I quickly descend from the perch.

"Vivian's not the bad part. End of name conversation. Does the dude have any money? I've been sitting on my ass all night fuckin' fighting with Fish over this stupid job. He's freakin' on me, dude."

I slide a tampon under the stall door. "He'll get over it. Or he can just move it on out. There's plenty more where he comes from."

"Fuckin'-A, right! Hey what happened with Jode? He seemed kind of pissed 'bout something."

"I don't know. I screwed it up. He left early."

"Yeah, the girlfriend was waitin' on him. Fish was sayin' she's real uppity. In an annoying way. Kinda plain, but doesn't give him any grief, I guess."

The girlfriend reality rears its ugly head.

"Good. Maybe it won't last."

V exits the stall tucking her boobs into the one-piece string dress with open midriff.

"So, what's this dude look like?"

"Salt and pepper hair. Nice suit. Tightly wound. Heavy wallet. Probably somebody you met in Vegas. He's at the bar. Want me to go with you? Freak patrol?"

"Yeah, why not. Maybe we'll double him…both make some cash-ola!"

We walk toward the bar and it hits me. I completely forgot to tell her about Helga…and Evan!

"Oh my God, I forgot to tell you! Evan came in and—" V halts abruptly at the sight of the man at the bar.

"Fuck! Dude, hide me." She pushes me in front of her, ducks down, and tries to move us in another direction. The guy at the bar sees us and yells.

"Vivian!"

"Fuck," she says not-so-quietly from my lower back area. He approaches us.

"Vivian, please. I just want to talk with you."

She stands up and faces him. "What are you doing here, Dad? I told you to leave me alone!"

Holy shit! Time for me to leave. I try to go. V grabs on to the back of my mini-dress.

"Stay!" she orders.

"I didn't want to believe it. I guess I just had to see it for myself. Please come home, Vivian. Your mother wants you and the kids to come home. She's very upset."

"Yeah, I've seen the mama drama for…I think…about twenty years too long…when it was convenient for her to talk to me, of course." V says sarcastically. "No thanks. We're doing just fine."

Dad tries to stay composed, but I sense his pain. He reaches in his interior coat pocket and hands her an envelope.

"Fine. I put some money in a college fund for the boys. Since you won't let us help *you*, at least we can provide for our grandchildren." She hesitantly takes the envelope.

"I don't know why you want to make your life so difficult, Vivian." He turns toward the door, then turns back. "For what's it worth, your mother's women's network is hosting a benefit at the Bonaventure next month. She's speaking on the issue of teen pregnancy. Something you're somewhat of an expert about." V rolls her eyes and looks away. He continues.

"She'd like you to be there and offer your personal experience to help save a few teenagers from becoming as angry as you are. You'll be well paid for the lecture, and if you could set aside your hatred for us just this once, I'll never ask anything of you again."

"That's a really great offer for a fuckup like me and all, but I think I'll have to take a pass on exploiting my adolescence so Mom can have less guilt about her deficient parenting years." She waves him off. "'Bye, Dad. Maaaavalous to see you. Do come to our fine establishment again. Ta Ta." She walks from him, leaving the uncomfortable moment for me to deal with.

I smile at him then do a quick curtsy and say, "Nice to meet you...and thanks for the wine."

He gives me a patronizing "Charmed," then leaves holding his hands over his ears, blocking out the blaring vocals of Creed's lead singer. I catch up to V and pull her into the bathroom.

"What was that?"

"What was what, dude?"

"Hello? Your dad comes here. Sees you in your underwear seducing men. Begs you to pass on your vast knowledge and *eloquent* speaking abilities to America's youth, offers you money, and takes care of your kids' futures? I don't get it. That anyone would employ you to influence young women is baffling on its own, no offense of course. But even more of a mystery is why you wouldn't accept his albeit feeble attempt at an apology for I'm not sure what, *or* his financial support at a time when you're taking your clothes off for society's greatest disappointments!"

She stares at me for a few seconds. "Are you done?"

"I'm not sure!" I yell, then go to the sink and rinse my face. "This day...it's unbelievable. High highs and low lows. I'm so exhausted!"

"Not everybody had a perfect childhood, dude. My dad was a drunk. Mom—a professional pill-popper. They never noticed me until I got pregnant. I was such an embarrassment. Oh, how they talked at the country club." She mimics her mom.

"They tried to force me to get an abortion, put me under lock and key like a fuckin' animal, and decided they'd chaperone every minute of the rest of my life. So I bailed. Then they cut me off to manipulate me back in, and I told them to go fuck themselves. That's pretty much where it's been for the last few years, and…I'm over it."

"Wow. Sorry." I dry my face. "That comment about you passing on information was not because I don't think you're smart, it was just the whole, you know, compulsive profanity thing."

"No worries, dude. I got it."

I reach out and give her a hug. "You're a survivor, Vivian-with-the-mystery-last-name. Everything's gonna work out. Your parents…they'll come around. They just got to see you for who you are and not who they want you to be."

She pulls back and composes herself. "I'm tired of being the black sheep, you know? You hear it so many times, you start livin' up to it."

"Yeah. Conditioned response. You got to break the cycle. Show them what you have to offer the world, and if they still don't get it, at least you know you tried and gave your kids an opportunity to know their family. You got to do that, ya' know. For the kids."

She shrugs rebelliously. "Dude, I don't even know what I'm doing or what I have to offer. I hate the nursing thing. Doesn't feel right. Fuckin' bedpans? Seriously, I can't do it. I tried this time, I really did. But I'm not exactly the nurturing type."

"I would never have thought that." She's not buying it. "What did you want to do when you were little?"

"I don't know. Be in a band."

"You're musical? What do you play?"

"Guitar, piano, sing. Ten years of fuckin' lessons."

"V, that's great! You got to do it. You got to follow your dreams! I don't know why you won't just kiss and make up with your parents. Let them pave the way for you for a while. Maybe if you told them what you really want to do, they'd understand you better."

"Doubt it. Besides, too much water under the bridge already. They wouldn't believe I could do it. Yadda yadda…it'd be the same old shit."

"You could blow their minds and show up at the benefit. Insist on a clean slate with them, and I'm willing to bet they'd totally support you. I really sensed your dad's need to make this right."

"Yeah, guilt is pretty powerful. I'm not doing it. What would I say to a bunch of troubled teens anyway? *Don't be stupid, you'll end up with a fucked-up life like mine?* That can't be good for my self-esteem."

"You can relate to these kids. They'd believe you. Whatever you say, however you say it."

"I'm not good at public speaking. It freaks me out. And you know…cussing is a regular part of my vocabulary. Something could slip out."

"You only said *fuck* maybe six times during this whole conversation. You could do it," I say jokingly, as we exit the bathroom, both having evolved a tiny bit from the last half hour of our lives.

"You're a good motivator, Alex, and thanks for lettin' me vent, but I can't do it. Shit! Forgot my fuckin' purse." She runs back in.

I said tiny.

> *Dear Diary,*
>
> *Why does it seem life is one big misunderstanding? Nobody communicates. We end up in relationships for all the wrong reasons with the wrong people, and don't act on the right situations when given the chance. It's as if we're all afraid of being in something good. Because then there wouldn't be anything to fix. Change becomes too much work. Easier to chalk it up to wrong timing or eternal screwed-up circumstances. I'm not copping out anymore! Risks have to be taken. Time is moving fast.*
>
> *Too much analysis…need to have fun. Club life getting old. Desperately need to move on. Mom called with annoying maternal instinct. She relieved me of Thanksgiving pressure, but applied new tension on staying focused on goals. She sensed I was drifting. Suggested listening: Lee Anne Womack's "I Hope You Dance." I love my mom, but I hate when she's right.*

12

Interception

It's Saturday morning. The effervescent morning-after. Of course, I'm being sarcastic. The cabaret, although semi-successful, was more of a disaster. The events of last night are still floating around in my mind as a possible and hopeful nightmare. I haven't had my coffee yet. We all crashed at Trina's after the cops finally broke up the party. The call was made a good hour before they arrived and their tardiness forced us to do the very thing we said we weren't going to do. No one else is up yet. I need aspirin…and a pen. It's productive for me to write things down right after they happened. Gives an accurate perspective when recalling the event later.

High points:

— My standup routine. Unanimous approval of the bit on men's continued confusion of what is sexy for the woman during intercourse: "Any guy thinking his lady is enjoying her legs pinned behind her ears like Bugs-fuckin'-Bunny needs to rent *When Harry Met Sally.*" I stole the Bugs Bunny line from Dice Clay…no one noticed. Crowd howled when I assumed the position, and demonstrated the fake O.

— Trina breaking out in song after eating "special brownies" V brought for uninhibited motivation. Crowd booed until she flashed her boobs. Bobby threw trench coat on her, quickly ending her budding singing career.

—When on a break trying to figure out what to do next, Ava found Kodak moment, took camcorder into crowd, and interviewed mutts on why they go to strip clubs. Unknown female videographer wearing clogs taped the rest of the show to use as footage in mockumentary.

—V played a Jimmy Hendricks guitar solo wearing mesh, see-through underwear and bra, thigh-high boots from Halloween, and a purple shawl. She was adamant about appropriately representing the era.

—Bought time with complaining audience when more than half of show was over with no skin other than swift glimpse of Trina's boobs. My impromptu silhouette dance behind dressing screen in flesh-colored body suit quieted crowd momentarily. Camera caught Jode in awe of my seductive moment. Didn't know he was there. Music choice was key: "The Art of Love" by Toni Braxton. Brownies aided in stage jitters. Note: Get recipe from V.

—Final dance sequence felt good. We looked great. Everyone in sync. Bluesy version of "You Shook Me All Night Long" had roomful of numbnuts singing and chanting. Classic cabaret number seemed appreciated until...it was over.

Low points:

—Transvestite cross-dressers, called in as gap fillers, result in stage full of pizza and egg yolk. Crowd came prepared.

—Clinefeld in too-tight sequence elephant pants flops on stage and insists on demonstrating advanced pole work. Flimsy pole. Ambulance called. CPR performed successfully.

—No applause at end of most rehearsed dance number of the night. Forced to unveil full monty to avoid riot. Fade to black immediately. Butts run off stage through strategically placed spotlight. Never should have given Fish lighting controls.

—Cops actually showed up when called, but blended in with audience unnoticed. Apparently liked show more than jobs. Could have saved us from overexposure.

—Many attempts to get to Jode sabotaged by anxious regulars demanding free lap dances for hundred dollar entry fee. He left early. Lost opportunity again.

"Morning." Ava startles me. I put down my pen. "Coffee made?"

"Yep. Just finished brewing."

"Writing so early? How tenacious." She yawns, then saturates her coffee with sugar and vanilla soy milk.

"Just making a few notes from last night. Didn't want to forget anything. Too much cheap champagne."

"Ugh! Don't even say that word. I think I drank two bottles myself somewhere in between fifty-odd lap dances." She arches her back, then reaches forward to touch her toes. "My back is killing me."

"Mine too." She prompts me to get on the floor and stretch my lower back. I bend one leg and pull it across my body to give myself an adjustment. "Whose idea was it to hand out free dances anyway? Probably Trina's, since she's the only one that didn't do any."

"I made the call. Had to. During the transvestite bit, they were pounding me for their money back."

I contort into a half backroll, and flip my legs over my head to stretch my hamstrings. "Please tell me the freebie groping was worthwhile, and I never again have to put on a fake smile and talk to a man that reeks of onions and stale farts, only to be bounced off his lap with a pelvic thrust worthy of a bull riding medal!"

"Gross! I danced for that guy, too!"

I sit up to ask the dreaded question. "So, what was the bottom line?"

"Trina's doing a double check, but I think we're still short."

"How short?"

"Three thousand dollars short." Trina enters wearing a white silk pajama set that probably cost more than my car. She opens a lower cabinet and pulls out a bottle of Baileys Irish Cream to dress her coffee with.

"Sorry to be the bearer of bad news so early in the morning, but I counted three times, and compared our funds to the budget. We're a little over three thousand short, actually. I rounded down." She sips her morning cocktail.

"No fucking way!" V's up. "All that bullshit and we still can't put this thing in production? Dudes, c'mon. I want to help, but fuckin' A! I can't do any more shows...or trainin'...or any shit or whatever! I am officially partied out! My kids—they're startin' to call the sitter *Mom*. You gotta figure it out, dudes. This is going on too long!" She throws her coat over the jeans and T-shirt she slept in, and slams the door on her way out.

"Can't talk to her before noon. I forgot to warn you—not a morning person." Ava clears that up.

"Really?" I say sarcastically. "Who woulda thunk it."

"Don't get pissy with me. I'm equally frustrated. I got a deadline on this project, and if we don't get the money we need, it's gonna suck. And my graduation present—a membership to the jobless filmmakers' association. A hundred and fifty thousand members strong! And growing every day!" She slams her coffee cup down, them mumbles on her way out of the kitchen: "Be fuckin' dancing 'til my tits are dragging on the floor!"

Trina sits at the table and opens the newspaper.

"Sounds like everyone needs to take a chill pill and stop worrying about it." She pops a pill in her mouth. "I'll have money again soon. If we have to wait, we have to wait."

"Didn't you hear what she said? She has a deadline. It has to be done this month. She needs the money now or she can't finish shooting it. This is for all of us, you know. You might be back to your old life soon, but *we* all want something more than we've had, and I thought that's what you wanted, too." I dip the top of the newspaper down so I can see her eyes, and give her my best guilt look. She lifts her eyes slowly, then sighs heavily.

"I...do. You know I do. These last few months have been eye-opening for me. I want to do something constructive with my life. The money never made me happy. A little more content, slightly less worried, but never happy. So what do we do? What's the next plan? It's not really that much money."

I noticed the sports page while Trina was justifying her prior existence. The horses are running at Hollywood Park. I grab the newspaper and turn it around, so she can see the day's lineup.

"Alex...we can't! If you lose, Ava will freak out!"

"Then I guess I better not lose. How much cash do we have on hand?"

"Almost five grand. It's all from last night, but Ava's expecting me to deposit that money into the account today. We can't do it."

"Where is your faith? You know I used to be a good handicapper. In fact, I distinctly remember making you and Evan twelve hundred dollars on your anniversary one year."

She pours another Baileys and coffee while reminiscing. "Ahhh, the romantic marital celebration at the track. How could I forget? Anniversary dining at its best—corn nuts and a processed cheese plate. Should have read the signs then."

"Traditional romance wasn't exactly his strong suit. But didn't he give you the twelve hundred?"

"Hell no! He got all fired up thinking professional gambling was his next career and took off for Vegas the next day. He lost all that money plus another fifteen thou. Thank you very much."

"Ok, bad example. That's not going to happen to us. I can do this. I can double the money, and we'll get it in the account by the end of the day. Ava will never know. We'll tell her we got it from some guy at the club. Or that we took all your clothes to one of those secondhand places, which we could do instead of going to the track?"

Trina gasps at the mere suggestion. "Can we hang out in the Turf Club and lunch with the rich?"

"Absolutely! Wear a big hat and your favorite Chanel suit. We're gambling in style today!"

"They're in the gate…and away they go." The voice of the track announcer blares as we prance past the grandstand-level patrons onto the exclusive Turf Club Members Only escalator. We paid the daily membership fee of fifty dollars apiece to place our bets alongside the elite wagerers. Not having to listen to Trina snivel all day about the filthy vagrants in her personal space at the all-you-can-smell betting counters makes the hundred bucks a flea market bargain.

It's been a while since I've played the ponies. I think the last time was one of those document-babysitting days at the law firm, during which I was paid thirty-five dollars an hour to escort a box of damaging documents from point A to point B. Point A being a senior attorney's office that *mistakenly* received the box that should have gone to the shredding facility—point B. I had decided since I was obstructing justice, the firm surely wouldn't mind financing a quinella or two, and a few trifecta wheels.

I had always been an exotics player. That term was reserved for the gamblers that took the highest betting risks. Exactas and quinellas are simple standard bets—picking two horses to finish first and second either in exact order or reversible order. Those bets seemed kind of boring, and the payoff usually wasn't high enough for me. I was there to hit the big one! The score that would change my life.

Trifecta wagering is a bit more challenging to handicap, and has the potential to yield a high return on a mid-level investment. You have to pick the horses that will come in first, second, and third...in that order. To pick it cold is a near impossibility, unless you're related to Lady Luck, and she likes you. I'm sure there are some extreme opportunists that have bet their two dollars, and sat back and watched as the three horses they picked crossed the finish line in the exact order depicted on their ticket. However, most gamblers spend more money to increase the odds of nailing the positions utilizing a wheeling system.

I never did figure out why it's called a wheel, but the concept intrigues me. There are many different ways to wheel the race. What seemed to work best for me was to pick one horse that I was sure could hit the board. That's track talk for placing in the top three. Then, wheel that horse in all three positions with four other horses that were likely to come in around it. Whatever position the key horse didn't occupy was left open for one of the other four, assuming another horse from the field didn't get in there and mess up the whole wheel. That, of course, is the gamble.

While handicapping at Turf Paradise in Phoenix, I had designed a system that would tell me, statistically speaking, which horses would break out first, which preferred to be closers and make a stretch run for the finish, and which horses liked to be pacers and hang out in the middle of the pack. Although one must remember that the jockey is controlling the horse, and his/her win record and ethical reputation should most certainly be considered.

There's a lot of other factors that come into play when choosing on your picks, and the handicapping process can be a frustrating experience when the fifty-to-one long shot beats the two-to-one favorite. My general rule when they all look good: two medium-long shots, the race favorite, one semi-favorite, and a reliable pacer that relieved himself during the pre-race parade, as the key.

I had played at all Southern California raceways: Santa Anita, Hollywood Park, and the prestigious Del Mar Race Track in San Diego, where you can eat, drink, gamble, pitch a lawn chair and bag rays, and the horses will run around you. Del Mar is indisputably the nicest track in the country, but I do like Hollywood Park for its easy access. I'm probably one of few women so familiar, so comfortable, and in her element at the track.

"So what are we going to do? How do we bet?" Trina fumbles with the racing form, laying it across the table open to race number six at the Lone Star Track in Texas.

"Ok, first we need to look at the statistics from the horses that are running at the track we're at." I say, patronizing her in a loving tone, then flip the form to the Hollywood Park pages.

"We're gonna bet one race. That's what the professionals do. They find the best pick of the day and pound the hell out of it. It's sudden death. Make it or break it."

"I'm not sure I like the sound of that. The word *death* in a description of a business venture designed to change our lives not only doesn't sound profitable, but in fact has a negative connotation which alludes to a killing of one's dream. Can't we call it *sudden wealth*?"

"You've been listening to self-help speakers again, haven't you?"

"They're very informative and helpful. You should try it sometime."

I think the combination of the hat, the suit, the martini, the expensive hors d'oeuvres and the group of high-society folk gaggling over which horse is prettiest has brought back Katrina, the pompous Rodeo Drive lunch goddess.

"Why don't you go mingle with the privileged Rotary Club over there while I handicap the race. I need some space so I can think."

"Well, if you insist." Trina sashays into the group eagerly. Had to twist her arm on that one.

I spread my materials out on the table and begin the statistical calculations for each race. I'll handicap each race, and narrow it down to the best pick of the day. One race! Sudden wealth.

I'll spend up to a thousand dollars on the trifecta, then put five hundred across the board on our key horse. Even if we miss the trifecta, we'll have a chance at recovering the investment if our key wins, places, or shows. Not that I'm planning on losing. I never begin a gambling session with any thoughts of losing, but since it's not my money, and Ava will have a conniption fit leading to a mental breakdown if I put us further in the hole on the project, I better have a backup.

For the next hour, my head is buried in small print surrounded by clusters of illegible notes unidentifiable to any non-gambler. I, of course, know exactly what every number, dot, arrow, highlighted statistic, and scribbled abbreviation means. I've decided the seventh race is our best bet. Lucky number seven. It's a large field, which allows for increased possibility of catching a long shot in the mix. I will have to compile a more sophisticated wheel utilizing many horses, and hope and pray I peg the right positions.

I glimpse over my shoulder and catch Trina assisting one of the socialites in a bump and grind maneuver. She's got her hands on the lady's hips, swaying her from side to side, then demonstrates the front and back pelvic thrust, motivating the rest of the group to follow. Nothing surprises me anymore, but in my opinion the Turf Club hustle is happening way too close to the buffet!

I give her a strange look from across the room, perplexed at this bold exhibition, and what I assume is a public advertisement for the next lap dance semester. I was joking when I said we would do it again, but apparently Trina has a knack for rallying women to empower themselves through sensual movement.

I certainly understand the feminine need to be perceived as sexy, and what that power over men can do for one's self-esteem. These last few months of mastering the art of seduction have taken me to a level I never thought possible.

When I was younger, I wanted to do a sexy dance for one of my boyfriends, but I was way too scared and embarrassed. Even though I had taken professional dance classes for many years, I was inhibited and fearful of being laughed at. I can only imagine what goes through the mind of an average woman not having any dance training or sensual background whatsoever. Why would she ever put herself in a position where the odds of ridicule are so high? Even if her guy is respectful, she would know he's silently embarrassed for her, thus destroying any chance of accomplishing the intended goal.

Like anything that you do over and over again, the business of exotic dancing has taught me to get past my fears. Men are very forgiving about the flaws we women obsess over, and won't even notice them if you accurately blind them with your assets. I find that my personal experience in the club has opened me up to all the passionate moments readily available throughout everyday life. I can easily slip into my own sensual world with little more than the right motivating music.

I interrupt the seduction instructor by making eye contact from a distance, and let her know I'm ready to make our bets. There's plenty of time before the seventh race, but I want to be able to go with my first instincts, and I know from past experience that if I wait too long to head to the betting window, I'll change my mind…numerous times. I missed many jackpots because I changed the bet at the last minute, then had to face the old track gang, and tell my *almost* story to a group that had heard it all before.

I feel good. Strong about my picks. For some reason, taking this risk with OPMs (other people's money) doesn't seem as scary as I thought it would be. For whatever reason, it feels like the right thing to do. I like living my life as a risk taker. That's why I was so miserable at the law firm. I was playing it safe. Afraid to step out of what society dictates as the norm.

I used to tell my mom that when I die, I want my tombstone to quote me saying: "Regrets, I have a few…but then again, too few to mention." It's from my favorite song of all time—"My Way." Elvis' version. He sings with so much passion, it brings me to tears every time I hear it. No matter what happens as a result of my life's choices, I'll at least have peace in knowing "the record shows, I took the blows, and did it…My Way."

"I want a twenty-dollar trifecta wheel—the seven over the one, two, four, nine, eleven." I dictate my wager to the teller like a true professional.

"I want a twenty-dollar part wheel: the one, two, four, nine, eleven with the seven, with the one, two, four, nine, eleven." I got lucky with a competent teller. She types fast and completely understands the bet.

"One more time, same bet—the one, two, four, nine, eleven, with the one, two, four, nine, eleven…with the seven." The teller looks up at me like I'm crazy.

"You know these are four hundred dollars apiece?"

"I know. I'm not done. Give me a hundred dollars across the board on the seven."

"Anything else?" She enviously eyes my fat wad of hundred dollar bills. I reluctantly count out fifteen.

"No that's it." I hand her the fifteen hundred dollars. She hands me the tickets, then smiles.

"Lucky number seven."

"Let's hope so." I walk away from the teller with a ironclad grip on my tickets, thinking to myself I must be crazy.

What did I just do? This better work or I'm going to have to go into hiding. A witness protection plan or something. Ava could completely wack out, attack me, or even try to kill me. I'm sure no one would blame her one bit.

"This is great. I love the track." Trina prances her way back to the table. "Those women are really interested in what I have to say."

"I'm glad you're enjoying yourself, but I need you to focus on what we're doing. I made the bet. I'm a little scared. What if we lose?"

"No, no, no, no, no, no. There'll be no negativity!" She scoops the tickets into a pile and pulls them closer to her, as if to bless them. "Positive thoughts. Lucky money coming our way." She strokes the tickets like a pet. "Everything's about energy, you know. Attracting the right energy when you need it." She snaps her fingers at the waiter, lifts her empty martini glass, and indicates she needs two more.

"I don't want a martini," I say.

"I didn't order you one." She sucks the gin-soaked olive off the pointy little stick.

"Can I hold the tickets, please? I'll put them in a positive place, I promise." I fold the tickets and put them in my wallet next to the wad of cash. Maybe the energized money will procreate in a private environment. "I got to go to the bathroom. Ten minutes 'til post." I'm so nervous.

I leave the table and head for the ladies' room. I feel like throwing up. I know better than to gamble on scared money. You never win. There's something to that energy business. Somehow the Universe knows when you're taking irresponsible money risks that often result in hard lessons being learned.

My old boyfriend, Michael, had this group of track buddies that were gambling gurus. Some of them didn't have jobs, and made their living betting horse and dog races, sports games, and playing cards. They'd come over after a rough day at the races and swap *almost* stories, get drunk, and wallow in the desperate financial scenarios they'd put themselves in. I'd hear them talk of credit card advances, second and third mortgages, and loans up the ying-yang.

Occasionally, I'd butt in and make an off-the-wall suggestion about getting a *job*. They'd look at me like they never heard of that word. The mere mention of stopping gambling or even tapering down to hobby status was forbidden conversation, and they thought Michael should oust me from the group for lack of loyalty and nourishment for the addiction. Instead of Gamblers Anonymous, this was a support group of Anonymous Gamblers. You don't call your sponsor when you're about to gamble; you call only when you're having thoughts of quitting. One person goes through a losing streak, the others organize an intervention and pull funds together to front the effort of getting him back on track…or in this case, back *to* the track.

"Did it start yet?" I yell out to Trina, and hurry to our table.

"No. They're getting into the…thingamajig. What do we want to happen here? I gotta know who to root for."

"We need the seven. Everything around him is moot if he doesn't get there." She grabs my hand, as we anxiously await the final horses being steered into the starting gate.

"No matter what, we'll figure out the money. Everything's going to be Ok. I feel it."

"Yeah. Just promise me you'll visit my cave in canyon country where I'll be rotting out the rest of my natural days hiding from Ava." She laughs, and downs the backwash of her fourth martini.

"And away they go!"

Trina and I watch the race from completely different perspectives. She squints at the tiny TV on our table trying to distinguish one horse from the other, unable to follow any of them. I, a seasoned horse-race fanatic, watch every move from the horses we need. They're all crammed together. Number seven lingers in the middle of the pack, close to the rail. He's in a good position, but better start making a move soon or he's not going to make it. My palms are sweating as the horses round the second corner, and our seven still doesn't break away. Our other five horses are all at the front, intertwined with a couple others. It's anyone's game.

"C'mon seven. Move! Move now! *Puh-lease!*" I look up to the sky and beg. When my eyes focus back on the race, it appears like the seven is moving up, but it's not fast enough.

"There's no way he can win! Our best bet is gonna be third!" The energy is high as they careen down the stretch. People around us yell out their numbers. My face is glued to the TV. The seven makes a late run for it. I scream at the top of my lungs.

"Go! Go! Run! Faster…Faster! Go! Go!" I'm not even watching the other horses. Nothing matters if this seven can't make it up for third. Trina slaps her hands on the table and screams out in slurred speech, *"Run, you beautiful hunk of a horse!"*

I glance at her for a quick second, not quite understanding her comment, then run to the window to see them cross the finish line in person.

"Ahhh! Nooo!" Six of them cross at once. I couldn't tell who was where. The seven was in there somewhere. I bolt back to the table to see the replay.

"We got a chance! He could have made it!"

The unofficial results post number four as the winner and number eleven running second. It's a photo for third. My wheels are turning so fast as they air the replay over and over. It's hard to tell. Sometimes it comes down to a head bob when two horses are at the finish line at exactly the same time. Third place is between the seven and the five. My eyes move quickly from the score board to the TV. Results, still unofficial. Photo-finish sign still flashing.

"I can't take the suspense. I'm getting another drink. Want anything?"

"No."

Trina walks toward the bar. On second thought, I yell out to her.

"Hey, get me a Margarita. Silver Patron and Cointreau." I took my eyes off the screen for a second. The crowd bursts into a gaggle. Immediately, I look at the scoreboard.

"Seven! Yes! Yes!" Trina runs back, and jumps around in circles screaming.

"How much does it pay?" she asks.

"I don't know. It's not up yet. Still unofficial. It'll just take a second. *We did it! We did it!"* We dance around and are joined by the rich ladies who bust out in a *hammertime* groove.

Under the celebratory vocal clutter, I hear a gasp echo through the crowd. I break away from our group and walk slowly toward one of the big screen TV's. I stare at the screen. Stunned. Trina joins me.

"What is it? What's wrong?"

"There's an inquiry. See that flashing sign that says 'Inquiry'? There's an inquiry." I repeat in disbelief.

"What does that mean? Did we win or not?"

"I don't know. It means the stewards are examining the videotape of the race to see if somebody did something wrong."

"Like the jockeys?" she asks curiously.

"Yeah, or the horse. Oh God, no!" The number seven in its third position flashes on the scoreboard. "The inquiry's about the seven! This can't be happening. We were so close." I mope back to the table.

"I'll go get the drinks." Trina suggests the cure-all.

I plop down in my seat. Bury my head in my hands. The track announcer comes on the speaker:

"A stewards' inquiry has been issued against number seven, Private Dancer, for alleged interference with number five, Mister Leprechaun, during the stretch run."

He directs our attention to the video screen on which they will now play and replay the part of the tape the stewards are examining. I can't bear to look, but I do. They were all running so close. I don't know how they can tell anything. I look around the room to see what the general consensus is. A few people seem as concerned as I am, but I seriously doubt any of them have as much riding on this decision as we do. Trina comes back with the drinks.

"How long do they usually take to figure it out?" she asks.

"Not that long. Could be a couple minutes. I've seen it be as long as twenty. How can we lose with a horse named Private Dancer?"

"Will you stop saying that! We haven't lost yet!"

"It wasn't right. Gambling with the investment money. I deserve this pre-torture to the full-blown torture I'll be going through in a matter of minutes." I fold my hands and drop my head and say quietly, "God, please let us win this one, and I promise I'll never, ever gamble again." The gambler's prayer. Heard openly at most gaming institutions.

"Hey, we still have lots of cash! If we lose, we might as well go out with a bang, and bet the rest on the next race!" I look at her openmouthed, then glance up as if *He* prompted her to say that.

Screams from the crowd! I look at the board.

"The seven stays! We won! It's official!" Tears roll down my eyes. Trina hugs me hard. I glance over her shoulder to look at the trifecta payoff, then start laughing louder than I've probably ever laughed, as I calculate our winnings in my head.

"Ava's gonna freak! The good kind of freak! We just won…eight thousand, two hundred and twenty-three dollars!"

"Oh my God!" Trina screams out loud, and clomps on me, nearly knocking me over, then we run to the teller jumping up and down like school kids at recess time.

"I've never actually seen this much cash before. It's all only been on paper…and…and…was never in my name!" Trina remembers that ominous marital flaw.

The teller prepares the paperwork for us and begins to count out the money with her supervisor overlooking her shoulder. We sign the tax documents and hold out our hands like kids at Halloween—*more please.* I stuff the huge wad in my already weighed-down purse, and follow Trina back to the table to take the last swig from our drinks. She hands me mine, and raises hers to toast.

"To you. Crazy dreams. Unconventional means. And an indestructible spirit!" She clanks my glass hard and chugs. "Track Chick Productions…is open for business!"

Four days until Christmas, and I've done no shopping at all. The girls and I have been working around the clock for the last three weeks on the mockumentary. Ava was so excited when Trina and I showed up with a shoe box of hundred dollar bills, which we said we found under a loose floorboard in Evan's den. She immediately set up the locations to finish shooting so we could move in post-production as quickly as possible. We've been spending most of our nights in the editing facility at USC helping create the masterpiece.

The project is coming along famously and surprisingly ahead of schedule. Ava wasn't so keen on the name of our production company at first, but Trina and I convinced her that the money we found was from that anniversary she and Evan spent at the horse track, and Evan must have forgotten where he put it. We owed it to him to incorporate as *Track Chicks, LLC*. She was ecstatic about the money, I don't think it ever really mattered what we called ourselves. We could have been The Areola Entertainment Group, for all she cared!

None of us have worked much this month. We each took a cut of the money to live on while we worked on the project, and have put in a day or two at the club each week. I'm going in tonight, but only to cash in on Christmas presents from my regulars. The week before Christmas is supposed to be a great time to be at Mitzie's. The guys are festive and more generous than usual. Of course we prefer cash, but gift giving is always welcome, as long as it's limited to gift certificates for stylish clothes stores and/or electronics that can be exchanged for cash.

My regulars had been well trained in the past, and pretty much stuck to the recommended etiquette, except for Jim. I had effectively avoided the loudmouth, narcissist, egomaniac the last couple times I saw him in the club, but this time he cornered me with an armful of wrapped presents, so I made an exception.

I should have known he was baiting me into one of his ridiculously juvenile pranks when I opened the card, and got hit in the face with a three-dimensional penis. At that point, I tried to get up and leave, but he apologized and insisted I open a second gift, which would undeniably vindicate him for his poor judgment at the Hallmark store. I didn't have anywhere else to be, so I humored him and opened the gift hesitantly, holding it far from my face. I dug through the decorated tissue paper to pull out what I thought was some kind of ceramic vase, but when held in the light, realized it was yet another penis in candle form.

"Something is wrong with you!" I yelled at him, and I made my second attempt to leave the booth.

He stopped laughing for a millisecond, and pulled me back toward him, issuing a final plea to open a third gift, which was the only one that he really intended me to have. He said he bought the card and candle for someone else, but she wasn't there, and I just happened to walk by. I knew I should have taken the long way around the club!

"I'm not going to fall for this again! Move!" I tried to push by him. He blocked my way, and dangled a Tiffany's gift bag in front of my face. "Let me guess…sterling silver penis?"

He laughed and shook his head, then gave me a puppydog pout and begged me to please open the bag. This guy is such a manipulator, and I totally knew better, but by this time I was curious as to how much time and money he spent buying these offerings for his own humorous gain.

"You must be really bored!" I said, then snatched the bag from his fingertips and dug through it thoroughly expecting what I found—a nine-inch rubber dildo!

"Has anyone told you that you should be institutionalized? Something is seriously wrong with you! Who gives someone three penises…for Christmas?" I grabbed the penises and the wrapping paper, and forcefully piled them high in his arms.

"Thank you, but no thanks! I have all the penises I need!" I stomped off as he feverishly laughed at me. I turned back to scoff at him one more time, and saw Trina pick the dildo up off the floor.

"I could use a few more penises," she said, apparently having heard the tail end of our conversation. Didn't ask. Didn't want to know.

I cut my night short after the penis incident, and decided to use the gift certificate Marty got me to shop for presents for my family. I love the Bed, Bath & Beyond stores. I try hard not go in there very often. They have cool little *things* that I can always seem to make a case for. The store in the Beverly Center is way too close for comfort. Walking distance from my apartment. Which means I can have a glass of wine or two, then go shopping...for free! Any girl's everyday dream.

It's California law that pedestrians *always* have the right of way, but I decide to wait for the signal to cross at one of Los Angeles' most congested intersections. My first inclination was to join the holiday homeless who solicit money in the middle of the Third Street rush hour. If anyone would bother to notice them at all, the traffic may stop long enough for me to get across. Upon second review, I realize they may have a death wish. I'll just wait for the light.

The store is crowded. Everyone cramming in their last-minute shopping. People maneuver carts through narrow aisles with the usual L.A. courtesy. I've never shopped with a buzz on before. It's a whole different experience. No one bothers me. It's quite humorous to people-watch. Everyone else is in a frenzy, and I have all the time in the world to get...whatever I'm getting.

I browse up one lane after another and end up in the kitchen area. They have the coolest utensils here. This may have to be a shopping excursion for me after all. As I fiddle with the latest in spatula technology, I hear a voice the next aisle over. A man's voice. Deep. Somewhat raspy. Sexy. Talking on a cell phone about moviemaking.

Normally I wouldn't think anything of it. You can't go anywhere in this town without overhearing conversations about what agent is botching up what project, whose writer is f-ing up the script, or what money has fallen through on what theoretical ironclad deal. This conversation is different. The voice is familiar.

I'm wondering if I'm hearing things because I want it to be him. No matter how much I try to put him out of my mind, he's always there. I haven't seem him since the cabaret, and heard he's been MIA from the club. He's probably doing something with the girlfriend's family for Christmas, and I'm totally imagining that I hear his voice, but I decide to do a drive-by with my cart just to make sure.

I follow the unmistakable vocals and position myself at the outside edge of the hamper/garbage can aisle where I can see him, but he can't see me. His back is to me, and I honestly can't tell if it's him. It sounds like him, but for some reason the physique doesn't look like him. He's wearing long shorts, a baggy shirt, and a baseball hat. Ok, it's not him. *But it sounds like him!* I need a closer look.

I drive my cart around to the other side and do the nonchalant quick-look pass-by, then keep going. The guy looks right at me. It's not him. Definitely not him. Kind of looked like him, really sounded like him, but not him. I must be losing my mind!

I continue with my spree, perusing around picking out an array of potential gifts for my sisters ranging from shower head filters, bath pillows, talking picture frames, three-dimensional wall art, peculiar oil and vinegar bottles, and yoga videos. Just as I'm deciding the fate of an ionic air purifier, a sexy man on a cell phone walks toward me...smiling. I'm not crazy after all.

"I thought that was you," Jode says, clicking off his phone. "How are you?"

"Good. Fine. Just doing a little shopping." Duh! Why else would I be here? He makes me so nervous.

"Me too. Trash can. The stuff is flowing over the top..." The man is sexy even when talking about garbage.

"Yeah, that could be a problem. How've you been?"

"Good. Busy. Taking a little time off for the holiday, though."

A twenty-something woman with brown hair and an annoyingly spunky voice pokes her head around the corner. "J-o-d-e? White or gray?" She holds up two garbage can lids.

"Doesn't matter. You decide," he says, slightly irritated he's being consulted on this issue. She walks toward us.

"It does matter, honey. It's going in your house. Hi," she says to me. "I'm Peggy." I start to introduce myself. Jode takes over.

"This is Alex. Old friend of mine."

"Hi. I'd go with chrome...with the foot pedal, but if you're going to choose from those two—white. Goes with everything."

She's mildly amused with my input, then offers an extended explanation of why the gray one matches the kitchen appliances better, but she really can't decide and might have to buy both to try each one out for a week or so, then bring one back. She looks to Jode to see if that would be Ok.

"Fine. Whatever works. I just want the trash to stay in the basket," he says, a little embarrassed she's making such a big deal out of it. She skips off with the lids, then looks back and yells to him.

"Don't forget, we have pottery class in half an hour. We should leave in..." She checks her watch. "...six minutes. Parking is limited. 'Bye. Nice meeting you." She waves at me, and disappears into flatware. I was going to try and resist the urge to say anything negative, but I couldn't.

"Pottery class? Sounds exciting. Can't have too many vases and ashtrays, right?"

He rolls his eyes boyishly. "She's into it. I told her I'd go this one time. Kind of a Christmas crafty thing for her family."

"I'm sure it'll be a...fun time," I said as genuinely as the moment called for.

"Hey, I heard you guys made that short film, the docudrama?"

"Mockumentary," I correct him. "Yeah, we got kind of...lucky with the funding process, and were able to get most of it done this month."

"That's great. I'm happy for you, really. I...I wanted to talk to you at that show you put on. You guys did a great job with that by the way. I didn't know you were such a good dancer." He's really been paying attention in the club.

"Oh, thanks. I wanted to talk to you that night, too, but when I finally got a chance, you were gone."

"Yeah, I had to...uh...be somewhere." He nods in the direction of the girlfriend.

"Probably better that you left early. The end of the show didn't turn out exactly as planned." He laughs like he knows what I'm talking about.

"So...are you happy...in your situation? 'Cause my offer still stands. The one where I pled my case to know you better." I'm not passing on any opportunities anymore.

He smiles, then breathes deeply. "I'm content. She's a great gal. Lots of energy. Not a jealous bone in her body." Strange qualities to praise, but I try not to react.

"Good. Good. Well, if things don't work out, you know where to find me." I hate this part. Leaving him with no plans to meet again.

"Good luck with everything...the mockumentary...and everything." He gives me a tight hug.

He smells good. I breathe him in. Where is that pesky girlfriend? I don't want to let go, but I pull back within timely etiquette.

"Let me know when you're going to screen it. I'll bring some industry friends that might be able to help, you know, get it where it needs to go," he says.

"Thanks. I will." We stand staring at each other...again. Both ignoring the obvious physical chemistry we have. "Well, you better get to pottery class. Those artsy-fartsy teachers can be vicious if you're late." I have no idea what I'm talking about, but I want him to leave first.

"Yeah. Take care of yourself." He walks off, then looks back. "Seriously, call me if you need me." And he's gone again.

What's that supposed to mean? *Call me if you need me.* Of course I need him! I need him every night I spend alone in my bed! I don't get this guy. The attraction between us is so thick, you could cut it with a Ginsu knife. Maybe there's something wrong with him. Maybe he has a penis issue, an erection problem. That would keep a man from acting on such a strong physical appeal. No, that can't be it. I distinctly remember no deficiency in that area when I danced for him at the Halloween party.

I don't know. I'm done trying. What else can I do? Maybe he really likes Betty Crocker garbage can lady. Who knows? I shouldn't have to sell myself so hard. It's his problem if he doesn't see my potential. Time to move on. No more Jode thoughts!

> *Dear Diary,*
>
> *Am I the only one that thinks it's important not to settle for a passionless relationship? Maybe that's why I'm still single. I should take the easy road. Seems like everyone else is. "Just find a nice guy...someone who makes money...who'll make a good father...the attraction will come in time." Motherly advice.*
>
> *I can't believe he thinks her most marketable quality is that she doesn't have a jealous bone in her body. Who says that about their girlfriend unless they're out screwing around all the time? But if he's such a big player, then why isn't he jumping on me...literally! I promised myself I would stop analyzing this situation, but...he's a wine drinker...RED WINE even! Archetypal sign of a passion seeker!*
>
> *We'd be so good together. I know he knows it. Why can't he see beyond the stripper stuff? It's not like I'll do this job forever! Timing is key. It'll be just my luck that when things take off in my career, he'll be getting married! Although...I am lucky. I should have told him about the track. Dammit! Oh forget it! I give up.*

13

Touchdown

Thank God the holidays are over! Without kids and a hubby they're really a drag. Totally obligatory. I breezed into Phoenix on Christmas Eve, and stayed through the twenty-sixth. I did my daughterly duty. I guess it wasn't that bad. No uncontainable brawls, no uninvited guests, decent food, and I didn't have to do any of the work. But I'm still glad they're over.

New Year's was uneventful. Just like I like it. The whole night is totally overrated anyway. I've done the Vegas routine—five hundred thousand drunken amateurs screwing up the tables, cluttering up the streets. No thanks. Did Tahoe one year with Alan and three other couple friends of ours that didn't know each other. Someone had the brilliant idea we all stay in the same cabin! Actually, I think it was mine. Momentary lapse of intellectual clarity.

The best New Year's I can remember was my first one with Alan. We arranged blind dates for two of his law school buddies with Kathy and Liza, my Phoenix friends. The six of us were going to attend a murder mystery dinner in Hollywood. We got a fully stocked limo for the night, and everyone was looking forward to it, until the last minute when my girlfriends bailed out.

I can't remember exactly why, but I'm sure it had something to do with breaking in the New Year with a complete stranger they may have felt obligated to tongue-swap with at midnight. They guys were disappointed, but were already dressed and in the limo before Alan and I broke the news.

Since I was going to be on entertainment duty for three guys, we got the champagne flowing early and kept it coming.

By the time we burst into the all-quiet, clue-searching moment of the dinner, the four of us were completely hammered. We stormed the event laughing out loud, offering our mystery solving theories to everyone who dared cross our path. The other sleuths were deeply into the suspense of it all, and didn't quite appreciate our contributions.

Things were getting a little dry during the whodunnit sequence, and I needed another drink promptly or risked losing my absolutely necessary buzz. I saw one of Alan's buddies talking quietly to a waitress, probably still trying to muster up that New Year's date. I stumbled over to them and recited my order to her, then patted her on the butt to move her along, illustrating my thirst urgency. She looked at me with sheer disgust, then at Alan's friend whom she was beginning to like, then threw her nose in the air and stomped off. When Alan's friend stopped laughing, he told me she wasn't the waitress, but opposing counsel on a case he had in the past. Who knew? We laughed about it all night, and the encounter made that New Year's one to remember.

"Oh shit!" I took a wrong turn.

I hate driving through downtown L.A. Every other street is a one-way, and the spectator-slowing is suicidal for tailgaters. Admittedly, I'm contributing to both catastrophes. There's so much to have to pay attention to—the homeless jetting out in front of cars, tourists with limited peripheral vision, and the new spectacular high-rise hotels going up on every corner.

I've got my Thomas Guide open to page 634 and am trying to thumb down to G-6 to find the nearly invisible side street that Faye: Psychic to The Stars, lives on. The other night at work, I traded a hundred dollar gift certificate from Strings By Judy, the best stripper clothes store in town, for a session with this well-recommended psychic and spirit medium. I may end up with the short end of the deal, but I figured it was a step in the right direction. No point in buying more outfits if I'm not going to be dancing much longer. I'm practicing that positive thinking stuff.

Ava screened the mockumentary at a small independent theater on Sunset last week. We invited everybody we knew in the industry including a bunch of people we didn't.

Clinefeld lent us her mailing list in exchange for a private lesson on what young girls are doing with their men these days…sexually. She feels she's behind the times and needs some new insight on "hand/penis coordination" and "new millennium fellatio." I told her I couldn't help with these requests as I'm stuck in a time warp myself, but Ava and I graciously volunteered V's expertise and Trina's slide presentation as long as she needed them.

I sent postcards promoting the screening to every mid-level theatrical agency in town and a few of the heavies. It's the best way to secure a good agent, and it was painfully apparent I didn't have one. My auditions had become few and far between, and the ones I got sent out on were for jobs I hoped I didn't get. I wrestled with whether or not to invite Jode and his people, and ultimately decided I would be too distracted if he was there, and it was likely the night would end in disappointment, so I opted for *not*.

The mockumentary had come out pretty good, considering we rushed it to finale. Ava had to turn in by the end of the year in order to graduate, and we knew it didn't have to be perfect. The purpose was to showcase her as a producer and director. I got writing and lead-acting credit, and V got featured actress, and wardrobe and makeup credit. Trina was billed as technical coordinator, and co-executive producer, for helping pull together money. I thought it was best not to fight for credit from our gambling contribution, since no one knew the truth about it.

The audience seemed receptive and laughed when they were supposed to laugh, and a few times when they weren't. We edited the piece from the cabaret when Ava went out into the crowd and asked a bunch of guys for the one main reason they go to strip clubs. It came out pretty funny.

"To see naked ladies!" (chanting) "We want bush! We want bush!"

"Sometimes, I just want to talk to a pretty girl." Marty rocks nervously.

"What do you enjoy about this kind of entertainment?" Ava asks an East Coast visitor.

"What's not to enjoy? Youse beautiful girls. Great music. *Big, huge, va va va va-luptuous—*"

"Feet. I love feet. A women's foot is so—"

"…rancid! Smelled like the VIP room in Vegas during COMDEX!" Jim! I hate that guy.

"Why do I come here?" Bobby boasts. "To get laid. It's so…challenging. Are we on camera? Shit! Trina, I love ya', baby!"

"I like to drink a lot, and I don't know why, but women won't drink with me anywhere else," Fat Joe from the bikini bar comments. "I think it has something to do with the lighting."

"Dipshit!" Henry punches him in the shoulder. "Is that thing on? Get it off me! My wife thinks I'm at the Laker game!"

"We candy-coat it a lot of different ways, but when it comes right down to it, men want passion as much as women do. If we can't find that one woman who makes our blood boil every time she walks in the room…we come here." Profound words from Jode that I didn't even know were on tape until the screening.

Ava thought it would be a great surprise for me. She was right. Just when I was getting him out of my mind.

There were a lot of laughs, enthusiastic clapping, and an after-soiree which seemed promising. A few people gave us business cards. I was asked for my acting resume from a couple agents, and everyone wanted to talk to Ava.

The best scenario for her would be to get a real producing and/or directing job out of it. I'd be happy getting even a mediocre acting agent, so I could book enough work to not have to dance anymore. I'm so over it! Now we wait.

I pull up to the psychic's house. I'm ten minutes late. I wonder if she knew I was driving the wrong way down a one-way street. This is probably going to be stupid. I don't know why I even came. I've seen psychics before, and I guess have gotten accurate information, but nothing life changing.

I've always been interested in metaphysics. Drawn to spirit mediums that channel the dead. I saw James Van Praagh a few years back on one of his big touring events. People seemed to believe that he was communicating with their relatives. I don't know. Call me crazy, but I'm intrigued by the possibility of knowing what's coming your way.

"I feel you need this reading for more of an immediate situation." The psychic begins in her Polish accent.

"Sometimes people come to find out about things way in future. You have a lot going on right now. Lots of energy around you. Yes, this is more of an immediate situation. Drink the coffee." She hands me a tiny espresso cup and explains it's Turkish coffee. Very strong, and very intuitive.

Intuitive coffee? Whatever. I sip the java until it's gone. She takes the empty cup, places it on a saucer, and tilts it on its side.

"We look inside later."

"What will we find in there?" I ask stupidly.

"Ahhh, secrets. Animals, numbers…don't worry, honey, I tell you everything." She hands me a regular deck of cards, and tells me to shuffle and concentrate on what I want to know about, then she leaves the room.

I shuffle the deck and look around at all her stuff. Her house is nicely furnished, a lot of expensive antiques. The psychic business is doing well, I guess. There's a gift basket and flower arrangement on a marble table in one corner of the room. Both have cards attached. Risking the possibility that she knows exactly what I'm doing out here, I creep over to the table and cop a peek at the cards. One says, "You're truly gifted. All my love, Goldie." The other says, "Thanks for all that you do. Brad."

"My regular clients." Faye startles me. I fumble the cards back where they were.

"I'm sorry. I was curious. They told me you have a lot of famous clients."

"Most of them not so famous when I first met them. I taught them to believe."

"Believe what?" I ask stupidly again.

"That all things are possible. Come, sit down. We have work to do." She takes the cards from me and deals them out in an octagon-like formation.

"I see a lot of men around you. They're everywhere. Do you have a lot of boyfriends?"

"Not exactly."

"Well, you could. They would all be willing."

"Not all of them," I say, immediately regretful for giving her too much information.

The phony psychics talk generally about things that everyone deals with, then they follow your leads into specifics.

"You will have marriage. He's a wonderful man. Brown hair, not too tall…green eyes. Very nice-looking man. Also in entertainment. You two will complement each other well. Have you met him?"

I'm freaking out a little bit here. "Uh, maybe. You're describing someone that's unattainable for me. How did you know I'm in entertainment?" She smiles at me, then closes her eyes, takes a deep breath, and looks at the cards again.

"Something that you're doing will generate a lot of money. I don't see you without money right now, but whatever you're working toward will bring lots of money. Huge money. I don't see money being a problem for you, honey. Not to worry." Again she closes her eyes.

"This sounds strange, but I'm getting something about a toilet. They keep showing me a toilet. Does it mean anything to you?"

"Um, just that it's where my life's been for the last year," I say jokingly.

"I don't know what it means. I just keep seeing it. I've learned not to try and interpret everything I get. Just give it out, no matter how strange it sounds. Let's move on. Shuffle the cards again." She swoops up the cards and pushes them to me.

I'm not saying anything. I wonder if she's reading my mind. That coffee is churning up my stomach. I hope I don't have to poop in the middle of her revelation. Maybe that's the significance of the toilet!

"The man is afraid of you, honey. He will come. Men get scared when they feel love. Better to be without than to risk losing, they think. I see you two in a courtroom."

"That can't be good. Divorce court—I haven't even met him yet!"

"Don't worry. You worry too much…analyze everything. You're protected out there, honey. You have strong spirit guides that watch over you. Very lucky energy." I glance over my shoulder thinking I see a shadow. "Do you understand what I mean about spirit guides?"

"Sort of. Like dead relatives of mine?"

"Not exactly, but they could be. You have to believe, honey. They can influence you to take action that's right for your life here, but it's harder for them if you don't believe."

"O-k. I'll work on that." Didn't know I was going to have homework. "I believe there are no coincidences. That people come in your life for a reason, and that you are where you're supposed to be at any given time."

"Not everyone is where they're supposed to be. Free will, honey, creates havoc for some. I don't want you to be afraid about things. That which you fear most in life has already happened to you. Past lives."

"That would explain my fear of being restrained under water! Maybe I drowned in a past life?"

"I don't think anyone likes to be restrained under water, honey, but you're on the right track. Believe in yourself. You've taken a great risk, and you will be rewarded." She stares off blankly as if she's watching a movie or something inside her head, then blurts out confidently, "Two friends of yours will marry each other. It will be good. Do you have any questions for me before our time is up?"

"The money. When is it coming?"

"It feels like soon, honey, but I've learned that time as we know it and Universal time are different. In the spirit world, a whole lifetime here could pass in a very short time there, but it feels like soon. You will have money soon." She picks up the coffee cup, puts on her glasses, and studies the shapes the leftover coffee has left on the inside of the cup.

"Elephants." She laughs. "Lots of elephants. You are very lucky honey. Incredibly lucky. I've never seen anything like it." She squints to see into the cup. "You need to get out of your own way. The Universe keeps trying to bring you luck, and you keep stopping it from reaching you. Open yourself."

With that as her final words, she gathers the cards and patiently waits for me to pay her. I give her the gift certificate and a ten dollar tip.

"I don't know what the proper etiquette is for tipping a psychic—" She grabs the ten.

"Good read. Good session. I'm not worried about you," she repeats as she opens the door for me, letting in her next client whose face is covered with a scarf and dark sunglasses. "Everything is changing, honey. Believe." She closes the door behind me.

Wow! I'm tempted to run out to the track and put that lucky money stuff to its true test, but I did make a divine promise not to gamble after winning the trifecta. Or maybe, I should employ a private acting coach to get a head start on what might be coming my way! My adrenaline is racing too fast. I've got to watch where I'm going. It's rush hour, and I still have to figure my way out of downtown.

That was the shortest psychic reading I've ever had, but I gotta say, she piqued my interest. I like what I heard, except the part about the toilet. What the hell is that supposed to mean? And what two friends of mine are getting married? Maybe V's a lesbian, and she and Ava will get together! Or Trina and Bobby! But Bobby's not really my friend. I hope Trina's not a lesbian. It could be Liza—but she hates men! Uh-oh, the Turkish coffee is kicking in again. Shit! No, don't say shit! I've got to pull over.

I take my next left into an entrance parkway of one of downtown's swankiest hotels. What am I going to tell the valet? *I'm just going to use the facilities at your five-hundred-dollar-a-night hotel. Here's my keys?* I'm so embarrassed.

"Good afternoon, ma'am. Are you here for the Step-Up symposium?" the valet cordially asks as I hurry out of my car.

"Uh, yeah. But I'll only be a few minutes. Keep it up front, will ya'?" I run past him slightly doubled over, and heel-toe it toward the revolving door.

"Down the hall, first room on your left!" he yells out, obviously knowing where I need to go.

I race through the lobby of this gorgeous hotel eyeing every door on my left.

"Where is it? C'mon! I'm dying over here!" I say under my breath with my jaw clenched tightly. I reach the end of the hallway and plunge through the last door on the left side. "Finally!"

Oh my God! I feel like I just entered the twilight zone! It's a quiet banquet room full of young girls that all look at me as the heavy door slams behind me. I try to back out discreetly, and realize the door I just came in only opens from the outside! The commotion prompts one of the event coordinators, I presume, to jump out of her seat and lead me to the back whispering.

"All of the literature is back there on the tables." She indicates an area where a few women are gathered drinking coffee. "There'll be a short break between speakers in a few minutes if you want to find a seat." She gives me a little shove in the direction of the tables.

"Thank you, but I'm just trying to find the—"

"*Alex!*" I turn toward a stern voice at the dessert table. V grabs my arm and aggressively pulls me out of the limelight.

"What are you doing here!" she whisper yells. "I can't believe Ava cannot keep her fucking mouth shut!" Two girls turn around sharply and shush us.

"I don't know what's going on. I have to go to the bathroom!" She looks at me completely confused. "I just stopped here on my way home from the psychic!"

"You got to be fucking kidding me? You didn't know I was here?"

"No! What is this? And why are you so…so…cleaned up?" V wears a classy black pantsuit, no piercings, and her hair has a little wave to it, replacing the usual straight, wet, persecuted look.

"Dude, I took your advice and kissed my parents' ass. Things were taking too long, you know. I had to make some changes. Can't dance anymore. My body hurts…and I'm startin' to hate everybody!" I know the feeling. "There's no place for me in you guys' project. My dad's gonna front me some cash to get together a band." She's embarrassed. I sense her disappointment for selling out to them. "I had to do it, dude."

"V, that's great! Right? I mean, they'll stay out of your way…and…you won't have to dance anymore!" This was my idea, and I'm hoping I didn't butt in where I wasn't supposed to. I do that sometimes. "I'm right there with ya', hating everybody at the club. Something's gotta give."

The crowd applauds the exiting speaker, and a woman takes the podium. She's gaunt, anorexic-thin, and proper. She'd like everyone to believe she's got it together. Covered head to toe in expensive conservative wear. Pretty much how I pictured her.

"Is that your mom?"

"Unfortunately." V washes down a bite-size brownie with her last sip of coffee.

"You didn't make those brownies, did you?" I ask cautiously, glimpsing the possibilities if she did.

"No, but I should have. This thing is boring as hell!" We laugh quietly. "Listen. The witch will speak." We direct our attention to the podium.

"…and I have so many people to thank for helping us keep this organization strong. As you all know, we are happy to be a nonprofit association—" V coughs and says *bullshit,* then leans into my ear.

"She spent two days at one of those fuckin' rejuvi places after OD-ing on 'ludes when she first heard the words *nonprofit.*"

"You're kidding, right?" I whisper back. She shakes her head, and nods to keep listening.

"…enough about me. Without further ado, I'd like to introduce our final speaker of the day. She's my…pride and joy. My sole reason for living—" V puts her hand to her mouth preparing for the bullshit-cough again. I stop her.

"—and while she's not the smartest kid on the block, and certainly has made some *unimaginable* mistakes in her life, she's pulled it together and is here today to help you young ladies to keep from messing up *your* lives. Please welcome, my daughter. Ms. Vivian Marion Stifledorf…the Third."

I'm in total shock! Stunned! That a mother would introduce her own daughter that way was inconceivable to me, and to curse her with *Stifledorf?*—cruel and unusual punishment. It all makes sense now. I don't know how to react. Do I laugh, clap, or throw crepes and brownies at her mother? The audience turns to the back of the room where V and I stand.

V puts down her coffee cup, fake smiles, and mutters out of the side of her mouth.

"Condescending, and they gave me Stifledorf! That's way fucked up, dude!"

I concur. V hesitates before walking up to the podium. She's definitely looking for a way out of this. I watch her mom pinch her lips together hard, trying to smile, knowing V's on the verge of a bail. I look back at V. She buries every ounce of pride she has, and takes a step toward the podium. I grab her arm.

"Stifledorf *is* bad, and reason enough to never talk to them again, but not really their fault, and you can change it! What you can't change is your mom's bitter attitude. Doesn't have anything to do with you. She's mad at herself and nothing you do can fix that. I can't let you sell out. I know you'll regret it." She looks scared and relieved, then looks toward her mother. You can almost see steam filter out of her nose and ears.

"But what about—"

"Don't worry about her. She'll find somebody else to be pissed at before the day is over." I'm gambling this woman has been an uptight negative bitch V's whole life. Body language is very revealing, and she does a poor job of hiding her insecurities and need for control. "You got to take care of yourself and your kids now. It's time to grow up. Nothing you do is going to please her. She wants to be mad."

"You got her pegged, dude! She thrives on misery. Always has." V stares at her mom, takes a deep breath, then proudly shakes her head *no,* letting her know she's not going to win this one.

"Let's get the hell out of here before she blows!" She takes my hand and runs me out the door like a wild animal just released from confinement. We race through the lobby giggling, and plunge out the door into my car.

"That was fucking great! Did you see her face? I don't know what I was thinking! *You* are a lifesaver, Alex! Don't know how the hell you knew, but I'm sooo glad you showed up!" V hugs me hard.

"Just happened to be in the neighborhood. Purely coincidental. Now can we *please* find a bathroom…Stifledorf?" Her look of hostility tells me I should never mention that name again.

Who am I kidding? I'm always preaching that there are no coincidences! Maybe I entered bizarroworld after I left the psychic, or she put some kind of spell on me! What are the odds of randomly ending up there?

I've had déjà vu experiences before, where I was sure I was having a ground-hog day, but this was truly an irrefutably timely occurrence that could not have haphazardly come about.

You just don't stumble into a five-star hotel where your friend happens to be hosting an event you didn't know about, and save her from making a horrible life mistake! It just doesn't happen! But maybe it would more often if we'd accept the Universal leads that are given to us. The unwritten road signs right in front of our face that direct us exactly where we're supposed to go. I bet if I paid more attention to them, I'd realize I'm on the right path for my life, and give myself a break once in a while. It's like the psychic said, *Believe and get out of your own way!* I've got nothing to lose.

It's been a week, and I've been meditating like a peaceful crazy person. Three times a day with spirit-drawing scents and candles. Positive thinking, creative visualization, and a few white spells to help the Universe bring what's rightfully mine—money and love! I do feel a greater sense of energy around me lately, and I did get a call from one of the agents that came to the screening, so I must be doing something right. The agent represents mostly established actors, but said he liked my work in the mockumentary and would take a shot and submit me for a few of the new pilots.

They're technically not supposed to promote talent that haven't been signed on as clients, but they all do it. It's called hip-pocketing. They submit your pictures to casting companies they have relationships with, and if feedback is good, you *might* be considered for representation.

It's the same old Catch-22. You've got to book work on your own before a good agent will take notice of you, but you can't book the work without one. At least he was willing to hip-pocket, and he's reputable. I'll take whatever I can get.

I heard through the grapevine that Jode's girlfriend was moving in with him. I'm sure she had that planned when she initiated the trash can buying spree. How conniving of her! Why do girls always do that? Subtly redecorate one room at a time, discreetly adding a possession or two of their own. After a couple months, they convince the guy they're practically living there anyway, and might as well make it official. Before the poor sap even knows what's going on, he's got lava lamps in the den, tampons behind the bathroom mirror, pink satin sheets, and is now the proud master of an apricot toy poodle named Peppermint!

I guess I should be happy for him. I really do like him as a person, and I have to respect his refusal to compromise his relationship by jumping in the sack with me. By now, he must know I'd be willing to play second fiddle, but would have for only a short time. My plan was to lure him in with some very hot, passionate encounters. The *A* material—abundant impromptu lap dances, sex on the kitchen floor, fabulous dinners prepared by the naked chef, or maybe taking in a drive-in movie, and doing it in the car like teenagers.

After I sucked him in, no pun intended, I'd push him back to his lifeless liaison, prompting him to deal with the situation appropriately. Following a few weeks of Scrabble nights and pottery classes, he'd come crawling back to me begging for more. Single…and available.

But, as usual, my plan and the Universe's plan never seem to be the same. Things always felt right when I was around him, but I guess it's just not in the cards—or the stars. I'm sure if I open my eyes and my heart, I'll find someone else that makes me feel that childlike giddiness you feel when you're in the company of someone you could love. In the meantime, I have plenty of distractions. Super Bowl Sunday awaits.

"So things are better? With your dad and everything?" I ask a calm and more confident Marty.

"Well, not so much with him. I mean, he has Alzheimer's. They don't get better. But I have learned how to deal with things better. I started seeing someone…a therapist. She's helping me understand the meaning of life, my life."

"That's great, Marty. Really. I'm happy for you."

"She's not as cool as you are, or anywhere as nice to look at…and she wears a lot more clothes, but you know, she's a professional…and…she takes insurance," he says embarrassed.

"Marty, you don't have to explain. I'm just happy that you sought some help. Everyone can benefit from therapy. We get older, and somehow stop talking to people. I mean, really talking. Good friends become distant acquaintances as we move through life, and everything gets bottled up inside. I'm really proud of you." I hug him.

"She thinks I should stop coming in here. Doesn't think it's good for me to spend so much money senselessly. She says I should spend the money on clothes or other things that might boost my self-esteem."

"What do you think?"

"I don't know. I like coming here...most of the time. I know girls take advantage of me, but it's not like I meet a lot of women, you know? So I don't really care."

"Well then, I think you just solved your dilemma. A lot of people don't understand what goes on in these clubs. It's different for each person. Come here as long as you enjoy yourself. When it stops being fun, don't come in anymore."

"You always give me the best advice, Alex. Simple, and to the point." He stands up, gets ready to leave.

"Life should be simple. One day at a time, remember?" He kisses me on the cheek and walks away. I yell out, "Happy Super Bowl."

He looks back and waves goodbye. His pants aren't so frumpy anymore, and I can tell he's making a conscious effort to not look at the floor as he walks out. I have a strange feeling I'll never see him again.

I thought it would be more crowded today. I came in early to catch the pre-game rush. Nobody's around. My regulars seemed to have stuck to their New Year's resolutions to quit giving us all their money. I heard a few of the old-timers in the locker room discussing the annual bleakness in January. Just like the retail industry, the strip clubs suffer dramatically at the onset of the new year. I'm sure the customers will be back by Valentine's Day.

I haven't talked to the girls for a few days. I lost my cell phone and have been avoiding home a lot lately. I'm trying to keep my head clear. Taking long runs through the Beverly Hills parks, trying to put together my plan of attack for this year. My new agent has lined up a couple auditions for me this week. Pilot season is about to take off, and I really need to brush up on my acting skills.

You never know with pilots. If you stumble on one that gets picked up by the networks, your whole life could change. Look at *Friends*. Other than Courteney Cox, no one had ever heard of the other actors before. I'm sure they did a lot of discreet work, but nothing mainstream that would have created familiarity. That's the whole idea behind a new pilot. Making stars out of nobodies that the network employs cheaply for at least a couple of seasons. Then if the show becomes wildly successful, the new stars can command outrageous salaries. I predict the *Friends* clan will each make a million an episode if it stays on the air into the millennium.

"Alex, what the hell's going on!" Ava rushes through the locker room door and practically tackles me.

"What are you talking about?" Why am I always in the dark?

"I've been trying to reach you for days! Stuff is happening! People are calling!" She's so worked up, she can hardly talk. "Holy shit! I don't even know where to start!"

"Chill out. Sit down. What's going on?" I remind her we're not alone, and lead her to the wretched sofa that has resided in this locker room since sometime in the seventies.

"Why didn't you call me back? Jesus Christ! You got to stay available!" she yells at me.

"I lost my phone, and...I've been meditating a lot lately."

"Well, meditate on this! I sold the mockumentary!"

"No way! Already!"

"Way!"

"To who?"

"An Independent Film network on TV. It's a new cable station. Somebody Clinefeld invited to the screening!"

"Oh my God! What does this mean?"

"Some dough for us, for one thing." She pulls a check out of her purse made out to Track Chick Productions for $35,000. "Retire your stripper bag, babe! We're done here!" I grab the check out of her hands, and stare at it in awe.

"We did it. We really did this. Do you know what this means?" I ask her, knowing full well she does. "Snowball."

"It's already happening. The producers of the show hired me to direct a small feature they're doing!"

"Ahhh!" She screams with me.

"They're producing their own original films to air on the cable channel. It's called the IFC. Independent Film Channel."

"What's the film? Anything for me in it?" I ask, hopeful.

"Can you play a Chinese immigrant struggling in the toy business?"

"Ofcourseican!" I say in the worst Chinese accent imaginable.

"I'll create something for you. I am the director!" We laugh and hover over the check, in total disbelief this came about so quickly.

Ava fills me in the details as I pack up my S-bag for hopefully the last time. I come across some of my early outfits. The ruffles, the lace, the too-conservative, the vampire look, the unworn crotchless panties that some-how I thought would be a good idea, and V's infamous thigh-high leather boots.

"I don't know why I have these," I say, as I cram them in the bag.

"I always end up with her stuff. It's the only way her shit gets washed! Oh, I forgot!" She digs in her purse and retrieves a piece of paper. "Some guy called for you. Said he was from HBO, and met you in the bath-room?"

I stop and think for a second, then it comes to me. "Oh yeah, him."

"Did you screw somebody in the john at Clinefeld's?" she asks in a judgmental tone.

"Nooo! Trina did. I counseled a drug addict."

"Right. That's what he said. That you helped him, and he needs to talk to you ASAP."

"I don't have time for that, now that we have a new project. Especially for free. It's time I get paid for the counseling services. He was totally messed up."

"I think you should call him. He sounded Ok, and what if it's business related? He does work for HBO. I checked."

"The guy was snorting coke off the toilet!" I gasp. "The toilet! Oh my God! Give me that number!" I grab the paper out of her hand, toss every-thing in my bag, and run to the nearest pay phone.

Ava and I share the mouthpiece as the two-month clean-and-sober Dave details his proposal to present my idea about a comedy series set in a strip club to the heavies at HBO. He ran it by some creative assistants over there, and they thought it was a great idea. HBO is currently working on a live reality-based show where strippers wear hidden cameras and go about their normal work nights. The whole stripper show concept had already seeped into their programming. I told him I think our idea is better than that. He agreed.

He wants us to put together a pitch that includes a character break-down, a synopsis of the pilot episode, brief paragraphs of eight to ten future episodes, and my bio, designed to promote me as a potential staff writer and/or script supervisor for authenticity's sake.

Dave went on and on about how I helped him more than anyone has ever helped him. And his new-found sobriety brought him to the conclu-sion that he needed to give something back to people that have been there for him. I acted like I wasn't completely freaking out, and this kind of thing happens to me all the time, but inside I was losing it! Everything is happening at once. I can't even keep my head straight. I haven't even recovered from Ava's news, and now this! It's so exciting, and so unbelievable! I don't know what to do first.

He could have pitched the idea without me. Stole it from me. Actually, I can't believe he didn't. Hollywood is so cutthroat. Everyone out for themselves. I've heard so many stories about nobodies that got screwed because they gave their ideas to the wrong person. You have little recourse in battling the bigwigs. Even when you've protected your work, there is still a great chance someone you've exposed it to could take it to a producer, change a few minor details, and call it their own. Happens every day in Tinseltown.

I can't believe I made such an impact on Dave's life doing something so effortless like letting him bleed on my shoulder for an hour. People want to be heard. Nobody listens anymore. We're all too busy to acknowledge cries for help that would be so obvious if we'd only take a minute to notice. Normally I wouldn't have listened, but since I was trapped in the loo that spooky Halloween night, I got lucky *again*, and benefitted from yet another valuable life lesson. Coincidence? I think not.

14

Finale

*L*ife is so unpredictable. It seems just when you can't see the light anymore, extraordinary things become clearly visible. The thought of not doing this job anymore, and to have actually accomplished what I set out to do has created overwhelming and excessive happiness.

I guess there was a part of me, the hideous self-doubting force lying deep within, that didn't really think I could do it. I had always lacked a little self-confidence. Afraid I wouldn't be good enough to compete with professional entertainers. I'm still not sure I'm there yet, but what I do know is that I'm ready to try. Ready to dive into my new career headfirst. This is what it's all been about. Relocating my passion. Living my dream. The doors have opened. I took the risk.

I didn't hate being a *dancer*. It's kind of hard to, since my career goals coming to fruition was a direct result of making the choice to do that job. It did help me overcome some fears and build confidence. I still remember that first time on stage in Vegas. The guys staring upward at me, anxiously awaiting my ungarmented entertainment expertise. It was a humbling experience. Frightening, exciting, humiliating, and intriguing all at once.

It's different when acting, especially for film or TV. Everyone there knows that you're acting. It's not you who's being portrayed. When playing the role of *stripper,* and it is a role, you take your clothes off, try to do something different than the hundreds of girls that have gone before you, but the pressure is all on you and only you. You can change your name, your hair, your makeup, and your entire look, but it's still you, and you know it's you.

I can say honestly I walk away from the business of exotic dancing taking with me more than I went in with. And I don't mean money or an STD! The experience will stay with me forever. I opened my mind and learned so much about men, women, relationships, occupations I would have never taken the time to hear about, and the influence one person can have on another by killing some time and just listening.

After all the analysis, I conclude that I'll never fully understand why men spend so much time in strip clubs. I think it's different for each of them, but one unanimous contributing factor is that men are very visual. They can keep an image in their head alive much longer than women can. Testosterone creates a sexual need that must be satisfied one way or the other. It's a concept most women will never understand, and the best advice I can give is for all of us to stop trying.

They're pretty basic really. Quite primitive with their thoughts and actions. Most all disputes could be easily avoided and unraveled by nurturing their egos, and applying a simple strategy of TLC when absolutely necessary to keep the peace. Of course, one's personal values should never be compromised, and this method should be reserved for the good guys out there that are also doing their part. But that's a whole 'nother book.

My acting teacher had a saying at the end of every class that kept me going during some of those bleak nights when I sat in the corner of the club by myself, and wondered why I had put myself in an environment I didn't belong in.

"Don't give up on your dream five minutes before your miracle."

I recited it over and over when I'd begin to doubt my goals, and prayed for that miracle that I thought was my only chance of obtaining them. As it turned out, my miracle was happening the whole time. I did belong there. At least for the time it took for me to gain the experience, the confidence, and the perspective necessary to propel me into my dream world.

HBO is in final negotiations with my agents. Yes, that's a plural. It's amazing how many agents come out of the woodwork when you create the activity yourself. The network has agreed to produce a pilot and thirteen episodes of *Mitzie's*. The rest is up to fate.

I didn't get a part on the show, but they did agree to let me make a guest-starring appearance once I book a few more acting gigs, which shouldn't be too difficult since right now, I'm on the set of a new legal drama called *Family Law*. I landed a featured role for one episode with a possibility of recurring. I get to play a divorce lawyer who has an affair with her client. Big stretch!

I did secure a position as a technical advisor and script authenticator on my HBO series, despite the fact that producers didn't think I was qualified for any position. I cornered one of the young horny executives, brought Helga back, and convinced him to make a few slight adjustments, and create a job for me. He asks to see her every now and again.

Trina settled her divorce, got sole custody of the kids as expected, and was awarded seventy-five percent of the marital assets. The Court frowned heavily on Evan's attempted hiding of the money, and it didn't hurt that we had a female judge who was a principal fundraiser for the local MADD organization. Call it luck, irony, fate whatever you want, but the stars were lining up for us.

Instead of spending money on expensive shopping sprees, alcohol, and dinners on Rodeo every night, Trina was putting her money to good use. She decided to open her own strip club...excuse me, *lingerie bar*, as she constantly corrects me. There's no actual nudity, and in addition to the lap dancers, professional dancers will do *Flashdance*-type burlesque stage shows throughout the night. I think it's a cool idea, and L.A. is more than desperate to bring back a little of Old Hollywood. Besides, it's a great place for me and the girls to showcase some new steps.

Her other venture—a band called Rebels With Cause. Guess who's on lead vocals and guitar? It's a work in progress, but Miss Vivian, (we're allowed to call her that now), promises to stay focused and limit the profanity to twenty occurrences per song. It's in her contract.

Ava's been so busy lately, I hardly ever see her. A while ago, I hooked her up with my good buddy Phil to give her some producing pointers when dealing with the industry big dogs, and they are swarming around her. It's not all that common that Hollywood gets the gorgeous, the smart, the talented, and the dedicated all in one package. She really has an eye for what people want to see, and I suspect we'll be hearing her name read off an envelope by Jack Nicholson or some other celebrity dressed in formalwear one day.

The last couple months, Ava and Phil have been working on developing her next major production—their wedding! Yes, it appears the lesbian phase is over. I knew hers wasn't the genetic kind. Although knowing Phil,

I'd take two-to-one odds he encourages her to fall off the wagon every once in a while…as long as he gets to join in. Men!

I put down my pen and peek out of my trailer window to see if anyone is looking for me. The crew has been adjusting lights and cameras for the last two hours in preparation for my scene. I haven't left my trailer since hair and makeup were finished with me. I'm not sure when the next time I'll ever have my own trailer will be, so I'm taking full advantage of it, and hanging out writing in my *journal.* I prefer to call my memoirs journal entries now. It's a little more sophisticated than *Dear Diary,* but of equal substance. One never knows when the jotting down of life experiences may someday be voluminous and interesting enough to become a book.

"Alex?" The first AD knocks on my door. "We need you on set."

"Just a minute, please. I'm not ready yet. Could I get some fruit?" I'm totally ready, and I'm not hungry. I just want to be a prima donna for a few more minutes.

One of the production assistants brings me the entire fruit assembly off the craft service table. This is so cool. I eat a piece of pineapple, and ask him to napkin my mouth. He does without hesitation, then leads me onto the set.

I'm dressed in a short skirt and business-trendy suit jacket, hair wound up, but loose with long bangs framing my heavily made-up face. I tried to tell the wardrobe person that no corporate attorney would be caught dead dressing so sexy in the office, let alone in a courtroom addressing the judge on such a serious issue of child custody. My opinion was considered for about three seconds, and ruled against by all parties involved. Apparently the look is necessary to create my next scene, which is the post-court celebration bar scene where I throw myself on my client. As if!

"All right! If everyone could take their number one positions please," the Assistant Director barks out through his megaphone.

The director comes over to talk to me, and thoroughly explains my character's motivation, leaving few acting decisions to me. I pretty much got it. It's not going to be an Academy Award-winning appearance here, so I zone out on him a little while he talks, and stare at the cameraman's cute butt as he takes instruction from the DP (director of photography).

Wait a minute! That butt looks familiar. I know that butt! It can't be! He turns around and gets behind the camera, just as a crew guy blinds me with a light. Within seconds, somebody yells.

"Rolling. And action!"

It was the classic deer-caught-in-headlights shot, with a face of squinting confusion. The next thing I hear is, "Cut!" screamed through the megaphone, and the director is back in my face telling me that I must have misinterpreted the reaction he described. I assured him I was ready now, and knew exactly what he wanted me to do, then mentally eradicated all thoughts that thirty feet away a man I've obsessed over...and over...and over is watching me through a magnified lens.

Amazingly, I stay focused and get through the scene flawlessly. Again, not award-winning performance material, but another enormously necessary line on my resume. We shot the scene six times, and I maintained my professionalism each take, at least on the exterior, by not letting anyone see my attempts to identify the cameraman. The suspense was killing me, but the job was way more important, and I knew we'd be done soon.

"Check the gate!" The first AD announces they're checking to make sure they got the shot, and can move on to the next one. I'm baking in these lights, and the makeup person keeps running over to pad my forehead every two seconds, blocking my view of the camera activity.

I don't shoot my other scene until tomorrow, and if they dismiss me before the mystery is solved, I may have to lurk around and stalk the crew until I find out. I have to know. If it's not, no big deal. But if it is, it goes down in history as the greatest potential coincidence of all time. Not that I believe in coincidences (have I mentioned that before?), but this is getting a little eerie!

My normal complex analysis combined with the makeup person touching up my eyes and gossiping about the unusually straight wardrobe guy, somehow forced me to miss the announcement that they got the shot and would be moving on after the lunch break. A PA finally clues us in by rolling up some heavy cord under our feet, and thrusts us out of the way. I get swooped up into a gaggle of cast and crew hurriedly pushing their way off the set to get to the food line. I keep trying to look back to see if I can catch a glimpse of him, but it's too congested, and I'm going against the grain.

I get through the buffet line, scooping a little of everything on my plate. I'm not even hungry, but I can't think straight, so I'm doing what everyone else is doing...eating. I reach the beverage counter where a server awaits my order. Juice, coffee, sodas, water. What! No booze?

"The lady would really appreciate a glass of wine." A voice from behind me speaks eloquently. "Merlot, Chardonnay...maybe even a blush."

I turn around to meet my mind reader, but of course, I know who it is. The voice is unmistakable. I take a deep breath, and stare in calm shock. He smiles and nods back to the beverage guy.

"Two bottles of water, Sam." Sam throws them to him. "There's no liquor on the set." His whisper is so sexy in my ear.

"I know," I whisper back. We stare in each other's eyes for a few seconds. Both of us calculating the odds of such an occurrence.

"What are you doing here?" I finally ask him.

"Working. What are you doing here?"

"Working."

We take our food to a quiet table, and launch what I already know is going to be a beautiful, fun, exciting, and respectful relationship. There's no denying this kind of divine intervention. I felt it from the beginning, and was too scared to act on it. We always had a connection, but somehow couldn't get it together to develop it further.

This is one of those situations where the leader of our great Universe might have really wanted to clunk us in the heads and physically bond us together with super cement. Then at the last minute, he consults his people and decides, "We'll give them one more chance to do it on their own."

The experts say that we're born with an innate fear of falling, and a fear of loud noises. Good thing the loud noise issue works itself out with time, or new parents and their close friends and relatives would never procreate again.

Fear. It's a powerful phenomenon. We're frickin' born with it! How do we get rid of it? I'll repeat the words of the most accurate and categorically amazing futuristic forecaster I've ever seen (*psychic* has such a negative connotation):

"That which you fear most has already happened to you."

I don't know what that means exactly, or how it relates to my current life. But what I do know is I was afraid of change, yet driven by the need for change. That little voice in the back of your head that tells you you're not reaching your potential. It picks at you every time you make a life's choice against your true passion.

We all have a passion, at least one. Maybe it's a passion for science, or food, or protecting the environment, or for animals, kids, family, the opposite sex, to write, to dance, to play music, to teach, to learn, to right the world's wrongs, to love and be loved, or simply a passion for life wherever you are while in it.

We're not always where we want to be, and usually don't understand why we've ended up doing something we never wanted to do, or even thought about doing. But we don't have to settle! After experiencing what became possible from engaging in a stereotypically dismal occupation, I'll never close myself off from considering that all things happen for a reason. And eventually that reason reveals itself if you follow your heart, take the appropriate action, fight for what you want, and *believe* in yourself.

Find your dream! Live your passion! Wake up every day excited to do something. Don't let anyone skew your course. And don't ever, *ever* discount a plausible opportunity for life to imitate art…or vice versa.

Give the Gift of

The Stripper Diaries

to Your Friends and Colleagues

CHECK YOUR LOCAL BOOKSTORE OR ORDER HERE

❑ **YES**, I want _____ copies of *The Stripper Diaries* at $24.95 each, plus $4.95 shipping per book (California residents please add $2.06 sales tax per book). Canadian orders must be accompanied by a postal money order in U.S. funds. Allow 15 days for delivery.

My check or money order for $_____ is enclosed.

Please charge my: ❑ Visa   ❑ MasterCard

Name _____

Organization _____

Address _____

City/State/Zip _____

Phone_____   E-mail _____

Card # _____

Exp. Date_____   Signature _____

Please make your check payable and return to:

Tenth Street Press

2121 Rosecrans Avenue, Suite 2385
El Segundo, CA 90245

Call your credit card order to: 888-348-1010

tenthstreetpress@yahoo.com   **www.thestripperdiaries.com**